PERMUTATIONS: A WELL WORLD ANTHOLOGY

PERMUTATIONS

A WELL WORLD ANTHOLOGY

BASED ON JACK L. CHALKER'S
MIDNIGHT AT THE WELL OF SOULS

EDITED BY
DAVID BOOP

CAEZIK
SF & FANTASY
ARC MANOR
ROCKVILLE, MARYLAND

＊

SHAHID MAHMUD
PUBLISHER

www.caeziksf.com

ISBN: 978-1-64710-103-9

First Edition. First Printing. June 2025.
1 2 3 4 5 6 7 8 9 10

CAEZIK
SF & FANTASY

Caezik,. Phoenix Pick and Galaxy's Edge are imprints of Arc Manor

www.CaezikSF.com

Contents

FOREWORD
Neal Asher

When asked to do an introduction to this collection of stories based on Jack L. Chalker's Well World Saga I was a bit disinclined because it had been a while since I read it. I'd lost the habit of reading books through too much social media and constant work. It's a fact that when you're writing and editing all the time the editing head gets fixed in place and it then becomes difficult to read uncritically and recapture that sensawunda from our early reading of SFF. But because I've been pushing myself to get back into the habit, I thought, why the hell not, and picked up *Midnight at the Well of Souls*.

The first thing that struck me was bloody hell, I did read this a long time ago. My copy has my parents' address stamped inside. The rubber address stamp was an acquisition to assist in the process of submitting short stories to small presses and synopses and sample chapters to big publishers, in the days when all that was done by post. I also vaguely recollect that rather than this book being included in a bag of books from a secondhand shop, it was one I bought new. My edition was printed in 1977 so I was likely still a teenager when I read it.

Diving into the book immediately reminded me of how so much sinks into our unconscious and then surfaces later, its source forgotten. The first character we see in this book is Skander, a researcher on a Markovian world. I wryly realized then where those names had arisen from in my own work: Skander was a half-breed of elf and orc in one of my short stories, while the Markovians were a family that ruled Earth after a totalitarian regime in others. But in Chalker's future, the Markovians were an alien race that had taken itself to what would seem to be the pinnacle aimed for by any intelligent technological species. They had godlike control over their environment through advanced technology like the constructed brain sitting below the crust of the planet Skander is studying. But the Markovians have disappeared from the universe, leaving only these remains. This is immediately reflected in lines from the poem "Ozymandias" that Skander recollects, and which appear on page 2 of the book—a favorite of mine that may well have become so because of this book. The Markovians could create or change anything they wished. They had that good old "technology indistinguishable from magic," so why are they gone?

Skander and a brilliant assistant Varnett have just about cracked the secrets of the brain deep below their feet. They both want that power to change the milieu in which they have been born—Skander to reverse the horrible homogenization of humanity of the Com worlds and Varnett simply because "I am greedy and would like to be a god." Skander isn't inclined to share so commits murder to that end, but while attempting to kill Varnett, they both fall through a gate on their world and are swept off to the Well of Souls. And here I must digress because, for reading this as a teenager and lost in that sensawunda, I missed something about these books: politics.

I guess it's understandable. It took me until I studied for an A level in English at night school some years later before I realized that newspapers are politically partisan. In *Midnight*, human society has, mostly, gone the route of the socialist/communist nightmare. Though, I have to add here that this is vague and there might be other worlds under different regimes—a storyteller keeping his options open. Everyone has their place in the society depicted and is in fact bred for it. Varnett, for example, is one in a long line of clones from a brilliant mathematician. Obviously, the Com worlds are communist, which is something I suspect went straight over my head as a teenager.

One name that had stuck with me from my initial reading of the Well World books was that of the main character Nathan Brazil. For reasons not clear to me, I thought he didn't put in an appearance until later books, but there he was in the second chapter, and I got a bit of a tingle down the spine. Piloting a ship through a vacuum, he learns some truths about his three passengers, some of them quite nasty. The Com world woman Vardia is basically a deliverer of messages and a programmed diplomat. The man Hain is a drug dealer whose assistant, Wu Julie, he has enslaved to a drug that is destroying her body and mind. Brazil changes course to take Wu Julie to a world that is the source of the drug, where she can at least survive and where Hain will get the punishment he deserves. Along the way, however, he answers a distress beacon that takes them to the world Skander was studying. Finding evidence of murder and pursuing that thread, they too are swept through the gate to the Well World. And here is where things get seriously weird.

The world itself is divided up into hexes—each containing the environment of an alien race and members of that race—and they have arrived at a transfer point to those hexes. They are met by a chimera of snake and walrus called Ortega who, it turns out, was once a man and knows Brazil. Ortega explains the setup of the world to them. There is no way back for them and, upon being transferred out onto the Well World, the Markovian brain there will decide what race they are to become. The three passengers go through. Hain becomes a giant female insect in a civilization of the same, Vardia becomes a Czill—a walking tree—and Wu Julie, a centaur now free of the addiction that was killing her. Held back by Ortega after the departure of the others, Brazil is filled in on the situation about Varnett and Skander, and the disruption their arrival has caused. Then, when Brazil goes through, he ends up in a human hex unchanged.

It's an excellent conceit. I mentioned politics earlier, but I didn't find that intrusive. Chalker was obviously having a ball telling a convoluted story involving body transformation, cunning plots, and manipulation. I contend that he wasn't writing a book as a vehicle for homilies, but simply laying the groundwork to tell a thumping good tale and, as it turns out, many more such tales. However, as in any good tale, certain truths come through. This is the case with all good fiction if written honestly.

The contending factions on the Well World know that Skander and Varnett may have a way to access the power of the Markovians, but it's not something they can take off them until they actually obtain it. This is why they were allowed through to the world rather than murdered on the spot. Apparently, access to this power will be found only during midnight at the Well of Souls. From their various locations, all connive to find out where they need to go and to get there. Two groups result from this: Skander is a merman researching in an academy of the Czill—those walking trees—and is assisted by the transformed Vardia. They discover that the Well of Souls is a point on the equatorial wall separating carbon life in the south from the more exotic "Northerners," before they are kidnapped by Hain in his form of a giant insect, and a Northerner. Varnett it turns out is a bat-man, but not the Gotham City kind. He joins up with Brazil, who has snared up Wu Julie, now a centaur, along the way.

The two parties converge on the Well of Souls and, there's no other way to put it, have weird adventures along the way. At this point I have to mention one, or rather two creatures in a mutualistic relationship, who are also involved: the Northerner mentioned before called the Diviner, and the Rell. This combination consists of a floating strip with something poised on top of it resembling a glass chandelier. One of them is the thinking mind while the other provides the muscle in the form of energy weapons. This was the kind of stuff that got me as a teenager and still does now. Imagining centaurs, big bugs, and walking trees is no problem at all since they've been in literature forever. But I really enjoy it when depictions of alien life are stretched out of the norm and the known. And yet again, this is obviously something that lodged in my subconscious. One of my earliest short stories, published in a small press mag called *Premonitions,* was called "The Gyre and the Bibrat," which was a similarly combined mutualistic being.

The relationships between the characters and the courses they take are complicated to say the least. Wu Julie, who was drug enslaved to Hain, is in love with Nathan Brazil, or thinks she is. And Brazil it seems is looking for love from her, or maybe just acceptance. It has by this time been revealed that he is older than seems feasible, and as the journey progresses and his memories surface, older than seems possible. Meanwhile, Hain has been enslaved by one higher up in his insect civilization. The tree woman divides into two versions of herself, one of which is subsumed by a hive intelligence.

By and by, they all arrive at the Well of Souls, where Nathan Brazil lets them in to the levers of control while in the process revealing that he is a Markovian. Finally faced with the reality of what such power means, those who want it find that they cannot take it—that actually using that power is as far beyond them as computer programming is beyond a rat. It terrifies them when Nathan essentially hands them a gun and gives them leave to pull the trigger, and they demur. Thereafter, like some version of a judgmental god, he dispatches them off to appropriate futures. It is deus ex machina in the literal sense (in Greek plays, the gods were lowered on a platform to dispense justice to the players), but even so, this does not detract from a thumping good tale. Are you not entertained? I was, while I am also aware that the books that came after were even better.

One theme to this book, I would characterize as "be careful what you wish for." It's the defeating of expectations and the dispelling of illusions. Wu Julie, sure of her love for Brazil, is horrified by the reality of what he is—a Markovian—and that love is proven false. Vardia discovers that her Com world society is not a perfect collective for rulers still in place. Adding insult to injury, she finds the message she was to deliver was an introduction for Hain, whose organization, by dint of the drug they push, has been taking control of her society. All that Vardia saw as perfect is flawed. Hain, having been brainwashed by that higher-up in his insect society, wishes to be that one's mate and is so transformed, little realizing that his young will eat their way out of his/her body. Wu Julie and Vardia are dispatched to lives they could never have experienced as Com worlders, while others return to their new lives having learned the lesson of pursuing empty power. All of this is a reflection of Markovians. They got what they wished for in ultimate power over reality and found it empty at the core. They effectively extinguished themselves by becoming the races they created on the Well World and distributed throughout the universe. They started again to try and find what they had missed. And at the end of all, Nathan Brazil is once again alone.

But all the above resolutions are box-ticking endings to story and character threads, while we have enjoyed the story and those characters. The pursuit of goals and striving for perfection in the end are not what is important. The overarching theme of the book in a sense is more subtle, and what the Markovians missed, and can be summed up by a truth that came to be quoted from many sources, but in this case, Ralph Waldo Emerson: "It's not the destination but the journey."

In the spirit of that quote, here now in this collection are a few more journeys for you to enjoy.

Neal Asher 6/12/23

INTRODUCTION
David Boop

"**W**hy Well World?"

That's what people asked me when I told them I was doing a tribute to the seminal series by one of my personal favorite authors, the late Jack L. Chalker. And they weren't wrong to ask because certainly since his passing in 2005, Jack's name isn't mentioned in the same circles it once was. The flavor of today's fiction has changed a lot since *Midnight at the Well of Souls* first came out in 1977. Not all of Jack's writing could be considered to be "enlightened" by today's standard, and yet, in his books, he addressed many difficult topics such as drug addiction, fascism, gender identity, and religion.

So why, again, Well World?

It's not as simple an answer as Jack's writing inspired me as a teenager and I wanted to create worlds the way he did. Or that I was a huge fan who counts his The Quintara Marathon as one of the best trilogies I've ever read. I can't say I even got to meet him, as he passed before my first published work and my entrance into the world of fandom and publishing. From some firsthand accounts, Jack was—as I've been told—very opinionated and picked many hills to die on. Who knows? Maybe I'm lucky to have not met my idol. And yet his friends and family, many of whom were involved with this anthology, talk of how much of an intelligent and kind man he was; how they sorely miss him every day. So I *do* feel the loss of not having met him. I've met many of my idols, some who have become my mentors, and I would've loved that chance to meet Mr. Chalker and find out if we would've made fine peers and friends.

But none of that is the reason I chose to chart an untraveled path back to the Well World as my first official project with Arc Manor.

The reason came down to this. I love the ten volumes of Jack's Well World series *so much*, I didn't want to see them just end with his passing. I desired others—newer authors and readers who'd never been exposed to the previous books—to become fans of them, as well. I needed to be able to sit around conventions discussing Markovian ascension or Well World politics, as I'm sure my literary ancestors once did.

Truthfully, I didn't want to feel alone in Jack's universe anymore.

The first step was to find a few people just like me—authors who'd been inspired by the body-switching magic Jack infused into all his books. It wasn't easy, as authors are more inclined to mention Lovecraft or Asimov or Heinlein as their influences on their bios. I had to dig deep into blog posts, replies to fan groups, and online photos of Jack with his friends and peers. But slowly, I found them. And I got most of them, save for a couple due to scheduling conflicts. Two of Jack's dear friends— Catherina Asaro and S.P. Somtow—came aboard gratefully. Then, one of the most things incredible things happened! Jack's own daughter, Samantha Chalker, agreed to co-author with the also amazing Jennifer Brozek.

Like, how cool is that?

The dream was to have these authors write characters who were once human and have them waking up on Well World, the universe's petri dish, in a new body, and then having them solve a problem they were uniquely qualified for. Piece of cake, right?

Only, I didn't want my authors taking up half the story getting their protagonist to Well World through the godlike Markovian's transdimensional gates. So, I decided to write bumper stories. The first one would be a classic "How They All Got to the Well World" piece, and the other at the end would provide an epilogue of what happened to their protagonists after their stories ended.

This meant I'd be writing each of the author's characters into stories of my own creation. I worked directly with my "team" to make sure every word was to their liking and never betrayed the sense of the character or characters they created. The same goes for several of Jack's characters, including his "Wandering Jew," Nathan Brazil; and the six-armed, gruff, mustachioed snake-walrus known as Serge Ortega. I read and reread the first five books in the series over and over again to get the voice down, and ultimately, you, the fans of his work, will be the judge if I did Jack's creation justice.

This anthology takes place between *Midnight* and *Exiles at the Well of Souls*, the first and second books in the series. Jack left plenty of space for me to slip in this anthology (which hopefully won't be the last). On a planet of 1,500+ species, I feel there are many more stories to tell.

And if you come to love this world as much as I do, let's sit down at a con someday and talk of our favorite species over a drink (nonalcoholic is totally acceptable). Let's call forth Jack's spirit to join us, and we will all fellowship about worlds built—and lost—together.

D.B
12/02/2023

And now …

PERMUTATIONS
A WELL WORLD ANTHOLOGY

Chapter One:
ABOARD THE FREIGHTER STEHEKIN
David Boop

Near the Cerulean Corridor
100 Years After *Midnight at the Well of Souls*

Nathan Brazil sat on the bridge of his cargo hauler playing an unfathomable-numbered hand of solitaire, and he cheated, as usual. He didn't like to lose. Some would say he wasn't designed for it. But those people weren't there at the moment. No one was.

His freighter *Stehekin*—having just dropped off a bay full of cryogenically frozen produce to an outpost—now sat empty of cargo or passengers. The vacant corridors echoed with the noise of aging pipes, creaking welds, and memories. All needed an overhaul. Maybe after this job, he promised her, as usual. She held together well enough for now. Until something seriously went wrong, he, his cargo, and occasional passengers should be safe.

Notice of delivery came through the network directing him to Griiyama d to pick up a load of mining equipment for the Icolite Belt. Word was an asteroid filled with scandium, a much sought after mineral used in shipbuilding, had been discovered. Scandium was always in demand, and finding a huge deposit of it would make someone, not him of course, rich.

Brazil had never been rich. Well, not really in terms of how wealth was determined in the Confederacy these days. Back on Earth, a very

13

long time ago, he tried being wickedly rich, but it hadn't set well with him. He liked most people, but not the type who showed up when you had money. So, he went back to being poor and living a nomadic life.

That's why he "piloted" the freighter. The fully automated ship occasionally hauled very expensive cargo, so the shipping company hired a troubleshooter captain for each ship. It took a special type of crazy to spend most of your life alone, reading cheap pulps, and playing an unfathomable amount of solitaire.

It was also a good place to hide.

Not that any person actively sought Brazil. At least, not currently. The things he'd done before returning to his position as freighter babysitter were behind him now. Brazil didn't like to lose, and yet, in regard to fighting against the Com, he excelled at it.

The Com's manufactured society, which included manufacturing or converting humans into identical drones, was devoid of all the things that Brazil thought made people human: love, lust, laughter, trust, betrayal. They programmed their "citizens" to look alike, think alike, and have all their wishes and desires replaced by the Com's. You couldn't escape the Com when they took over your planet. More fell to them every day. The people who ran those planets were given absolute power to mold their society in a godlike way in exchange for selling out their citizens. Though, to be fair, Brazil considered, sometimes those leaders *were* blackmailed into signing over their world, usually through unwitting addiction to sponge. The only way to survive the deadly drug was by being given more of it by the Sponge Syndicate. Not enough, the victims became unwitting zombies until they finally died, so why not trade your souls for the small hope you'd be able to live out the rest of your life? Much as he wanted to, he couldn't stop the Com or their syndicate allies.

Brazil sighed—a long, weary release born from a long life and a longer list of failures that outnumbered his successes.

No, what he actually hid from on that lonely freighter was not the syndicate, the Com, the Fed, or even scorned husbands or lovers, despite there being quite a few. It was a force greater than anything in the known universe. It would someday find him—that was inevitable, no matter where he was, literally rearranging the foundation of reality to get to him. He'd known it to destroy entire civilizations to get his attention, and he'd give in like he always did, minimizing the long-term damage. But he could, during slow times like these now, lie to himself and pretend he stayed one step ahead of it. No sense of making it too easy, though, not when Brazil worked so hard to ignore his *other* job—the one in addition to cargo caretaker.

Nathan Brazil was the IT Technician of all existence. He maintained the computer that ran … everything.

Reality's custodian was in mid-shuffle for yet another game of solitaire when the freighter's alarm went off, causing him to spray the cards all over the console. He leaned forward in his overstuffed captain's chair to brush the sensors clean and turn off the loud, echoing gong.

A message scrolled across the screen:

DISTRESS SIGNAL FIELD INTERCEPTED. AWAIT INSTRUCTIONS.

"Damn. Why now?"

IDENTIFY SIGNAL AND MAGNIFY IMAGE, he typed.

A luxury transport came into focus on a small screen. Its engines were cold and it slowly rotated to the right. Flashes of internal explosions lit the port windows around the ship. So far, though, there'd been no hull ruptures. That meant they weren't trying to destroy the ship, but disable it.

Pirates?

The text of the call finally came through. The captain reported the luxury liner *Euphrates* had been sabotaged by anti-Com rebels, causing it to drop out of light speed. While Brazil certainly supported the idea of sticking it to the Com, the cruiser held thousands of innocent people who were now in danger of dying. The method of "breaking a few eggs" to win a war wasn't one he supported. Saving the Confederation's citizens from the forced indoctrination of the Com held a special place in his heart. Killing those same people? Well, Brazil had caused enough death in his exceptionally long lifetime. More than he'd ever make up for.

So, Nathan Brazil got ready to pick up what survivors he could. It would be a small drop in a large bucket of guilt.

By the time Brazil's freighter arrived at the coordinates, a mishmash of ships had also answered the call. There were other vessels, some Brazil recognized by their registration numbers. There were also a couple of Fed ships already docked with the luxury liner. Brazil suspected that'd be for troops hunting the saboteurs, not rescuing personnel. The Confederation's government, slowly being absorbed by the Com as it was, would prioritize arresting terrorists over saving its citizens … except maybe for a few VIPs. They'd be the first ones off, under a security escort. Otherwise, the Fed would rely on people like him to get the common folk off of the doomed ship.

After about an hour, instructions began coming through, lining up each volunteering ship to enter the loading dock or connect to an airlock. One by one, the larger freighters went in first, followed by medium-sized cruisers. *Stehekin* held twelve staterooms and had an empty cargo bay, so Brazil could take quite a few refugees. The coordinator set him at about six in of the eight waiting, which meant his passengers would be cranky and hungry from waiting for rescue. He took a quick assessment of his food reserves and cursed. He hadn't been prepared for people, so whoever he did end up with would still be hungry and cranky until they could reach a starport or space station.

Just as Brazil sat back in the chair, a part of *Euphrates* blew out into the vacuum of space. Shrapnel, equipment, and people floated away from the luxury liner.

"Holy shit!" came over the speaker via the coordinator. A barrage of voices talked over each other, and Brazil had a hard time figuring out what had happened or what was needed. He caught a snippet of a report that there were several passengers trapped in an emergency shelter on the other side of the exposed hull. There wasn't an easy way to get to them, or for them to make their way to one of the airlocks. If the ship's fuel reserves exploded, they'd be toast.

Brazil kicked his ship's engine into life, wincing as it protested going from impulse to full-throttle.

"*Stehekin*? What are you doing? Stay in line!"

He ignored the coordinator. The Feds might be content to let those people die, but he wasn't.

Nathan Brazil didn't like to lose, at cards or at life, and he knew exactly how to get to those stranded passengers.

Brazil cut the hard burn when he reached the right coordinates and spun the ship around to decelerate. While *Stehekin* drifted closer, he opened the cargo bay. Once, further back in time than he'd ever admit to anyone, a pirate named Serge Ortega talked him into being part of a jailbreak of one of his crew who had been arrested, sped through trial, and shipped off to a colony planet for hard labor.

The prison transport had self-contained cells, sealed using magnetic force fields, making them impossible to break out of ... *on* the ship. That security feature, however, meant that the whole cell could be removed from the ship without risking the safety of the person or persons inside.

USING *EUPHRATES*'S SCHEMATICS, CALCULATE THE LOCATION OF THE SHELTER ON THE STARBOARD SIDE, DECK 113, NEAR THE ENGINE ROOM, Brazil typed.

The ship did as commanded.

APPLY MANEUVERING THRUSTERS UNTIL THE CARGO BAY IS ALIGNED DIRECTLY WITH THE SHELTER.

Once lined up, *Stehekin* backed slowly up to press against the *Euphrates's* hull. Brazil donned his vac suit and pulled up floor plates until he revealed a large plasma cutter, which might have been modified outside Fed standards *and* actually would be considered illegal if ever discovered during an inspection. Brazil cut the gravity in the bay and picked up the saw. Carefully, he carved a large rectangle in the hull he hoped was the right shape to accomplish his plan. When done, he backed his ship up to let the shell drift free.

As predicted, Brazil could see across the interior of the transport all the way to the back of the emergency shelter. Like Ortega's crewmate's cell, the shelter had been magnetically sealed to keep whomever was inside from falling into space. Using the small propulsion pack on his suit, Brazil kicked off from the bay and swam over to *Euphrates* carrying a mag-cable. He attached the cable to the shelter and called to the coordinator over the network.

"Hey, tell those people in … ." He looked for some sort of marker. "Shelter 113-24 to hold on tight. It's a jailbreak!"

"Wait? What?"

"Just do it!"

Nathan floated back to his ship, gave his computer instructions on the amount of thrust they would need, and secured himself to a chair in the bay. This would either work, or he'd be responsible for the deaths of more innocent people.

The shelter slipped from the transport like pulling a thumb from a toddler's mouth. As they pulled away, the cube trailed behind them until they were well and clear of *Euphrates*. Brazil set the cable to reel in the shelter until it snugged into the bay, then he closed the doors and returned gravity to normal.

The shelter landed with a small metallic thud. Stepping over to the terminal outside its hatch, Brazil punched in a code given to him by the coordinator to drop the magnetic shield. Unseen to his naked eye, but felt through the hairs on his arm, Brazil felt the shield turn off.

He reached for the shelter's handle and pulled.

A cruiser the size of *Euphrates* normally had shelters that allowed for an equal number of passengers to fit inside, somewhere around thirty people.

Brazil raised an eyebrow in surprise. He found only ten people strapped in.

And a large stasis pod, which took up most of the rest of the space.

As one, they turned to stare at him, surprised that he wasn't a member of the Fed or even the Com. He knew what they saw: a small, thin man with brown-gold skin that suggested Old Earth Mediterranean heritage.

His Roman nose hung above a scraggly mustache and beard. Completing the image of a space-weary captain, he hadn't had time for a haircut in … well, years.

Brazil understood the disappointment on their faces. He had that same look in the mirror every day.

"Welcome aboard. I'm Captain Brazil, and you're safely aboard my freighter, *Stehekin*. Let's see if we can get you home. Anyone hurt?"

Other than shaken up, everyone inside seemed fine. Brazil stepped aside and motioned for them to come out. "I have enough staterooms for each of you. I actually expected more survivors."

Eight of the survivors turned to the nineth, who lifted a defiant chin.

"That would be my doing," said the woman wearing some sort of private security company uniform. She spoke with authority. "I'm a Confederation organ courier with a sworn duty to see my charge survive." She was tall and well-built, and Brazil doubted that she only did courier work considering she packed a weapon on her hip and probably had other weapons hidden on her tightly-wound body.

That started a round of accusations and insults, except for one woman, with bright red hair, who sat quietly, not joining the verbal tirade. Brazil focused on her, recognizing the signs of a broken loner. Slight and severe-looking in appearance, her passive posture and lowered head told him more than any question he could ask her. Hollow, brown eyes sought answers in a tragic past, and her chestnut-brown hair was in worse shape than his. He'd studied humans for such a long time, he rarely needed to talk to them to know their stories. At least, in part.

This woman hadn't wanted to be rescued.

Brazil quieted the cacophony. "Let's get you to your rooms. I'll need to report a manifest to the coordinator, so please give me your names as you exit the shelter."

The first strode out with an air of privilege.

"My name is Bennitt Grimbel, from Torus Electra, and I wish to protest these conditions. My man, Gerris, and I were waiting escort to the Confederation Battleship *Ukupanipo* when he shoved me into this shelter. Where is he? I wish to have words with him."

Brazil pointed to a portal looking out at the debris around the *Euphrates*.

"I think he's already been admonished enough for saving your life."

Grimbel swallowed hard, his eyes brimming at the edges. "No … Gerris …" he whispered and said nothing more. Brazil pointed him to a room he could recover in.

Next came a young woman of Hispanic origin, her head halfcovered in bloody bandages.

18

"Wow. Let's get you to the med bay."

But she waved it off. "It's superficial. I'll just clean up in my room."

Brazil insisted, but she stood her ground.

"Okay, Miss …?"

"Dina. Dina Ramos." She moved smoothly past Brazil and down the corridor, then vanished into the first stateroom on the right, and closed the hatch behind her.

"Well, then. Next?"

A lovely girl dressed in an outfit that reminded him of the late 2060s on Earth tentatively stepped out. "Um, is there any way you could *not* report me being here?" she asked, her voice and eyes pleading with Brazil.

"Whatever for?"

Brazil could not help but notice the deep soulful eyes of the teenager, and the way they pleaded with him. Her anxiety didn't match the confidence the dress—or lack of—was meant to imply, so Brazil figured her fashion was not her choice. Maybe no choice had ever been.

"I have nothing to go back to," she told him, clearly lying.

He understood the need to run from complicated relationships. Brazil had made friends of a couple—husband and wife—on Harvic's World, before it fell to the Com, and he'd been given a godchild to raise when the planet finally did. He could've taken the child on, a girl, but he didn't want to feel that close to another being ever again. He'd outlive her, feel that sting of her eventual death before closing himself off for another few centuries. Better that she go with someone who could protect her emotionally, as well as physically. Someone to teach her self-reliance and pain of life in a way he, being part of that equation, could not.

Brazil hoped wherever Marva Chiang had ended up, she was happier than he was.

"What should I call you?"

The girl paused, thought hard, and answered, "Lita. Just Lita."

"Okay, 'Just Lita.'" He winked. "Grab a room, and I'll check on you in a bit."

"Hi," said a young man exuberantly, and offered his hand. "I'm Jared Stencil."

He reminded Brazil of a stockbroker from Earth in the 1980s, back when it was in vogue to steal money and do lots of drugs. Jared's eyes darted around, scanning the cargo bay, Brazil, and everything else, as if he wanted to suss the situation to see if everything was as Brazil had said. Satisfied with whatever he saw, he nodded.

"Everything okay?" Brazil asked.

Jared nodded. "It is. You're alone on this freighter then?"

19

"Certainly."

"And do you own it, or does a third-party company?"

Brazil cocked his head. "It's sort of like a lease from the Confederacy's Department of Interstellar Shipping. Maybe I'll pay it off one day."

He could've paid it off centuries ago, but Brazil chose to "die" every hundred or so years, even though with the current success of rejuves, he could've played himself a lot longer. After dying, he'd pass along his debt to a relative who'd then assume it and pay just the minimum, accruing years of interest and thus increasing the debt. Having debt was the great equalizer. Everyone has it in some form, balancing the universe. People treated you like one of their own when you had bills to pay.

The answer satisfied Jared, who found a stateroom and slid into it.

With the next survivor, Brazil first took the odd contraption hanging on the man's chest to be some sort of respirator as they huddled in the back of the shelter, but as he … they, stepped forward into the light, he recognized the harness he wore wasn't a device, but a dog!

The corgi looked directly at Brazil, even though its owner refused to.

Brazil cocked an eyebrow. "I don't have a dog walk aboard. Hopefully, it's ship-trained?"

"Back off …" came the digitized, male voice emanating from the dog itself. "I will … piss on your leg … if you … insult me … or Conrad … again."

Conrad, who must be the dog's owner, managed to look both embarrassed and pleased at the same time, with a blush to his cheeks and a slight smirk to his lips.

"Randolf is special," Conrad explained, still looking at the floor. "Augmented intelligence and communicative abilities."

Brazil nodded. "I can see, well, and hear that."

Conrad unbuckled the canine from the harness and set him on the floor. The corgi barely came up to Brazil's knees, and he was small for a human. Conrad reached down and hooked a leash to Randolf's vocator collar, though Brazil thought it unnecessary.

Where was the dog to run off to on a ship this size?

Randolf, still eyeing the Captain with suspicion, spoke for himself, "I can take … myself to *the potty* … though nothing … I could do … would make this … ship smell worse."

That time Conrad did lean closer and, in a loud whisper said, "Randolf. This man just saved our lives. Can you be kind?"

Voice modulated lower, the small animal answered, "If he is kind … to you." Holding his head up defiantly, he continued, "I do not really … care what he thinks … of me."

20

Neither he nor Conrad believed that, the Captain surmised.

Brazil understood the dynamic now. Randolf was an advanced form of an Old Earth therapy or support companion. He knew some planets still employed such methods of treatment. Not on Com worlds though. They brainwashed all atypical thinking or emotions out of their citizens. At least, that's what they said on "paper." He knew more than one Com clone who hadn't had their mental challenges erased, just suppressed.

The Captain bowed slightly at the waist and, with a wry grin, said, "My apologies. You are both welcome aboard my ship, and I'll see if I can throw some fresh filters into the environmental systems to help with that smell."

When it came time for the broken woman, Brazil offered her a hand, which she reluctantly took, and walked through the hatch. She released his hand immediately and just stood there.

"Name?"

"Elida Silduun."

The Captain bowed again at his waist. "It's an honor to have rescued you, Miss Silduun."

But she would have none of his charm. "Which room is mine?"

Seeing conversation wouldn't be happening at the moment, Brazil escorted her to a stateroom, opened the hatch for her, and closed it after she entered.

Brazil turned around and discovered a young man, dressed in the uniform of the cruise liner's staff, standing practically behind him. Brazil—who took pride in not being snuck up on—started. "Yikes! Where did you come from?"

The young man shrugged. He had blond hair and a nose that looked to have been repeatedly broken and set poorly, giving it the impression of a lumpy radish.

"Willem Trake," he said quickly. Too quickly. "I'm a floor maintenance engineer."

Brazil did a quick head count. With Trake, that actually made nine in the shelter, not eight as he first inventoried. That sent the hairs on the back of his next tingling.

"A janitor, huh? That's a job I've done before and will probably do again."

Trake grinned. "I'm more than willing help, if you need an extra hand."

Brazil made note of Trake's eagerness. "Nothing really to be done. Ship takes care of itself, mostly. Why don't you take room 4? I'll let you know when we prep to land at the nearest station."

Nodding once, briefly, Trake went to his room without further comment.

Brazil decided that the strange youth needed following up on later.

That just left three: the courier and a man carrying a small boy. The boy seemed to be asleep, or maybe …

Brazil stepped over and felt the boy's cheek. Still warm. Brazil breathed a sigh of relief.

"Your son?" Brazil asked.

The man nodded. "I don't know what happened. He passed out during the raid. He … well, he didn't hit his head or anything."

Brazil grabbed a med scanner and ran it over the child. "What's his name?"

"Thorn. I'm Alyss."

"Is … was his mother also onboard?"

Alyss shook his head.

Brazil looked at the readings. "He seems to be perfectly fine, except he's in a coma. Something must have given his system a shock, and his brain chose to protect him. Electricity?"

Again, Alyss said no. "This type of thing, he's either going to wake or not. Could be in five minutes, could be in five years. What do you want to do?"

The father looked down at his son and back at the Captain. "I think … . I think I just want to hold him. If there's nothing you have onboard that will fix him … that is."

Brazil shrugged. "This isn't a rescue ship. It's just a freighter pretending to be one. You'll be comfortable enough in one of the rooms. Probably better than hooking him up to a bunch of monitors in the med bay."

Alyss nodded and Brazil assigned them a room.

When they had all entered their temporary quarters, Brazil stepped into the shelter and walked to where the courier had not budged from the stasis pod.

"And what's going on here?"

The woman drew a datapad and handed it over to him. "You'll see that I have all the proper clearances for transporting human remains in cryogenic stasis, Captain."

Brazil scrolled through it, not bothering to read anything but the name that signed off on it. "Councilor G'Tchen Muskamin? Even I've heard of her, and I don't do politics."

The courier nodded. "She's the head of the council that directly oversees the Department of Interstellar Travel, so it's expected that you would've."

Brazil tsk'd. "What happened to her?"

When she spoke, her explanation felt rehearsed, like a script that everyone had agreed to beforehand. "Councilperson Muskamin was poisoned at a charity function by whom we believe were anti-Com sympathizers. While she remains alive, the damage to her internal organs was intense, and she's in immediate need of a transplant."

Placing his hand to his chin, Brazil questioned, "Why haven't we heard anything about this over the newsfeed?"

Again, the courier gave a clichéd reply. "We are keeping the news from the media as Confederation security does their investigation. We don't want the terrorists to know how close they got."

"And the donor?"

The courier tried to look sympathetic, but her guarded persona didn't sell the words. "Poor thing. Young girl on a farming world fell off a tractor. Most of her was crushed, but her torso remained remarkably intact. A tragic, yet miraculous, situation."

Brazil nodded. "Yes, miraculous, indeed."

If there was a god above him and the Markovians, he doubted they worked in such ways. A god who would kill a girl with her whole future ahead of her to save a politician who'd probably sold her soul to the Com wasn't a god he'd ever want to meet, but then, Brazil had made difficult and tragic choices in his job, too. So, maybe he should go easy on the old deity, if there was actually one listening … which he doubted … but he also couldn't completely rule it out.

The courier studied him closely, gauging, he assumed, if he was buying her story. Brazil had little doubt that she could seize the ship without much effort, jettison their bodies, and pilot his ship to wherever Muskamin waited.

So, Brazil played along.

For now.

"Would you like to move the donor to the med bay so you can keep her frosty in there and not rely solely on the unit's power?"

The courier decided that was acceptable, so together they pushed the hovering pod to the *Stehekin*'s medical unit, where Brazil hooked it up to the ship's power. The woman then refused a room, saying she would be fine waiting next to the donor until such time as they arrived at their destination.

Brazil didn't think it was fine but chose not to argue the point. The body wasn't going anywhere, so why all the need for such security?

He returned to his captain's chair and pondered the mess he'd picked up. Did any one of them actually tell him the truth about anything? What had really happened on the luxury liner that drew these ten together?

23

And would there be problems he'd have to take steps to resolve before they arrived at their destination?

Brazil didn't think he had *good* answers for any of those questions.

The Confederation reviewed all video logs from every cargo freighter upon arrival to its destination. This was to keep the captains honest and establish who got the best assignments. Pilots who slept the whole trip were more likely to miss flight errors; the ones who didn't showed signs of space madness and were more likely to send their hauler into a sun. The Feds also recorded the staterooms, unbeknownst to the passengers, in case of illegal activities, the hijacking of the ship, or to later run facial recognition against a database of wanted terrorists. That feed couldn't be accessed by the captain for legal reasons, thus, Brazil couldn't spy on his passengers himself without a damn good—and semilegal—reason. Luckily, he'd had time to come up with ones the computer accepted.

He typed, SUSPECTED MENTAL TRAUMA IN RESCUED PASSENGERS THAT COULD LEAD TO SELF-HARM. SHOW ME CABINS 1, 2, 4, 5, 9, 11, 12, AND MED BAY.

The computer did as ordered, showing each room in order, making a note in the ship's log about the emergency request. He'd put Elida closest to the bridge, in case she decided to do something drastic to injure herself or others. She didn't sleep, despite all the events of the cruiser. She just sat at the edge of the bunk, staring into space, as if replaying some horrible event. Her occasional blinking was the only tell she was still alive. She posed no threat to herself, or anyone else, at the moment.

Grimbel paced like a trapped rat, nervous about being disconnected from the privilege he'd been raised in. He talked to himself, and Brazil couldn't help but turn up the volume to eavesdrop.

"Why, Gerris? Why'd you do it?" Grimbel spun. "I mean, not that I don't thank you, but really? Giving up your life for *me?*"

He paused. "And Father … you traded Mom's world to the Com for a piece of the sponge business? I'm the son of a drug lord?" Grimbel punched the air. "Dammit!"

That triggered Brazil to check in on Alyss and Thorn. The boy lay on a bunk, and the father had pulled up a chair. He held his hand and looked lost. Nothing to be done there, Brazil moved on.

Cabin 5 revealed very little about Jared. He lay on his bed, propped up on pillows, working on a datapad, and humming quietly to himself. Of all the passengers, Brazil thought he looked the happiest at the turn of the events. Not like he'd had something to do with them; he was too calm.

No, he appeared content, like a detour to an out-of-the-way planet wasn't the worst thing that could've happened to him.

Jared dictated into the recording app: "So far, no sign of Messier. Don't think he had anything to do with the sabotage. Looks to be anti-Com terrorists. That's another bullet dodged." He grinned, pleased with himself. "When the bulkhead erupted, I ran for the nearest shelter and barely got in. I managed to grab a lady who was walking toward the end of the hallway *toward* the tear." He puffed up like a peacock. "I don't know if she'd hit her head, or what, but I yanked her through the hatch with me just as it sealed, and we were all stuck there." Pursing his lips, Jared sadly said, "She never thanked me. I wonder if I should tell the Captain? She might have a concussion." He ruminated. "Nah, better to keep a low profile. He doesn't seem to be working for Messier, but I can't afford to be given attention, or praise, or even an award, for saving someone's life, grateful or not."

That explained a lot to Brazil, so he moved on.

Room 4 held the mysterious Willem Trake.

PAUSE. DO A FACIAL RECOGNITION SCAN OF THE OCCUPANT IN ROOM 4.

The computer replied that the subject showed signs of having had rejuve surgery on his face.

DECONSTRUCT AND RUN ACROSS CONFEDERATION NEWS FOR MATCH.

It took the computer a bit to complete the task.

"Calum Brach, huh?" Ship's captains, such as Brazil, regularly received alerts regarding missing people of importance. Brach was one that'd come across his feed nearly five years ago. The rich playboy vanished without a trace and became the talk of scuttlebutt at the various waterholes Brazil frequented because of the award attached to any tips to his whereabouts. Money didn't matter to Brazil, and he certainly understood what it was like to be on the run from your past. His only concern was if some sort of harm came to the youth. Transformed as he was, Brach had not been kidnapped by anyone but himself.

Brazil twirled it around in his mind. Maybe he would talk to the lad before they docked and see what he could do to help.

The camera went to the med bay next. The organ courier sat on a bench next to her charge. Brazil studied her, and the more he did, the more something didn't smell right about the story she spun earlier. Council members didn't normally have the type of pull to order replacement organs from across the galaxy.

PAUSE. BRING UP CURRENT IMAGES OF G'TCHEN MUSKAMIN.

Several pictures of the middle-aged woman appeared from different Confederation meetings and public appearances on various planets over the last several months. Brazil made an appreciative sound, as Muskamin looked good for an older woman.

"Well, I wonder how grateful she'll be when I deliver her lifesaving organs." He'd promised himself he'd stay away from younger women, but considering *every* woman was younger than him, it was more like a guideline than a rule.

He typed, HOW OLD IS G'TCHEN MUSKAMIN?

The answer made him whistle. Then it made him worried.

SHOW ME IMAGES OF G'TCHEN MUSKAMIN START-ING LAST YEAR AND GOING BACK EIGHTY YEARS.

It didn't take Brazil long to figure out why Muskamin stayed so young looking. It wasn't rejuves, which were more like microsurgeries to repair any failing body parts, from skin to major organs, mostly done by nano-tech. To someone who only saw her occasionally, they may not notice the specific changes, but as the images turned back time, Brazil witnessed a councilperson who sought immortality piece by piece. He growled because that meant the donor in his med bay was most likely not a willing participant, nor some random farm girl caught in a combine.

Cloning, in practice, was not illegal on most Fed worlds, and actually promoted in the Com, but there was a stigma attached to it, like plastic surgery on Old Earth. Any cloning for personal use was regulated by the Feds under the strictest guidelines and only used in cases of emergency. Brazil didn't think a tummy tuck and removal of flabby arms would be considered lifesaving procedures. He was sure now that there was no assassination attempt and that the body in stasis was actually a healthier version of Muskamin heading for final dissection.

He would have to do something about that, but he wasn't sure what, yet.

RESUME OBSERVATION OF CABINS.

When the computer brought up cabin 11, though, the screen was black.

RUN A DIAGNOSTIC. IS THE CAMERA WORKING?

After a moment, the computer replied:

THE CAMERA HAS BEEN DISABLED BY THE PASSEN-GER IN CABIN 11. A REPORT HAS BEEN MADE TO CON-FEDERATION SECURITY. PER CONFEDERATION LAW, NO PERSON MAY TAMPER WITH, DISABLE, OR DESTROY ANY RECORDING DEVICE INSTALLED IN ANY SPACE TRAN—"

Brazil stopped reading. He'd pegged Dina Ramos as a hardened fighter, but now he wondered if she was more than that.

He finally got a message to drop his passengers off at the Delarara Station, only a twelve-hour trip from where they were. He informed his passengers by intercom, not sure yet if he should confront Ramos about the sabotaged camera feed. If he waited until closer to arrival, he could theoretically trap her in her stateroom and turn her over to Confederation security upon docking.

Brazil typed a message. WARNING TO CONFEDERATION SECURITY ON DELARARA STATION: POSSIBLE ANTI-COM TERRORIST ABOARD. MAY BE RESPONSIBLE FOR EVENTS ON *EUPHRATES*. REQUEST INSTRUCTIONS. USING THE NAME DINA R—

The screen went blank. He tried typing again, with no results.

DIAGNOSIS.

COMMUNICATION ARRAY OFFLINE.

WHERE IS THE FAULT?

The onboard computer gave him a location back near the engine room. Brazil swiveled his chair around and made his way aft. He crawled down a ladder to where the array hung on the wall. Or, at least where it used to. Remnants of it lay scattered on the floor plating. Whoever did it did a thorough enough job as to make it near-impossible to repair. Brazil could spend the next twelve hours fixing it, which might be what they wanted, so they could seize control of the ship.

Brazil did a quick scan of the navigation array and, finding it un-tampered with, figured the culprit wanted to see his reaction to the communication disconnect before moving to stage two.

Would he tell the passengers?

Would he accuse any of them?

Would he lock them in their rooms?

He had no doubt that if he did lock the saboteur in, they had already figured a way out. He didn't have any special security installed. Maybe he should consider that in the future. However, what *they* hadn't counted on was that Brazil knew this game; played it for centuries. It was like sending a chicken into the fox house. He'd tear them apart before he'd let them hurt another person.

To start, he disabled navigation himself. This would've normally triggered an alert to the Feds, but with communications out, his ship would just scream voiceless into the void. They were already on trajectory, and inertia would keep them going in the same direction.

Next, he rerouted thrusters over to a remote device he kept in case he had to work outside the ship. No sense in letting them get control of those.

Finally, he rigged a deadman's switch, which Brazil always thought of as amusing since he couldn't die. Everything short of, but his heart would never fully stop. Many had tried, but the Well always found a way to keep his consciousness alive, sometimes without it connected to his body.

This switch would instead monitor his pain levels, and if he reached a certain state of torture, the ship would go dark. Everything would shut off save for life support. No heat. No engines. No thrusters. No communications, even if repaired. The refresher wouldn't work, and that's what usually got them in the end. When the shit got really deep.

Secure that no one was going to take the ship away from him now, Brazil climbed back up the ladder and waited for their next move.

When Brazil returned to the command deck, the warning klaxon reverberated through the ship once again. He had not disabled the sensors, since he might need to know if a Fed or Com ship flew out to meet them.

Or worse, the terrorist's friends, which is what Brazil hoped would not happen. He had no plan that countered a boarding party.

He shut it off and awaited the readout.

SUBSPACE ANOMALY DETECTED. COURSE CORRECTED.

Brazil pulled up the readings and cursed. "You've got to be kidding me!"

What he found was not a passing ship, but the worst form of karma he'd ever encountered.

Since returning to real space about a hundred years ago, Brazil had been on the run from the thing he feared more than anything else in the known universe. Now, it'd found him … and with a bunch of unprepared passengers aboard. His last trip to the Well, as with now, he'd brought a bunch of strangers along. But that'd been accidental, he having erased the painful memories of his past and his responsibilities. Brazil believed the Well had intentionally drawn him in to remind him of his duty. The Well wasn't sentient, per se, but close enough. It had a malicious sense of humor.

His "master" had made use of his amnesiac arrival and put him through hell before he finally remembered everything. Then, job finished, it dumped him back into the universe. Upon exiting, he adjusted a few things to make sure he'd never forget who he was again. He'd accept the guilt, responsibility, and paranoia for however long it'd take to find someone to replace him.

Brazil reminded himself that it wasn't paranoia when something *was* actually out to get you.

Here and now, the Well of Souls had caught up to him, and he'd have to respond.

How did a Markovian gate end up floating in space unattached to a planet or asteroid or anything?

Markovian gates couldn't be destroyed under any circumstance since they weren't made of the same matter as the rest of the universe. A two-kilometer hexagon, the color of the absence of light, hung in space like a portrait on a wall, and yet invisible to the naked eye. Brazil, though, had modified his sensors to warn him of any planet containing one. If he could help it, Brazil didn't ever want to step through one again, but the truth was, someday, he knew he would.

Brazil checked the star charts and discovered this gate had probably been on Dubpra b, which no longer appeared on any scans. A few dozen light-years away, though, a small asteroid field existed that didn't appear on the charts. It had about the right amount of material to match Dubpra b.

"Did you do this?" he asked the Well, knowing the computer couldn't answer, and wouldn't admit to it even if it could.

Nothing seemed to be going wrong on a universal scale that he felt needed to be fixed, but then he'd only been playing in a small part of it. He had an instinct about when reality-level threats happened, but other than the Com, nothing really threatened any civilization, corrupt as they were.

Then an idea crept into the dark part of his brain, the one he never listened to unless he'd been alone for too long. The gates often activated for a person who was at the end of their ability to deal with life. It was a way for the ancient creators of the universe to return to the Well and reboot. The Markovians. The evolved beings that had reached the pinnacle of life; gods whose every thought would be instantly made real. Bored deities who found that having everything didn't make one happy. So, they started over.

Had the Well detected someone on the ship needed that second chance? Maybe it wasn't here for him, but for one of his passengers. He could drop that person into the gate and not have to go through a journey to Well World again.

But which one?

There was no way to know for sure, so he'd just have to drop them all into the gate.

"Nonononono." Brazil leaned back, shaking the thought from his head. "Last time, those unfortunate souls were dragged through by accident. I'll have to give them the choice this time."

Brazil knew, however, none of them would choose to spend the rest of their lives on Well World, especially after what it would do to them.

He assessed the passengers, realizing that almost any of them could have triggered the gate. All save for one.

Mind set and jaw locked, Brazil worked out a plan.

This time, Brazil didn't silence the alarm gong.

One by one, his charges stuck their heads out of their rooms. Once again, Randolf was in the chest carrier, tiny paws flopping in the air as Conrad moved them quickly back to the hanger bay. This time, Brazil was acutely aware of Trake/Calum and noticed that the young man was just good at not being paid attention to. Nothing mystical or science-y allowed Trake to be actually invisible.

"What's going on now?" Grimbel asked, obviously perturbed.

The others echoed the question.

Brazil wore a worried expression. "When I pulled you from the *Euphrates*, my ship was damaged. Life support is failing."

Chaos erupted among most of the people, except for Elida, who looked relieved.

"What are we going to do?" the organ courier demanded. "I need to get this donor to Valloa Prime or Councilperson Muskamin is going to die." She bared her teeth, as if Brazil could just stop them all from dying with a thought. *If only she knew.* "We've already been delayed so much." Behind her angry eyes, Brazil found something else. Anxiety. He recognized it to be for her life, though, not Muskamin's.

"I can fix it, but I'm going to have to cut all life support." He sold the lie like a slight-of-hand con man. "I only have one vac suit, so I'm going to need you all to get back in the shelter, which has its own system, until I repair the *Stehekin*."

There was moaning, but Brazil continued the ruse until they all marched back into the cargo bay and returned to the box they'd arrived in. Dina Ramos gave Brazil serious side-eye, searching him for duplicity. Brazil spent too many lifetimes learning how to be whatever was needed in a moment, and he sold the act until she, too, stepped into the shelter.

Brazil went to the med bay with the courier to retrieve her stasis pod. Since it had antigrav lifts, she could've moved it herself, but Brazil offered to help guide it into the shelter.

"Thank yo—"

The tranq gun put her out instantly. Brazil moved her to a bench, then piloted the pod to the shelter.

"Where's that lady?" Ramos asked, immediately on guard.

"Refresher," Brazil lied. "Don't know how long it's going to be.

Grimbel said he wanted to use it, too, but Brazil just told him to "hold it."

Pod in place, Brazil stepped out through the hatch and smiled. "Don't worry. You all will be on your way shortly."

"Wai—" Grimbel shouted, just as Brazil slammed the hatch shut.

Brazil had no way of knowing what the reaction was inside the shelter when they realized he'd tricked them and they were being offloaded again. He imagined a lot of cursing, pounding on the hatch, empty threats, and so forth.

If Brazil was right, the gate would activate when the emergency shelter got close to it, and if he wasn't needed on Well World, then it would go inactive afterward. If it stayed open, then he would follow them and find out what the Well of Souls wanted with him.

The shelter drifted into the gate's field, then faded from existence.

Brazil held his breath.

The gate went inert, and he sighed in relief.

Returning to the med bay, he used a stim gun to wake the courier.

She shot up, immediately scanned the room, then put her hand around Brazil's throat.

"Where is she?"

Gasping, Brazil managed, "Where … Muskamin can't … part her … out … any … more."

The courier stumbled back. "What have you done?"

Rubbing his bruised neck, Brazil said, "Cloning people for body parts is just as wrong as what the Com is doing." He pointed at her and growled. "Muskamin's quest for immortality takes away choice just the same as manufacturing a perfect society does."

"ARRGH! Who are you to decide that? You've sentenced a woman to death."

"Wouldn't be the first time, but I assume there are other clones? How many more?"

The courier crossed her arms and said nothing.

Regaining his composure, Brazil matched her posture. "The way I see it, there are two paths we can take. Everything on the ship is recorded, including this conversation, including the scans I made of that clone. I can release all of this to the Feds or a news agency, and Muskamin's rep will be ruined."

Raising her eyebrow, the courier asked, "Or?"

"Or … you can answer my question."

Sighing, she admitted, "Two more, but they aren't ready yet for harvest."

The word *harvest* made Brazil cringe.

And then she relaxed her guard, releasing her anger, and gave Brazil the truth.

"The Councilor was slipped sponge. The syndicate wanted to use her as a puppet, but she found a work-around. A geneticist created a way to pool the sponge in certain parts of her body, which she then replaces."

Brazil had never heard of a treatment like that, but where there was a will and lots of money, there was a way.

"The drug takes years to build up again, which is when Muskamin repeats the process."

While Brazil had some sympathy for Muskamin's plight, he still didn't agree with the tactics she employed. He shook his head. "It doesn't matter. Someday, the syndicate will either dose her again, kill her outright, or her luck will run out. Meanwhile, how many defenseless clones will be no more than spare parts?" He looked the courier directly in her eyes, imploring, "What type of life is that for any person?" Brazil could tell her resolve had weakened, so he pressed on. "You're going to take me to the facility where they're being grown and help me sneak in."

The courier cocked her head. "Whatever for?"

Brazil turned around and hot-stepped toward the bridge. "We're going to destroy all of Muskamin's DNA material, then free those two girls so they have a chance at a real life, not just one of being dissected a piece at a time."

Not moving at first, she called after him. "And if I don't go along with this plan?"

"I have one vac suit and unlimited time. You can just hang outside the ship until you change your mind."

The courier, who Brazil later learned was named Alexis, capitulated and joined him on the bridge.

Chapter Two:
SOUTH POLAR ZONE, THE WELL WORLD
David Boop

In his office, Serge Ortega rested on his long tail, reading reports. They were spread all over his U-shaped desk. He needed no chair; his serpentine body worked fine for that. The words on the page, translated for his understanding, came from Umaiu, whose inhabitants were once again having problems with their neighbors, the Pia. The Pia, floating brains with big eyes and ten tentacles, hated the Umaiu with a passion. The Umaiu, Ortega recalled, were possibly what inspired the Old Earth legend of mermaids. Both water hex races shared space in the Overdark Ocean, and despite warnings going back as long as Ortega had been Ulik ambassador for the Southern Zone, sailors tried to slip through the Pia's hex quietly, only to incur their wrath each time. The high-tech hexes of Czill and The Nation often worked together on large mathematical problems, sending representatives back and forth across the sea. While Umaiu was the nonviolent, direct route, their hex had frequent, severe storms. Pia tended to be smoother sailing, though a longer journey. The Umaiu hired themselves out as guides and protectors for the various shipping companies, which angered the Pia to the point of war.

Ortega rubbed his thick, bushy eyebrows with one of his six hands while pressing his communicator with another.

"Is the Umaiuan ambassador in?"

The Ulik female who acted as his assistant that month replied, "Yes, sir."

There was no reason to ask if anyone was in the Pai's office. They'd never sent an ambassador to Zone.

"Tell them to come to my office later today. I hate to say it, but they're going to have to stop hiring themselves out. I know it'll cut into their economy, but until these attacks from Pia slow down, we can't risk them starting a war."

"Yessir," the woman said, and rung off.

Ortega's equally bushy mustache twitched, he dreaded the impending argument he'd have with the merpeople. He'd tried as much as he could to avoid direct confrontations in the centuries since his arrival to Well World. And having lived so long, he knew exactly what to do to achieve that under most circumstances. He kept a network of spies through most of the 780 southern hexes, and even a few to the north. Ortega had acquired enough blackmail material to get most leaders of a hex to bend to his will, and where he couldn't, he arranged for a "transfer of power" to someone more open to the Ulik's point of view.

The box on his desk buzzed. "What? Already get a reply?"

"No," the assistant said with concern in her voice. "Entries, sir."

And here Ortega thought averting a war would be the toughest thing he'd do that day.

Nine humans from the Confederation sat in a semicircle in Ortega's office, though one, a small child, was asleep in what could be his father's arms. Another hovered in a stasis pod at the back. The awake ones were confused, which was nothing new. Rarely did any Entry have an understanding of what had just happened to them.

One, a cocky kid, demanded answers, but Ortega had no doubt he wouldn't like them.

"My name is Serge Ortega, and once, a long, long time ago, I was as human as you are."

No surprise, a round of doubts and denials came.

"Many centuries ago, I was an old spacer working for the Fed when I stepped through a Markovian gate and ended up here."

"Centuries?" asked a calmer man, who introduced himself as Jared. "How can that be?"

Ortega laughed. "Oh, there are a few species on the Well World that can live to be older than that. My race is one."

And if the deal I'm making goes through, I'll still be alive long after all of you.

A female with skin tone similar to the one he'd had as a human challenged, "You said many species. You mean there are alien species here?"

"Well, to them, you'd be the aliens, but yes. All told, 1,560 species reside on the planet."

"Get out," another said, a young man Ortega didn't notice at first sitting in the corner. *How'd he gotten in here without me noticing?* "There's no way, mathematically, that many different sentient species could evolve on a planet naturally."

"That's because they didn't evolve naturally. They were created by the Markovians. We all were." Ortega waited for the expected din to stop. "Before I start from the beginning of time and catch you up to now, anyone hungry?"

Food suitable for humans arrived, and almost everyone dug in voraciously, save for one woman who just picked at her plate. When she ate, there was no joy in the act.

"Are you going to wake this kid to eat?" Ortega asked the older man, who'd forgone dinner and just sat in a chair with his son.

"He's not asleep. He's in some sort of self-induced coma. Thorn has always been … different. I'm hoping that this state is just part of that."

Not wanting to pry any further, the Ulik let the subject drop. Instead, Ortega lit a cigar with two hands and pointed at the stasis pod with another.

"What's the deal with that?"

The Hispanic female, who identified herself as Dina Ramos, shrugged. "We don't know. When we were rescued from the attacked cruiser, that came aboard our rescue ship with an escort."

"Courier," the quiet lady, Elida, said. She only gave her first name during introductions. "Organ courier. She's a donor for some councilperson who was dying." It was the most she'd spoken so far.

"So, the person in there is dead?"

No one knew for sure.

"So where's this courier now?"

Grimbel, the brash kid, answered, "No idea. Captain Brazil said she was using the refresher before he betrayed us."

"Brazil!?" Ortega reached into the secret panel under his desk and pulled out a pistol. "Nathan Brazil? Did he come with you? Tell me now if you want to live!"

The shock that rolled through the Entries resulted in spilled trays, and people falling out of chairs and scrambling to the back of the office. The only one who Ortega thought responded appropriately was Ramos, who dove to the side, rolled, and used the pod as cover.

"No," shouted Grimbel. "Like I said earlier, he tricked us back into the shelter then ejected us from his ship. He basically sent us here, and if I ever see him again, I'll have my father kill him."

"Oh," Ortega said, putting the gun away. "You won't see him again. Highly unlikely. There was a reason he sent you through the gate, but he won't show his face here again unless the Well calls him."

Grimbel, relaxing, brushed the front of his clothes. "My father is powerful, more powerful than I even knew. When I tell him about all this, he'll hunt that pirate across the universe."

Ortega sat back on his tail and puffed his cigar. "You don't understand. You're not going back. The Markovian gates are one way. There's no way back to the life you knew." He placed fingers in his flat ears and held up his others to silence the yelling. "If you'll let me explain, without interruption, it'll go faster."

So he went on to explain how the Markovians, the first beings in the universe, had evolved intellectually to the point they broke the code of reality.

"They built planet-sized computers that could materialize anything they dreamed up. Nothing was denied them. Every wish was fulfilled. And when you're given everything, well, you grow bored. Art. Invention. War. Even sex. They lost their joy in everything."

The Markovians figured they'd missed something in their evolution, so they decided to start again, but as new species. Many new species, Ortega explained to them, in hopes that one of their "children" would reach perfection, nirvana, and find true happiness that would be eternal this time.

"They built the Well World and tasked their greatest artists to use every twisted imagining they could dream up to create thousands of races. Then they dropped those species into hexes that had different environments, to see what types of conditions they could thrive in. They set up different tech levels, as well."

Jared asked, "So they created 1,560 species and what? Seeded the universe?"

Ortega shook his head. "Much more than that. They would fill all the hexes, seed planets, as you said, then start again. They did this tens of thousands of times, until the whole of the universe teemed with life."

The man called Trake whistled. Everyone except for the redhead and the woman of Hispanic descent seemed impressed.

Ramos questioned Ortega's logic. "Where are these gods now? Here? How did doing this help them solve their problem?"

The Ulik leaned forward, pointing his cigar at her. "That's the brilliance, or madness, of their plan. They turned off all their technology, leaving it inert, then devolved themselves to randomly become one of the species they created. The Markovians planned ahead, though. They made it so that if they didn't connect with the race they'd devolved to, they could come back to the Well World for a do-over. After reprocessing, some caught that species planetary seeding or, on rare occasion, snuck into another planet's seeding, thus creating some of the myths from Old Earth. But you only got one chance after your first. The gate wouldn't respond a second time.

"That's why," Ortega continued, "the gates respond to a desire to leave the prime universe behind. If Brazil found an activated gate, and it wasn't looking for him, it must have been triggered by one of you."

A very young girl with mischief and understanding in her eyes nodded. "So, that explains why we only see ruins on Markovian worlds and no relics. They're all gone and took their technology with them."

Serge pointed at her, smiling. "You get it. You can't evolve a new set of gods if you give them the old gods' tech."

"All gone. How could they just devolve and leave this place on autopilot?"

Ortega chuckled. "Well, all are gone, save for one. They needed someone to stay behind to make sure the computer, the Well, that maintains the whole of reality keeps running. A maintenance engineer. A Watcher."

"And he's here?"

"Nope." Ortega took a long pull of his cigar, letting irony flavor the smoke. "He's out there, in your galaxy, pretending to be one of you, living forever, hiding from the Well and his responsibilities. A god walking among men. You've already met him."

They all now understood why Ortega had freaked out at the name of their rescuer and betrayer.

"Yes, *that* Nathan Brazil."

Ortega let them rest for a while, having cots brought in for them to sleep, if they wanted. They hurt. They didn't understand why Brazil had pushed them through the gate without allowing them the choice. Ortega suspected, like an ancient tribal leader, Brazil had sacrificed them to the volcano to appease it.

To keep the awakened demon from claiming him instead.

The other possibility was that one of these people had triggered the gate, and Brazil didn't know which one, so he pushed them all through. Having spoken to them, they all had issues of some sort, whether spoken aloud or not. Serge wanted to give them time to adjust to what he'd already told them before he had to push them through a different gate, one that would change them permanently.

The greatest enigma was the stasis pod. Why would Brazil send a dead body through the gate? The Well of Souls was powerful, but he'd never seen it raise the dead. But then Brazil knew the system better than anyone, be he Markovian or not. He was the Watcher, after all.

Ortega slithered over to the pod. The torso of a young woman lay in state under the semifrosted glass. She had no limbs, seemingly surgically removed. Her head was shaved, but her eyebrows indicated she'd had dark hair once. Ortega thought it a shame.

Then he looked at the blinking controls and found a small digital line that had peaks and valleys.

"Well, I'll be damned!"

"What?" asked a couple of the Entries.

"This girl is still alive!"

They all gathered around the pod. Elida spotted a note inside it.

Ortega popped the lid and retrieved the note, addressed to him. "That old spacer summabitch."

He read them the note, quickly written:

Serge,

Sorry to drop these people on you. A gate activated, seeking one of them. I wasn't sure which, but my suspicion is it's this girl. She's a clone that was being processed as spare parts by some rich powermonger, and I felt her chances through the Well were better than a certain death.

"I was right," Ortega said under his breath.

To keep your life simple, I didn't come through with them. You probably remember what happened last time. Plus, as you know, I have my reasons.

The Entries made disgusted noises.

But the others aren't clean either. The one calling herself Dina Ramos is actually an anti-Com terrorist who was responsible for the sabotaged cruiser that dropped them all into my lap.

Five people turned as one to stare at Ramos, who backed up in a defensive posture. Then, faster than anyone could react, she ran to Serge's desk and pulled out the gun from the drawer he'd returned it to earlier. It was a simple enough design—point the small end, pull the trigger—that she had it aimed correctly and proficiently at Ortega instantly.

"Okay, now tell us the truth. How do we get home? I have … I have people who are counting on me."

Ortega sighed. "Go ahead. Shoot. It won't do you any good. That thing's coded to me. And if you, or any of you," he looked around the room, "came with any weapons other than a club, they won't work either."

Ramos tested his words by pulling the trigger. When nothing happened, she numbly let it drop. Serge understood that the reality of everything he'd told them since the beginning had finally hit her.

"What happens next?" asked Lita. "Are we going to be, as you said earlier about the Markovians, processed?"

The Ulik nodded. "Your life will begin again here. It's a chance to start over, to shed the weight of everything that held you down before." He looked at Elida. She had those hollow eyes he knew Brazil would've had a hard time resisting. Not sexually. Well, not at first, but Brazil had a well-known, and legitimate, god complex. He loved trying to save lost lambs. Too bad he wasn't really all that good at it.

"We'll stop being human?" asked Jared. "Will we look like you?"

"The prototype for humanity is here, but you don't want to be one of them. Centuries ago, they got into a nasty war with their large beaverlike neighbors called the Ambrezans. The furry bastards loosed a chemical into the air that turned all the humans into primitive idiots, then took over their hex. If you end up there, you'll end up stupider than a box of rocks."

A chill passed through the room, and as Ortega expected, the idea of ending up some sort of new species sounded better to the lot of them.

The one called Conrad was petting the top of his dog's head. The corgi sat patiently next to its master. Ortega learned that the human had been some sort of phenom programmer back in real space, but the pressure broke his mind until they'd paired him with Randolf, he thought the dog was called. Conrad reached down and pulled the dog into his lap, face to face. Randolf stood on his hind legs and tucked his head into the space between Conrad's chin and neck.

If Ortega didn't know better, the dog whispered something to its master.

"Will ... I mean, as far as you know, what effect will the Well have on an animal you put through?"

In all his years, he'd never considered that question.

"Well," he began, scratching his chin, "I mean, it's not like we've only had humans come through the gates. Many of the races on the Well World thrived out there, not all. And the gates are in every known part of the universe, so we've put other sentient species through these same gates, and they get randomly converted into something else, just the same as humans.

"But those were sentient species. I don't know if we've ever put a what? Animal companion through before? I could consult some records, but as long as your dog's not too smart ..."

39

That caused Conrad to rock back and forth and the corgi to howl. Tears flowed freely from both. "There's ... there's no way ... we get to stay together?" The rocking intensified, making the others in the room, and Ortega, nervous.

Figuring he had to say something, Ortega said, "Possibly there's a solution, but it's unlikely. See, the Well fills holes in hexes that have low populations and rarely sends more than one Entry to the same hex. If a hex is particularly low, it might send two there. That's happened before."

Conrad's rocking slowed. "Really?"

The Ulik nodded. "And the Well, truth be told, while not fully an AI, does have a mind of its own. Brazil always ends up in Glathriel, but with his full faculties, such as they are. So, the Well recognizes him. It's been known to choose the hex based on the Entry's hidden desires." The walrus head shook back and forth. "But it's not science. It's not even magical. It's chance. And luck."

That settled the duo down, and a glimmer of hope stopped their tears.

"So we will end up one of 1,560 aliens, then?" This from Jared. "That places the odds at ..."

"Not 1,560. Only any of the 760 carbon-based races here." Serge tried to be positive. He preferred to get these people through the Zone gate willingly. "And that diversity is unlike anything you can believe. You might be able to fly ..."

Lita grinned ear to ear. "I'd love that."

"Or be a water species ..."

Grimbel shuddered.

"You may even change sex, depending on the Well's determination of need."

That created another round of exclamations and refusals.

"Listen, you're going through whether you like it or not." Ortega slithered over to his desk and pressed a button that opened a different door than they'd come in through. "The question is, do you want to go now or after you've had a good night's sleep?"

Elida asked, "Will we remember who we were? Does it erase the past as well as our bodies?"

Sadly, Serge told her, "No. You'll be disorientated at first, but eventually you'll remember who you were, and what you were. You won't even lose Com basic, even though you'll be fluent in your new language." He tried to look reassuring, something he had been told many times he had no talent in. "I'll be honest, some hexes are horrible. And some even have what you've

40

been led to believe is magic from fairy tales, but the Well seems to choose your new race not only by statistics, but also by what you desire most."

"Really?" asked Jared. "You're not just saying that to get us through that door?"

Ortega shrugged all six shoulders. "That's what they tell me. So far, no one's ever come back for a refund, so there's that." He laughed in a way that suggested this was the end of his attempt at empathy. The strangers talked among themselves, then agreed to leave right then, except Ramos, who hung back.

"I'll wait."

Serge nodded and guided the rest through the doorway. A black Markovian gate waited there, still as void of color as when he'd been pushed through centuries earlier. One by one, they began to step through, with only Grimbel whimpering as he did so.

Next to step up was the father-son team.

"If I let him go through first, will he fall?"

Ortega shook his head. "No, he'll just wake up in his new body, wherever that is.

The man, Alyss he'd said, seemed happy. He stood the boy, Thorn, up next to the gate and gently pushed him through. He started to cry as he watched the boy be enveloped by the blackness of the gate.

He turned around to address Ortega. "Thank you. And if you should see Mr. Brazil, thank him as well. You've given Thorn a chance that he wouldn't have had under the Com. For that, I'm grateful."

Alyss reached into his pocket, pulled out something like a pill, and swallowed it. He collapsed right in front of the Ulik.

"What the ever lovin' …." The Ulik called for security and a doctor, but Alyss waved it away.

"I don't deserve … a second … chance." He exhaled his last breath and died.

Ramos stared down at the prone form. "It looks like he planned to do that from the beginning. No one just has a suicide pill in their pocket."

That sounded right to the old spacer. Whatever was going on with those two, why the boy was in a coma and why the father had planned to kill himself, he'd never know, nor did he care. He called for a cleanup in the gate room.

Conrad rocked back and forth, petting his dog reflexively. "We need to get out of here," he kept saying over and over. The dog nodded as if he understood. As Conrad held his companion close, the dog's head still on his chest, he prayed in a loud whisper, "Together. Together. Together."

And to Ortega's shock, the dog whispered along in a metallic voice, "together … together … together."

Baffled, Ortega then returned to his office.

"Why did you want to stay behind?"

Ramos, defeat clearly on her face, gestured to the stasis pod. "I attacked that ship looking for the woman who is the source of this clone." She looked down at the young girl's face. "I've lost everything because of her …. No, I lost a war because of *me*. She's my windmill."

Ortega burst into a wide smile. "Don Quixote, huh? And so you're going to what? Kill this clone before you leave?"

The terrorist shook her head. "No, I'm going to be the one to push her through that portal. It seems …. Well, it seems right."

Nodding, the Ulik let her do just that.

When they were all gone, he returned to his desk, looked down at the forgotten reports, and reached into his top drawer for a fresh cigar. He lit it and drew in a deep breath, letting the smoke fill his entire being, before exhaling.

"Damn you, Nathan Brazil. Damn you to hell."

Chapter Three:
IVROM:
THE WELL WORLD LOST
S.P. Somtow

vrom … ivrom … ivrom …

A memory.

A warm room in a wintry space.

Mia was his mother. Her voice was gentle, soft as a blanket on a cold night.

They galloped through the night, father and son, and the elf-king's daughter called to him … oh, father, father, don't you hear?

And in the warm room the winter conjured up.

"What's galloping?"

They were riding a horse.

"What's a horse?"

Something you ride, that runs swiftly on four legs, into the night.

"Like a teacher."

Yes, but not made of metal.

Thorn looked up from the bed. The warmth was from her eyes, not from the wind that shook the branches beyond the window. The moonlets hung in the night like bright baroque pearls.

"Why are you leaving?"

I have to, darling. It's conformity. It's more efficient. It brings us toward purity. At least, that's what they tell us.

"I don't want com-formity."

She laughed a little. *Com-formity*. A silly pun that he had heard from other children.

"Will you gallop away? On the back of an animal?"

You know they don't have animals anymore, my love.

"Except the storming insects. The ones that blow through the fields and eat everything in their path."

Yes.

"Sing me a song, mother. So I can remember you forever."

She sang. The moonlets shivered in the shimmering night.

Mia was his mother. Her voice was gentle, soft, and filled him with a sense of contentment, even though there weren't enough blankets, and the window was broken.

She sang to him of the ride through the forest and the song of the elf-king's daughter …

Dark is the dreaming, the song began, but he was already drifting into slumber.

Through darkness unfathomed, in the silence between the stars, they sat without speaking, riding a serpentine trail of light through a curtain of night that concealed more night.

Through the ordeal, Thorn clutched his parent's hand.

"You're not going to die," his parent, Alyss, said.

But Thorn knew better.

His world was being purified. The criteria of perfection were unyielding. And Thorn lived up to them all. He had beauty, as his world perceived beauty: his skin blue-black like a starless night, his eyes as purple as the hills when the twin suns set one behind the other. His intelligence, his analytic skills, his creativity were never in question. He was only lacking one thing …

But this congenital defect could mean imperfection, now that his world had fallen completely under the hegemony of the Com, and everyone was going to be made uniform.

"You're *not* going to die," Alyss said. "You *can't*. Whatever's there, it will save you, and it will bring you back to me."

But Thorn knew Alyss did not believe it. People who went to the Hill did not come back.

"To be pure," Thorn said, "is to be pure essence," echoing the words they now had to recite in the classroom every day. "To be essence is to be essentially pure." The words, in the language of an off-world society, made little sense, yet all young people knew them now, and most children with defects were happy and honored to contribute to the return of the world to the essential.

"Don't repeat things you don't even understand," his father said.

They emerged into normal space. Thorn saw, in the distance, the barren world they were headed to. It seemed an inoffensive planet. It had a ruddy, desert look about it. On this world was a place they called the Hill. The name came from a myth about the original homeworld, in which parents used to expose defective children on the side of a hill.

And the fairies would take them away.

"They'll take care of you," Thorn's parent said.

"You mean euthanasia," Thorn said.

"Where did you learn a word like that?"

"In purity class," Thorn said.

They sat in silence.

They were the only passengers in the private cabin. Theirs was not a cruel world, and the journey toward the inevitable end was not designed to be traumatic. It allowed the families to say goodbye, softening the pain, to travel in a luxury they could not normally afford.

Around them, the walls of the cabin had deopaqued to show a three-hundred-sixty degree view of space. The stars were not too different from the homeworld. They had traveled a mere two parsecs, hardly worth the expense of FTL. They had spared no expense. And Thorn's demise would be conveniently far away from their normal world.

Other cabins, no doubt, held other abnormals and their relatives, large families come to celebrate these last mournful moments. Thorn only had Alyss. And still, he clung to Alyss's hand.

As the world came nearer, Thorn heard the voice again.

A wail …

Alyss said, "You're doing it again."

… above the sighing sea …

"You don't hear that?"

Alyss sighed.

That was Thorn's imperfection. He saw and heard things that were not there.

That's what they called it, but they *were* there. The things he saw and heard existed somewhere *between*. It was natural to him and madness to others.

"What do you hear?" Alyss said.

"A high-pitched voice, calling to me over the sound of water."

"You always hear these things. They're not real."

"But it's different now. It's getting closer. Alyss, it's coming from the Hill."

"There's nothing but space between us and the Hill," Alyss said. "There can't be any sound."

And Alyss gave Thorn the "look." The look of frustration, outrage, and pity that he had become so used to. *This wouldn't have happened,* the look said, *if you'd only kept quiet.*

That was Thorn's handicap. His brain didn't process sound like other people. He wasn't deaf. He heard what everyone said, and everyone understood him, to a point—he tried to avoid saying complicated things with too many emotional subtleties. But there was so much *more* sound that he could hear. Tones within tones. Harmonies piled on harmonies. Sometimes these extraneous sounds were so painful he could not think straight. And sometimes they were beautiful, and that beauty was a kind of pain, too, because no one else could hear the music.

This was one of the beautiful times. He could *see* the melody, flitting across the close air of the ship's private cabin. The song had shape. It had color. It almost had—Thorn could almost hear words.

Come to me.

"It's calling me," Thorn said.

Thorn knew by now how this must seem to other people. His parent gave him the look again. He sighed. No doubt he was thinking: *A child lost in a private world.* Or mulling over some psychiatric term, perhaps, like *fugue* or *solipsistic withdrawal.*

The voice came again now, filling his world.

He almost let go of his parent's hand. Then he clutched harder. He was disoriented, afraid. He closed his eyes, afraid to look, imagining them hurtling toward the planet while inside, he felt only a kind of desolate stillness. He imagined the planet splintering, the stars scattering ... and himself the still center in a whirling universe.

Then—

"*Alyss!*" he screamed—

A voice: one everyone could hear now: *Anomaly. We are being intercepted. Abandon ship.*

Thorn screamed again and felt his parent's hand seemed to melt into emptiness—

Because his parent was fading into the storm of light. Thorn saw flashes of other images. Other children teasing him. A flurry of insects devouring a field of crimson grain.

The woman sang to him again, and then there was nothing to see at all; the woman's voice was the whole world.

A woman's wail above the surging surf…
We have no "women." We have no "surging surf."
Then what is it I hear?
Your own crazy self. And echoes of a past you may no longer touch.
I'm still hearing it.
That is not permitted. There are standards. Do not speak of seeing or hearing beyond the limits of uniformity.
I'm trying not to hear it. But I can't turn it off.
Be quiet! Don't let anyone think you are different. Or you know what will happen.

The darkness did not give way to light immediately. But Thorn became conscious of warmth, a warmth that had a ruddy hue to it. He did not know how much time was passing … time meant little here, it seemed … but at some stage he became aware that he was weightless, floating in some kind of fluid that seemed to nourish him as well as keep him buoyed up. He tried to move and the fluid was viscous. It flowed around him, somehow attuned to his inner rhythm.

He could not see very much. Somehow, he could breathe. The sound of the singing woman was somehow part of the amniotic liquid he was floating in. But all he could see was a kind of reddish glow. It would be much longer before he could make out anything other than the vague light.

Thorn remembered …

… a flurry of insects in a crimson field …
When he was four, he had run from the school, screaming.
They had called him a freak too many times.
The tall, bright-red grain called *haya* grew wild in the fields beyond the edge of the town. He knew the way there, through ancient tunnels beneath the school, a place unmapped in the teacher's memory but known to many of the children.

Over the next few years, he came there often. It was here that the voice started coming to him, sometimes above the whisper of the grain, sometimes behind the wind. Most powerful when it melded with the sound of water, for Thorn's world did not have vast oceans, as some others he'd been told of. Yet he still knew it, as though he existed simultaneously in more than one world.

There was another child who came there sometimes. The child's name was Eth, and there was something wrong with Eth, too. Because while Thorn heard and saw things that everyone said were not there, Eth often missed seeing or hearing the things everyone said *were* there. They called Eth stupid, and idiot, and dumbfuck.

Thorn knew he could find Eth wandering alone in the field sometimes, not too far from where the tunnel emerged—if you wandered too far, you could surely get lost in the billowing scarlet.

Sometimes he would spend all day in the fields with Eth. They rarely spoke. Sometimes Eth would hug him, and Thorn would not know why. They were friends, Thorn thought, even though neither of them had friends.

And today, Eth was there as well. He stood in an irregular clearing that the grain stalks had missed. One sun was at high noon and the other at the northeast horizon, and Eth cast two shadows, one deep purple, the other black.

Eth said, "They tease you again?"

"Yes. You?"

"Worse. I've been *picked*."

Thorn said the things you always say when you hear this. "Don't be afraid, Eth. You'll be with friends, and when they fix you up, you'll be with us again."

"Thorn, they don't fix you up."

And this was something Thorn had heard as well. It was something the adults whispered about. And every discussion always started with what things used to be like, before *they* came. *They* were, of course, the Com.

"I'll come with you," Thorn said. "They won't split us up. We'll always be together."

Thorn took Eth by the hand and led him through a maze of man-tall crimson. A high wind sprang up and the grain whispered and wuthered. "Do you hear it?" Thorn cried. "Above, *entwined* with the howling of the wind?"

"No," said Eth.

That was when the teacher came to fetch him. The teacher, his rusted arms squeaking as he clawed his way along the earth, was shrieking Eth's name. Thorn's parent was with the teacher. He was riding the teacher's back, man-thing mounted on metal-thing, ripping great holes in the waves of grain.

The teacher's jaws opened and spewed out a silvery net that caught Eth in a swingle swoop and lifted him into the air.

Eth screamed, "You're not going to fix me! You're going to *kill* me!"

The net shimmered, shivered. Its strands were semisentient, able to tighten the mesh.

"You'll crush him!" Thorn said. "Alyss, do something!"

Thorn's parent dismounted the teacher and came to Thorn. Thorn embraced him. "Teacher's squeezing Eth to death!" he said.

But at that moment—

A cloud of insects filled the sky. Their buzzing drowned everything. They were storming through the field, devouring the grain, blistering the stalks, eating and mating in mid-flight.

There was nowhere to run.

Alyss unwrapped his cloak and threw it over himself and Thorn. The two of them fell to the ground in a heap. The insects roared. He could feel the weight of them, millions of them.

And just as suddenly, they were gone, and there was silence.

Thorn peered through a fold of the cloak. He struggled to his feet. His parent took even longer to get hold of himself.

The teacher, like a silver crab, held the net in a pincer up to the sky. Both suns were starting to set. The net was empty.

"They ate him," Thorn said. "You just let that happen." It happened so fast, perhaps Eth did not even know he was being devoured. Thorn hoped he had not been conscious.

The teacher wheezed, "It made no difference."

"You're going to kill me too, aren't you?"

Alyss said, "No, Thorn. You are different, but some of your differences … it seems … the Com would like to study you a little."

"Humanity betters itself in imperceptible increments," the teacher said. "Your life may give other lives meaning."

"So it's to be medical experiments," Thorn said softly.

"Yes," said the teacher. "They have decided to send you to the Hill."

Thorn could see now. He could more than see.

The liquid he floated in was filled with points of light, of wormlike shapes, creatures that swam and wiggled and cavorted in a landscape of shadow-shapes. He had eyes. He had a mouth and, when the creatures swam near, each one was a tiny *pop* of tastiness. It was food. It was *tiny* food. As he started to focus, he realized that this was not seeing as he used to see. His vision could fine-tune to the microscopic level. He could see into the infrared and ultraviolet. He knew this because there were colors he had no names for.

He tried to wade in the fluid he was immersed in. Now, able to see beyond what encased him, he realized this was some kind of oval tank. He could not reach the top or bottom or the perimeter; the fluid was viscous and resisted him, but he wasn't frozen in amber either. He could drift a little.

He tried to raise his arms, and that's when he saw that he didn't have arms. He wasn't quite sure what they were. They were jointed like an insects', but they ended in human-looking hands. He stared at his hands for a long time before realizing that he had six of them. Or, perhaps, they were legs.

Controlling the middle pair was tough. It was like getting his stomach to twitch. But suddenly, he felt them jerk. Getting them to do what he wanted took a supreme effort. He tried moving his six limbs sequentially and found out he could steer himself around the tank a little bit. That was when he bumped his head and realized his head wasn't a head. He had more arms growing out of his back, too. No, not arms. Something else. He tried flapping them, and they scraped against the side of the container. The music crescendoed, too; it was as if the voice were directing him, telling him to fling himself from whatever was confining him.

Then, for the second time in what seemed like only hours, or days, his world exploded.

They were wings and now he was flapping furiously and thrashing against something solid. The liquid was sizzling, seething.

And then the solid thing shattered.

He stood in a pool of viscous liquid. The place could have been a really large room, or something natural like a cave. All around him there were hundreds of the oval tanks, and they were all starting to shatter. Each pool of liquid was enveloped in a purple mist, and as Thorn watched, the little mists were dissolving and revealing … creatures.

The flurry of a million insects through the crimson grain …

Were they insects? Were they fairies? They looked around, bewildered, seeming to have emerged from a long sleep. When Thorn gazed at them, and looked at his own appendages, his body, he saw that he was one of them, too. Something like a locust, and something like an angel.

Other creatures, more insectoid than the hatchlings, somewhat like beetles and much larger in size than the emergent ones, were moving in and among them, sucking up the pools of nutrient. There were others, too, resembling giant worms or larvae, lapping up the liquid.

Overhead, other creatures flew. Their wide-spanning wings glowed fluorescent green, and it seemed that their function was to illuminate this hatchery.

I ought to be terrified, Thorn thought. *This is worse than any nightmare. It's worse than the night they made our whole planet into one-parent households.*

But there was a deep, calming music that echoed in the chamber. It seemed that the entire community of insect-creatures had a kind of rhythm, that the little noises they made blended into a massive subliminal murmuring that sounded like i-*vrom*, i-*vrom*, i-*vrom*. And all at once, Thorn could understand. *This is what we are,* he thought. *We are Ivrom.* Thorn was not human anymore.

Had the Com done this?

Had they snatched him away just before landing? Was this one of the medical experiments they were using him for? But even the Com couldn't turn you from a human into an insect.

And then there was the music …

It rumbled beneath the threshold of hearing … i-*vrom*, i-*vrom*, i-*vrom* … yet he could hear it perfectly. He had *always* been able to hear it.

On his world, it had been faint, inchoate. But here the sound was the fundamental harmony on which all other communication was founded. It was the life of the hive.

This *was* a hive. He was part of something. He felt truly home for the first time.

Sing me a song so I can remember you forever.

In the warm room, in the winter, the moonlets through the open window …

She sang about the elf-king's daughter, taking a child to the other world …

Once the workers had siphoned away all the nutrient fluids, there was no food. Thorn saw a little puddle and skittered over to see if he could find some sustenance. Two others beat him to it and started fighting each other.

As Thorn stared, another boy-insect sidled up behind him.

"Let them fight it out," said the other boy.

Thorn thought of him as a boy even though he was a slender six-legged thing with diaphanous, phosphorescent wings. His face had something human about it.

"Did you look like me before?" Thorn said.

"Yes. I was sent to Kragenfort for the child tax. Were you picked for the child tax?"

"No. There's no child tax where I come from."

"Why, then?"

"Imperfection."

"I don't get that," said the other one, lifting himself in the air and flying circles around his head. "I'm perfect. That's why I was picked. To be part of the child tax is a great honor. My town gave me a parade."

"Mine shipped me off to be used as a medical test subject."

"Then why are you here?"

"Something happened—who knows? Ion storm, string anomaly? But someone intercepted us, and I was unconscious for a long time and I woke up inside the tank."

"The *egg*," said the other boy.

Yes, egg, Thorn thought. That was it. He still was who he was before, he still knew the same things, but he had become something else. *I'm a changeling,* he thought, remembering whispered stories from his childhood, stories his mother told him at bedtime, in the days when people still had mothers.

Children being snatched away by the fairies.

Maybe *we're* fairies, he thought. "What's your name?" he asked his new friend.

"I gave it up just before they sacrificed me."

"You don't have a name? I'm Thorn."

The other flapped, agitated, soared straight up like a rocket, then plummeted, unfurling his wings. He started making a noise that sounded like howling and laughing at the same time. As he settled back down to the ground, Thorn realized that it was a kind of weeping.

"I thought you were perfect," Thorn said.

"I hated giving up my name."

"Well, what was it before? I could still call you by your name."

"That's the problem," he said. "They excised it with a psych-scalpel. I don't know what it was. I just remember losing it. And I miss it. I'm hungry for it."

"I'm hungry too. Isn't there any food?"

"We feel hungry, but that's from the past. You don't know anything, do you? You have some kind of aching in your abdomen, beneath that glistening black carapace of yours. But it's not real."

There was something missing. Thorn tried to swallow, but his biology was all wrong. There was an emptiness inside him, but it wasn't the lack of food.

He had no stomach.

"We're males," said his friend. "We don't eat."

"Can I give you a name?" Thorn said. "It's weird that I can't call you anything."

"It would just be make-believe."

"Then I'll call you Eth, because he was my best friend, and he would have wanted to be here with me."

"Why didn't he come?"

"He was eaten alive in a field of grain," Thorn said, "by a million insects."

"Were you scared?"

"I felt … a kind of love."

They gathered all the males together, in a crimson field, much like the one Thorn had left behind. All the ones that had hatched during the season. There were hundreds of them. There was tension in the air. He did not know why yet. He stayed close to Eth, learning from him how to catch the air swell and skim the drifting wind. They circled. They danced.

Trying to keep up with the others, Thorn remembered the swarm of insects on his homeworld. In this new body, he had no sense of size or distance. Was he as small as the insects who had eaten his friend? There was no objective feeling of scale; he could only measure things by how big he felt he was himself. *We are all giant bugs,* he thought, as he figured out the rhythm of his wings—he had four of them—timing the flaps to the crosscurrents.

Now he and Eth were circling each other, flying sideways, doing figure eights around other flyers. Thorn exulted. He almost forgot the gnawing hunger.

Overhead, a vague brightness shone evenly; there was no star to illumine this sky. What kind of world was this, where the sky had its own innate glow?

Presently, the thundering *ivrom … ivrom …* crescendoed. It seemed to be coming from the planet itself. The very air shook with it.

Above the roar was the sound of the woman singing. And they all heard it. Thorn was not the only one anymore. The melody wove in and out of the rumbling ostinato of *ivrom*. If *ivrom* was the foundation, the roots of the song, the voice of the woman was the fabric that connected everything together. And Thorn realized that he was *meant* to be in this place. This was what he had heard as a child. The song that his long-lost mother seemed to know a few fragments of when she lulled him to sleep at night.

Now, interspersed with the melody, there were clear words:

Come to me … love me … dance through the night with me …

The song of the elf-king's daughter!

The male hatchlings ceased wheeling and circling and alighted in rows on the ground. A group of large females, warriors perhaps, came and made the young males stand in precise rows according to the time they had hatched. Luckily he and Eth were across from each other and could still talk.

An impressive warrior, larger than the others and with a golden carapace, reared up and began addressing the males. Her voice was interlaced with the surging music, and the words were not so much in a spoken language, but in sequences of frequencies. But Thorn knew what she was saying. He had always understood this language.

"You are so fortunate," she said, "to have been created for just one purpose. You have grown from egg to boy in the briefest of time, and soon, you will embark on the quest that keeps the world in motion. Perhaps you will be the one who will evolve from boy to man in the final moments of your destiny. In a few moments, I shall give the signal. In a few moments, you will hear the song of the beginning and end, and you will fly to the west, braving the perils of our world to conquer the Hill. Oh, you will soar, you will sing, and you will love as we workers and warriors can never love. All future generations will be in your debt, and your name will be added forever to the song of the Ivrom."

One male, towering over the others, cried: "I'll be the winner! I always won every race where I came from. *Aiya-ha-aiya!*" It may have been some kind of war cry, but Thorn immediately named him Aiya in his mind. Aiya's wingspan was twice as wide as anyone else's. As he shouted, others cheered him—perhaps they came from the same world.

"That one is trouble," Eth said.

At that moment, the sky shattered.

It had not been a sky at all but some kind of dome. Above they could see storm clouds swirling. Above them was a nightmare of churning wilderness, foreboding and forbidding, lit only by streaks of crimson light.

And yet, beyond the storm, he sensed, something was calling to him.

"You are to follow the song to its source, children, and become one with the eternal music of our world," the golden warrior insect intoned.

Would the golden warrior guide them? he wondered, but his thoughts also wove themselves into the music and blended with the thoughts of others who must have wondered the same thing.

"We are flightless," said the warrior. "It is only to the young males that is given the glorious power to soar above our world. Now … I will give the signal. Find the cold hill and make her warm. Kindle the fires of rebirth. Now go!"

The young males, in a single movement, took to the air.

He was part of it, a shimmering sheet of living creatures angling upward to pierce the clouds. He soared. In a moment he was choking as cut through the lowest layers of cloud.

The clouds were heavy with noxious fumes. He could see the others dropping. He dared not stop in his upward flight. But he could see them, by their thousands, plummeting from the sky like golden hail. Some were in flames, brilliant comet-tails sprouting from their carapaces.

They fell out of the sky, and Thorn felt he should be falling with them, but then he saw Eth up ahead, and he knew he could catch up because even though Eth had had all the foreknowledge of this destiny. It was Thorn who heard the music most clearly.

But way ahead of the pack, Aiya flew, sheltering his body from the assault of the wind with his huge wings.

Thorn fought the falling boys, shoving them as he pushed his way upward on a rising current. Their lives, like pinpricks, smarting, brief. He could feel the wind surging, felt like giving in to it and letting himself fall—

"Thorn!" Eth shouted.

Eth reached out with a hand and, with a supreme effort, Thorn kicked against the thick wind and rocketed up and seized the hand, and now they flew together, perfectly in tandem. Their wings flapped exactly in time, left right up down and 'round again, catching the swift tide of air.

How many remained?

Thousands had already fallen. Hundreds remained still. They formed pairs, like Eth and Thorn, discovering the formation by instinct. All headed west, although Thorn did not even know what *west* really meant on this world. All Thorn knew was that he was flying toward the song.

They flew together in this formation for a long while, no one breaking out. Thorn knew the journey would be long, but not how long.

The crossed a lake redder than the field of grain. Beyond it were foothills.

The surviving males were slowing, getting ready to land in the hills.

"We should rest." Thorn said, gasping.

"No, we have to be the first to get there."

But still, they found themselves drifting, losing altitude.

Some of the others were already falling into the lake. As they fell, flames leaped from the water to engulf them. As they descended, dangerously close, Thorn could see they were *literally* tongues of flame, whipping out from the mouths of monstrous amphibians, roasting their friends into tasty morsels.

And Eth was slipping from Thorn's grasp, about to plunge into the lake. Thorn could see the amphibians gathering, their tongues darting.

Descending now, trying to hold onto Eth, Thorn could see bulbous eyes beneath the ruddy foam.

Zeroing in on where Eth was going to fall, the tongues made a circle of flame surrounding a crimson circle of death. Eth was gasping, losing the will to fly on. With a supreme effort Thorn flew beneath Eth, snatching him skyward.

Thorn flapped his wings harder now. Eth was thrusting desperately. They linked three of their hands to make a double engine and managed to push higher for a few moments. The music roared. Thorn tried to gauge the direction of the wind. Some of the others had escaped the fiery lake only to dash and expire against the escarpment.

Got to clear the cliff ....

Thorn soared. The weakened Eth was dragging him down, but Thorn flapped harder, caught a lucky current, managed to skirt the escarpment and brought them down, bruised but not too damaged, on a heap of dried foliage. Thorn let go of Eth and shuffled over to the edge. He looked down. Hundreds of young Ivrom were still hurtling into the abyss.

"You saved me," Eth said.

Thorn turned to look at his new friend, whose face had a burnished glow. His compound eyes were deep set. Eth was, Thorn began to see, in the way that his new species saw others of their kind, beautiful. His wings had purple striations against a shimmering, shifting pattern of blue and gold. Thorn wondered what he himself looked like. Perhaps he would never know.

"If we don't go on," Eth said, "we will never make it."

"And if we leave now," Thorn said, "We won't stand a chance." He knew this from the music ringing in his ears, because his attenuated senses knew exactly how far he still had to go.

"But she's calling us," Eth said.

"She's only calling *one* of us," said Thorn. "And I doubt that you or I are destined to be that one. It's probably going to be that bully, Aiya."

"But I'm perfect," said Eth. "I was *chosen* for this."

Thorn said, "And yet *I* saved your life."

"You did."

"Yet, we should both be wishing for the other's death, because only one of us is going to finish this quest."

"It can't be true," Eth said. "You are my friend, my *only* friend."

"How can I be your only friend? You said yourself, you're perfect."

"Where I come from, it costs to be perfect."

"Whatever our fate is supposed to be here," Thorn said, "I won't wish for your death. You know, I had a friend called Eth, *my* only friend. I didn't have friends, you know, because I was *not* perfect. I did not even know there were any downsides to being perfect."

There was so much to be learned about Eth's former world, and about the one they found themselves in. And so little time. The music was surging in him, its rhythm one with the pounding of his heart.

"Let's promise each other," Eth said, "that we won't betray one another. No matter what our fate is. We're not even going to finish the quest, are we? They say that some seasons, *nobody* finishes the quest at all."

"Then what do they do?"

"I think the hive becomes very weak. The Queen conserves her strength as best she can. Few are born, and those that live must work much longer to sustain the community. You see, everything depends on us."

Thorn tried to pay attention, but he could hardly hear, let alone understand, above the sinuous strands of music. But he was aware that Eth needed some kind of reassurance. "Yes," he whispered, "I'll promise."

He turned from the cliff and looked instead at the way forward. The sky was growing dark. There were only a few stars, and they glowed red, angry, through veils of cloud.

It was cold.

Thorn watched as Eth built a fire, piling up dried leaves and rubbing his hind legs to produce a spark. Eth truly knew the world far better than Thorn. Somehow, he had known he would be coming here. He had been taught its lore and trained in the world's secrets.

He knew when we hatched, Thorn thought, *that almost all of us would die in a matter of days.*

"We can sleep for a few hours," Eth said. "Some of them will leave earlier, thinking to get an advantage, but once the hail hits, they'll be too weak." Eth pulled out some more vegetation and made a crude bed.

"Do we even *have* sleep?" Thorn said.

"Not really," Eth said. "But being still can help us stay strong."

The sky was darkening. Even the red stars dimmed as more clouds gathered. The fire burned, deep blue, though it gave off heat, it had a cold light.

Thorn moved closer to Eth. Eth spread a wing so Thorn could lie closer. Thorn turned, some of their legs entwined; the closeness lent them an alien warmth. Eth's wing tingled, sending more heat through Thorn's body.

As Eth predicted, Thorn did not sleep. But he did enter a kind of disembodied state, and into his inner world came memories ….

… the day the teachers came to the house to conform the family …

They ran to the lake's edge, Thorn and Eth, to see the ship leave for the South. If a set of parents had one child, mothers were selected for reassignment, and for the most part, they left willingly. The alteration process was not as intrusive.

Eth's mother had chosen not to relocate. But her vaporization had been painless and swift. Eth's father stood by, weeping into a washcloth. He watched her dissipate into the wind. Thorn had been there, as well. He and Eth were the only children on their street, so many neighbors came to watch as well. It wasn't often that the whole stately panoply of the Com presented itself in such a remote part of the world.

Eth's case being rather different, the teachers had offered a dual termination, promising to find a decent parent for this rather special child, but Eth's father refused, and went instead for the alteration to sole parent. They led him away as soon as they had finished with his wife.

Alyss had not wept at all. Thorn thought he was too numb. They took him away for alteration, promising it would only take a few hours.

Thorn and Eth stayed by the water's edge, and that was the first time Thorn heard the singing woman.

No, of course, he had heard Mia sing. But Mia was real.

This was a voice than came from inside.

"Don't you hear?" he said to Eth. But he knew that Eth could not.

They stayed together until the suns both set. They did not speak. He heard what Eth could not hear. He listened to the song, and something stirred, something that was telling him, *Come away … there is a better place … come dance with me, come love me …*

"My mother's dead," Eth whispered.

Thorn envied him that. At least Eth knew for certain where she was.

"Wake!" Eth was fluttering, trying to extricate his wing. "My wing's all numb now."

Everyone had left already. They were the last ones left on the escarpment.

But the song was strong in Thorn's consciousness. His tiredness slid away as he stood up on his hind legs. A cry escaped his thorax. He gulped the air, knowing it had no sustenance.

"I am powerful! I am crafty! I will finish the race!" he shouted, exulting.

"Save your energy," Eth said urgently.

They took off together. The song was strong in Thorn's soul, in Thorn's body. He rode the shape of the song, swerved upstream with the upswing of the song's smooth shape. He was mighty. He was powerful. And Eth took strength from his strength. They formed a double wingspan to skim along the sharp edge of the wind shear into sheer plummeting.

They were catching up.

The next test was a pelting hail of jagged ice pellets. As they reached the main body, they could see hail ripping through wings, causing many to lose their balance and plunge into a sea of ice.

"Sideways!" Thorn shouted. "They won't puncture the wings that way."

How had he known? *The music told him.*

Turning themselves ninety degrees, they became two-dimensional strips, letting the current carry them. They were inching toward the next resting place. As they drifted along, the hail abruptly stopped. They landed on a narrow plateau. Behind them was a sea of ice; ahead of them a wild volcanic landscape, spewing fountains of lava.

Why so abrupt? Thorn thought. It was as if this world had been constructed somehow. No natural planet could have such sharply delineated regions, bounded by rings of cliffs.

The world was an artifice, but whose? And how far did it extend? Was this even the real sky, were the cliffs and volcanoes and hailstorms simply conjured up from some alien imagination?

He wondered what Eth knew.

"What did they teach you about the Ivrom?" Thorn asked his friend.

"That it's a higher plane of existence. That it's an honor to be chosen."

"How do you get here?"

"We are sacrificed," Eth said. "We have a funeral procession and everything."

"But you're alive," Thorn said.

"We're alive … when the high priest throws us into a fiery portal." Eth had come with a purpose. Thorn being here, as far as he could tell, was an accident.

Who was still in the lead? Aiya, of course, though his wings had pinprick holes from the hail. And who else remained? No more than twenty or twenty-five, out of thousands. The group, clumped together on the plateau, chirped and shrieked aggressively at one another.

Aiya did not stop to rest. He set off right away. As soon as he took to the air, the others fell silent. There seemed to be a sense of inevitability about who the victor would be, who would be celebrated in song for a thousand years. At first no one followed. Two of the males dueled right there on the plateau, flying at each other, ripping at each other's wings with jaws and claws.

"We'll never do that," Eth said.

There had been a lull in the song. But now, little by little, the chant *ivrom, ivrom* came up from fissures in the ground. Behind them the ice sang. Ahead, the lava roared. Above it all, the twisting sinuous melody. It was the elf-king's daughter's song from his childhood. It was a lover. It was a mother.

The two fighting males were slumped down on the rocks, their frail bodies ripped apart.

Thorn felt weak, paralyzed by hunger. And yet his spirits lifted. "Come on," he said, dragging Eth up from the ground. The whole world was singing now.

Holding on by just one hand, Eth was going limp. But Thorn persisted. He turned and prepared to leap once more into the wind.

He was crazed with weakness, yet he held on. Presently Eth's strength returned, and they soared together now. The others were dropping. Sulphurous fumes would choke them if they flew too low. Too high, and the air was so thin they had to gulp the wind to get enough oxygen.

And now they saw their goal.

It was a hill unlike the others. Completely smooth, glistening. Oval. Like the body of a mountain-sized insect—It was a single carapace. Thorn's intuition told him that this had taken generations to create, billions perhaps of the Ivrom sacrificing themselves to grow

When he saw the hill, Thorn's heart leapt. The hill itself was singing …

Dark is the dreaming,
bright is the flame
that glows within
the dark heart of our world ….

Aiya still flew ahead, but they were gaining on him. The song was like a road that arrowed across the swirling air. Thorn gave himself to the sweep of the music and found himself speeding in a straight line through the air, even as he held on to Eth.

He was getting closer to Aiya now. A tingling twist of melody suggested that Aiya might not waver.

The shining hill was directly below. Aiya was decelerating, reading to swoop. Thorn saw the goal now, a tiny dark spot at the summit. The passageway to the dark heart of the world!

As they started to descend, Thorn saw countless geyser-emanations bursting from the hill. They were being engulfed in a kind of steam … no … clouds of particles. No, not particles exactly. No. Tiny wiggly particles. Each particle had a note of its own, an individual resonance. Each particle sang. and Thorn realized each note was an individual pitch and color with its own unique overtones, and each note formed part of the symphony that the hill was playing, and he knew that these trillions of notes were waiting for the upbeat that would begin the song, the note that would start creation, the sound that would give birth to the universe.

And I have to be that note, Thorn thought.

They plummeted together. And now they landed, with Aiya just seconds ahead of them. Aiya turned. Ferociously, he shrieked, he flapped his wings to attack them. Death and desperation were in his eyes.

Aiya threw himself at Eth, the weaker. Eth clawed and bit. Aiya ripped through the fabric of Eth's forewing, and Eth stumbled.

The music was strong in Thorn. Unthinking, he swerved and rammed Aiya, leaping again and again and crushing Aiya's abdomen into the surface.

Aiya began shaking, shivering as the segments of his body separated. Thorn watched. Aiya was sinking into the gleaming substance that coated the hill. The carapace was *eating* his body!

Thorn looked down. One pair of his feet rested on the ground, and he already felt the flesh liquefying. He darted up quickly.

"We can't stand still here," he said. "If we don't keep moving, this place will devour us."

They moved on. Eth clung to him. He held Eth close, as though he were a parent. He could only fly a little bit at a time, and time he tried to land on a different foot before launching himself upward again, trying to lose as little flesh as before.

There was almost nothing now but the music. He saw the last of Aiya being consumed. Aiya gasped … he was not even entirely dead when he was sucked completely under.

They moved through swarms of wiggly creatures, and Thorn knew what they were: *My sisters,* he thought. *They are larvae, and the inside this hill is the mother of us all, the creator, the Queen.*

Closer and closer, they came to the opening. Down there was destiny. Only *one* male could mate with the Queen. He understood the song. *And I'm going to defy it.*

"Together," Thorn whispered. "Together. We'll fertilize the Queen together. You are my friend. I won't leave you here. I left my other friend to be eaten alive. Not you."

He held his friend tight with his middle arms, against his upper abdomen, letting him hear the pounding of his heart, if it was a heart. With his last reserves of strength, he positioned himself above the darkness, and prepared to drop.

The abyss yawned. It was a perfect darkness. The music rose to a climax and, in that final moment, he knew he would betray the only person in this world he loved.

"I love you, Eth," he whispered, and flung his only friend to one side as he fell.

He heard Eth's body smash against something hard, metallic.

At that moment, light exploded. There was an absolute joy that came from the instantaneous conjunction of death and life. Thorn was filled with love. He loved this world. He loved his parent, his teacher, his old world, he loved the universe, he loved himself in the moment of losing himself forever.

Time had ended. Existence had ceased to be.

Yet, there came, in a moment that was not a moment, another kind of reality.

There was a planet and on this planet there was a hill, and on the hill there was a building. Outside the building, someone was waiting.

Inside the building, Thorn was standing by the front door. He had found himself there, not knowing how he had come. It was up to him to open the door, and he could only open it when he knew the time was right.

And at long, long last he did, and he stepped outside.

His parent was waiting, but somehow, he had become a father again. Mia was there, too. Mia, his mother. And they both smiled at him.

There were many suns, and a gentle wind played with his hair. He came down the steps. Eth came running out from the grain fields that swayed in the breeze. The wind whispered; beyond the building and all the way down the hill stretched field upon field of crimson grain. Like home, but more beautiful, more perfect.

"Are you real?" he asked his mother.

"There's so much I could tell you," she said. "About the Markovians, the makers of many worlds, who are the gods. They made the elves and the insects and blended them into one. I could tell you about the ship that brought you here. About the storm in the fabric of spacetime. About the rescue."

But, Thorn thought, *I must have died*. For he had become the trillion cells that brought life to the Queen's children. He had become father to the world. And in this place that was an echo of the real world, it was reality that was the echo. This place had been given him to dwell in for eternity, or at least as long as he cared to have some physical nature.

"So, I suppose, we're ghosts," said Thorn.

"What is a ghost?" Alyss said.

Thorn knew then that this place was neither real nor imagined.

In the world the gods had created, Thorn too had become a god. There would be new verses in the song of birth and rebirth.

The dream was darkest
as the thorn first entered
but when the truth triumphed
the thorn flew true ...

"They fixed me," Eth said, laughing.
"There was nothing to fix," Thorn said, and he hugged his friend.
"Come home now," said his mother. "I'll teach you a new song."

Chapter Four:
WUCKL:
NEAR MISS
Keith Olexa

I

hate the Well World; it's full of cheats and false promises! They say second chances …. Second chances? What kind of second chance is running for your life from a four-beaked hairy bag, all stork legs, rubber limbs and a bobbling head, who is trying to kill me!

You wouldn't think such a silly-sounding creature would be scary, would even be dangerous? You would think, were I to tell you nothing about me except that I was young and active, that I could handle a giant beanbag stork … but I'm all wobbly limbs and bouncy bird head just like him, just like this Wuckl, this crazy determined-to-end-me bird thing is …

These Wuckl aren't even supposed to be dangerous; they're healers, the whole bunch of them … but I get stuck with the one crazy Wuckl who's got murder on his mind. It's so unfair. I used to be Bennitt Grimbel—and I wish I was still!

I look across a long expanse of rock and shrub-strewn flatland … maybe only yards from the tall electric fence that separates the temperate and forested hex known as Wuckl, named after the hex's inhabitants— my race now—from the desolate plain of hot, dry terror, the hex known as Ecundo.

The scrub and heat are nothing compared to the inhabitants of this land ... also called the Ecundo. I saw one only two days after my arrival. Giant bugs ... like earth scorpions, softer looking but no less nasty—all claws and legs and that evil stinger. They're larger than me and able to tear a pig-rodent thing called a Bunda into bite-sized bits in seconds. I almost retched to watch them eat, something that wouldn't have fazed me before, when I was still a person—a human— over this thing that I am now.

Only a week as a Wuckl ... seems like a lifetime ago, but Viveu said it would be like that, as did Ortega. As did that death-dealing doctor, Brantecore. He said it just before he reached out to me ... put his hand through me ...

I shrug off the disturbing thoughts. I travel light, carrying only a stun rod and a pouch with some food and water. I have a communicator, too. I need to make it to my rendezvous quickly before ...

But neither that nor the rod will work in Ecundo. Nothing that needs electricity works in Ecundo; it's very strange ... . Viveu told me to go north, parallel the Wuckl's security fence until I get to the Rolga border, and there I could find help. Another hex, another nation full of aliens. These inhabitants of Rolga, the Rolga, aren't likely to help me—most races tend to keep to themselves here, water races especial-lym which is what the Rolga are—but my tech stuff will work in their hex regardless, and so I might possibly be able to call for a ship from yet another hex for help. It's my only chance. This doctor Brantecore is crazy but has power, too; he's influential. He's framed me for *his* crimes, and I don't stand any chance against him.

I'll ask the Rolga for help. They might help me, or at least transport me to the Ambreza or another hex where I could find friends and defend-ers. I won't know justice in Wuckl. Not with this Dr. Brantecore and his reputation in my way.

I run gingerly from rock to rock. I don't think the Ecundo would ... eat ... me, but I don't know. They look nasty, and they eat nasty, and rela-tions between the Wuckl and Ecundo don't seem to be good right now.

If those Ecundo don't get me—or don't just get in my way—the doc-tor will get me. He's out there, he's hunting me. He hates me, called me an infection. He's crazy, but he knows this world, and I don't.

It's so unfair. Why am I even here? What misfortune led me to this Well World? One moment I was a well-off son of a merchant from Torus Electra, now I'm a—monster! A monster pursued by another monster on a crazy world of hexes filled with a menagerie of monsters!

Viveu thought it was a good thing that this all happened. Where she was concerned, I would almost agree. She has an interesting philosophy about things—a variation on that old human expression *any crash you can walk away from is a good one*—but she's wrong. This isn't going to end well; it's just going to end. I'm a starship about to explode on takeoff. A missile without a guidance system on a direct course into disaster!

II

I recall bitterly the circumstances that trapped me on the Well World .... I was on the star transport *Euphrates* when it all began. It started with pirates! I think it was pirates; that's what everyone else thought. Not sure I trusted the other passengers on the ship, though. I planned on a luxury cruise, but many people onboard were not ... the kind of people I typically mingled with.

I planned the trip to see my estranged mother, or so the story I told my father went. Neither he nor my mother, honestly, were thrilled with my plan. Gerris backed me up, of course; this was all his idea. I said it was a vacation, one I had coming. But no, it was an escape. I had to get away from my father, from the illicit life I didn't know that he—or I—led.

I idolized my father. Affluent, quite successful, a generalist and speculator, he seemed a great man to me, but no longer. I was taking this trip because of him. After I learned what he had done, how he made his wealth, I couldn't live with him anymore. I was heading to the inner systems to see my birth mother, who was vacationing on Mars. The thrill of being so far from home, so deep into the heart of the Confederation, did mitigate some of my anxiety and sorrow. I loved starships. I studied navigation in school, enough to know things but never enough to fly a ship on my own. It wasn't enough to dispel the terrible truth of my life, though. Bennitt's father: sponge dealer.

Sponge, that terrible life-form that produced a drug, highly addictive, that reduced its victims to apathy, idiocy, and eventual death. That's my life, never able to have good things for long. Eventually, the bad comes home to roost. It happened when my older brother died during the Argosy Riots, or when my mother left my father, despite my pleas as a child, for a life deep in the Confederation's heart. Now I finally understand why my mother left, how my father maintained our great lifestyle—so unfair.

My best friend and travel companion Gerris traveled with me. A good man, athletic, smart, and good looking, but not as well bred. I liked him and would never admit the fact that his presence always made parties better and women more receptive to enjoying a lower hanging fruit when they found Gerris too high to reach.

Gerris didn't indulge in the system as I had. He was no armchair space navigator—he could actually pilot a ship. He waxed heroic; I thought it was impressive but too idealistic—too foolish. I was always taught to keep my head down and follow instructions. My vacation involved a cruise through Saturn and races on Titan. I didn't want that ruined. I would just quietly enjoy my time … and there was thunder and the ship rocked like it was coming apart. An attack? Pirates? I didn't know.

Confusion bloomed into panic. We were being rushed out of our suites and into chaos: people running around madly, then that terrific explosion. I called out for Gerris, and he was there. He never left my side, except that one final time. Klaxon sound, mingled with assorted burnt smells, fried circuits,   and the hard vacuum of space. My mind raced hysterically, and I made for the stern of the ship, toward the escape pods. Gerris dragged me away, screaming that part of the ship was gone. He pushed me wildly in a different direction, to a vast room. Too scared to think, I rushed in. There, a woman interposed herself between me and Gerris, all to move some unfamiliar piece of equipment into that room … then more chaos, the closing of bulkheads and a violent thrust—the whole room moved laterally from the ship as further explosions churned our chamber this way and that.

My first realization once the tumult had died down was that Gerris hadn't come with me.

He was gone.

III

My life was in ruin. I had been saved, but not Gerris. He was dead; he died saving me. Terrible, and even worse, I was now before this scraggly captain of our rescue ship, who looked no better than the pirates, who would have at least ransomed me.

A flame of rage welled within me. It was that woman! That terrible, officious woman with her strange cargo … that stasis pod. She chose some pod over the life of my best friend. If we had been allowed to go our way, Gerris might be alive. I might now be in the hands of the Com, or even pirates, either of which would have been better, either of which would have eventually sent me home.

But to what? I wouldn't return to my father. He did this, too. His sponge dealing ruined my life, and I hated him for it. And what of my mother? Would she, who surely left my dad for this very reason, who lacked the care or desire to take me or my brother away with her, would she take me in now?

I had hoped that our grizzled pilot, this Nathan Brazil, would take us back to civilized space …. I thought he should dock with one of the Confederation ships right there! But no. He put us all in squalid cabins and left us to our thoughts and miseries. I didn't think it would get worse, but I was wrong.

"WAIT!" I screamed, as the treacherous Nathan Brazil again imprisoned me with the menagerie of survivors from the cruiser … hardly a luxury ship, from the *range* of people stuck in it whom I had the misfortune of being repacked with again. I realized from the first I didn't like any of them, only this Stencil character seemed like people that I knew on Torus, but there was something of my father in the way he behaved that made him as unpalatable as the rest. But it was all of it—having my choices removed, my comforts—that ate at me … and these people hadn't washed, and we hadn't eaten in a day … and I really had to pee. I felt like hell, and I cried out that things couldn't get any worse.

I needed to stop doing that …

What followed, for me, was something between a dream and insanity. It had to be one or the other, or both! It couldn't be anything else. I felt so detached from the madness I was currently embroiled in that I became a guest in my own head … watching myself go through motions that seemed reasonable, or as reasonable as could be expected, in a situation utterly bereft of reason. Bushy-mustachioed walrus-faced serpents just can't introduce themselves with human names and try to make sense of a situation. We were in a totally new space, too, a large room … teleportation? Madness! I railed at this creature's—this thing's—calm demeanor and demanded answers, ignoring the fact that he was endeavoring to provide them. This snake-being, Serge Ortega, he called himself, told us a long, involved tale, one that began to get through to me once he said the word *Markovian*.

The Markovian gate, this Ortega had said, and that got through to my rational brain. I had followed the scientific history of these enigmatic Markovians, who left the universe with dead, empty cities, planets covered in artificial crusts, and nothing else but questions. Ortega strove in this moment to answer those questions, and I didn't think he was doing a great job. He spoke of his human past, his change from human into what he was now, and of a planet of thousands of aliens living on thousands of lands—a planet called the Well World.

Change from human? Well World? I had fallen into stupefied silence by the time Ortega finished talking and let us rest.

Some of my senses returned after a restless sleep. Ortega told us more about our situation, which enraged me so much I swore my father would seek vengeance on this crusty space scoundrel who led us to this fate—feeling flushed with shameful grief at saying it, knowing I would never talk to my father again.

Ortega diffused my—and others'—various distresses with an involved digression on this place called the Well World, which became anything but a digression when it became clear what it meant for our futures. For on this world of some-odd-thousand aliens, the actual descendants of the original Markovians, with their powers sufficient to warp reality itself, had surrendered their entire godhood to begin again when they found omnipotence left them wanting.

That all seemed fine, ludicrous but fine, until Ortega added that those who passed through the Well gates, as did the Markovians of old, would likewise be transformed. We, too, would have to pass into this Well of Souls to be reborn as something else. Something alien.

Ortega tried to allay our fears, saying it would seem natural to us, or that this device tended to place people where they could restart lives as they should have lived them, or something like that. It fell on united deaf ears. I immediately railed against the very suggestion of the idea, and an extremely taciturn woman named Ramos tried to use a weapon she stole from Ortega against him. It failed, demonstrating our utter powerlessness in this situation. I collapsed inwardly as the magnitude of this truth struck me … there would be no father to hate anymore, no mother whose anemic love I feared I would fail to curry. There would be no more joys of Torus Electra or star travel to Mars or Earth or Villanche or anywhere. No Com anymore, no grand future. No Gerris. Just this. We were taken to a black gate as lightless as my future—I could barely keep myself composed as I stepped to this gate, touched it and …

And then I was somewhere else.

IV

I found myself on my back on a perfectly manicured lawn. That was a good start, a manicured green lawn suggested civilization. At the edge of my vision there appeared to be tall white buildings … a city! Even better.

Getting up made me feel a little like a newborn giraffe … very wobbly. I shrieked upon looking at my hands … my arms—and my *legs* …

maybe stork or crane was a better animal comparison. My shriek definitely sounded birdlike.

I was shocked, but I wasn't furious, or wildly terrified, or insane … unless calm in the face of this was a kind of madness. But no, I *was* scared, I was uncertain, I was worried, but I also felt … normal.

The area around me looked like a park of some kind or a glen, very large and grassy. A pond or small lake was immediately before me, and behind … my head felt a little like a balloon on a very dexterous string … but behind me was what looked like a city, a very modern city. If I were Gerris, I might start feeling optimistic. But what was there to be optimistic about? I have no skills; I have no family here. And I was some beaked, rubbery horror!

I dared looking into the pond … noticing a tall fence on the far side as I approached … the peaks that rose shallowly beyond that fence were very yellow and bare compared to the gentle rolling grassy hills to my left and right.

I gasped for a moment upon gazing into that watery reflection … what stared out was not my face. A bird, indeed, like a stork, looked out from the silver-black water … the gasp revealed that the beak—*my* beak—opened up and down and also side to side, four ways. My eyes were large, shoulders narrow; I had a body like a hairy potato sack.

I only gasped, though, nothing else. Funnily, I got this sense that as alien as I was, I knew—knew—I wasn't bad looking. My eyes weren't too large, the beak pointed down gently in just the right way, with the tiniest gap in the lower pair that might be seen like a cleft chin … was this that acclimation Ortega described?

I also realized I was naked, which I didn't know was the norm or not. I had to think differently now. Ortega told me all hexes were familiar with people coming from the gate, so this had to be normal for them.

Normal? Maybe. But were they all accommodating? I had to risk it …

Then I saw my first two other Wuckl … and saw what one was doing to the other.

The first Wuckl I saw was the doctor—and I know he saw me. He would be hard to miss, unlike many of the other Wuckl I've seen since; his head feathers were stark white, and he bore a crest I came to know was a healing icon. He was unusual in more ways than that.

A hex like the Wuckl hex, I would come to learn, was civilized, had laws … and had a long, long history of pacifism. Wuckl were vegetarian, they hated killing and hated death, so much that they excelled at healing … a race of doctors, I would later joke.

I clucked at the irony … a Wuckl laugh. My nemesis was a doctor—Dr. Brantecore—but when I ran into him, he wasn't healing.

How can a creature put his hand inside another creature and heal it? And the spasms, the expression on the face of that prone Wuckl, all four beaks open in a silent scream. And … I could feel it. I could feel something, like an electricity, a vibration, from both of the Wuckl, Dr. Brantecore's erratic, but strong, spiky, and painful, and the other on the ground, erratic, uneven … then fading, and then gone.

Then Brantecore, satisfied seeming, rose … only to finally see me, and say, "It's the drone plague again, call …" before he scrutinized me more carefully and added, "Oh, but I can see you're another new arrival, aren't you?" His tone became kind; I stood silent and still.

"That blank expression … and no identification, no crest, how could you be anything else?" I noticed then that the dead Wuckl was as naked as me. "It must have been some big event out there," he went on, kindly, inching toward me. "Forgive me. I'm Dr. Brantecore, this little town's resident physician. My, we almost never get arrivals to our hex, but here … two in one day. We're so … fortunate." Unnervingly, he turned his head on his neck like an owl's head on a string before looking back. "That poor soul? Don't look troubled. There's a disease going around—called a drone plague. It's terrifically fatal. I couldn't—couldn't save him. No wait—"

I made to move. Brantecore was lying; even he couldn't make his story work after what I saw. It made me think, suddenly, terrifyingly: he's never been caught flat-footed like this before … *before?*

"You must be quarantined!" Brantecore said with authority. "This disease only appears when new arrivals come through. You mustn't be allowed to spread it."

I didn't believe a word he said. I might be a brand-new alien, with no experience of how this body, or this new world, worked, but my instincts were fine … no animal needs to be told what to be wary of and what to trust. My instincts said flee … find other Wuckl, not him. This one only meant ill for me.

That meant I had to get around this Brantecore, however, who stood between me and civilization. I made to move right—

And he was instantly on me. Evidently, we Wuckl can jump very far very fast.

"Ah, that's better," he said, his beaks slightly open in some Wuckl version of a grin. "I'm very fortunate. I found two of you diseased fiends today. You all new arrivals are sick sick … you *are* the sickness! Time to get rid of the infection …"

71

Grabbing my neck with one hand, he set his other on my hairy bean-bag chest. I felt a weird flush and then terrible pain that started where a heart might be and spread all over my body. I was almost knocked out by it. It felt as if he put his hand right into my body and was squeezing the life out of me.

He meant to kill me, right there, but he paused as a voice carried over the air. "*Dr. Brantecore, Dr. Brantecore!*"

This mad creature gave a gurgled squawk, like an expletive. "*That Viveu is a burden! But okay, okay ...*"

This Brantecore was strong. He hauled me quickly over to the body of the other Wuckl. Then using that strange ability, he grabbed my own hands and put them into the chest of the other Wuckl.

In my daze, it seemed as if I put my hands into clay. It was quite gentle, and they went in like a leaf falling through the air ... but then he briefly stopped what he was doing ... and again, I felt a pain, in my hands this time. I felt as if they had burst thick balloons inside this dead Wuckl ... it was sickening.

"Sloppy, but it will have to do," I just heard him say. "You will have to be purged in a more traditional manner." Brantecore removed a short metal tube from somewhere in the folds of his body, and with a flick it extended out ... it looked like a truncheon. He put it into the hand of the dead Wuckl and placed the end of it in on my chest. "Your infections can keep coming, but I will keep working to keep the Wuckl hex pure!"

I felt a terrific pain, electrical, before I felt no more.

V

I awoke with a start. I thought I was rising in my wing suite on Torus Electra ... but my wobbly head and bony lips brought me back to my terrible truth. Not human, Wuckl, not in known space, but on the Well World.

But ... alive.

The last moments of my life came flooding back, and I leapt from my bed ... far, too far; Wuckl really can jump very far. I was in a room, dark and drab, and another Wuckl was with me. I made to strangle the creature, but when it turned, it screamed shrilly and, when I got a better look at it, I froze. Smaller, female, this was not Dr. Brantecore.

Her shriek and backstep were benefits to both of us. I think I might have hysterically attacked her anyway, but her fear of my action calmed me some.

"Who are you?" I squawked. "Where am I?"

She moved to me, but gently, her expression one of concern and also fear. "Please, *speak softly*."

She moved me back to bed. I let her; I was feeling very tired, very sore, and slightly sick.

"I'm Viveu," she said, "a student aid of—of this clinic. You're in an unused room, a utility room, I think, in a sublevel. I brought this bed in …"

"Why?!" I hissed.

"Because despite what Doctor … ." Viveu paused. "Despite what Brantecore said, I didn't think you were dead. I needed—I needed to prove that."

"How …?" I asked, incredulous, but more riveted by Viveu; she was wary, genuinely scared.

"You're new here," she said quietly, "new to Wuckl. But we're excellent healers here, natural healers—" She wiggled her fingers at me in a way I found very disquieting. "It's said we're the best in all the Well World. I sensed life still in you. I had to try …" Viveu sounded more than a little desperate.

"Well, I-I'm grateful to you … ." Then more came back. "But that Brantecore, he's a doctor? He tried to kill me!"

Viveu's eyes widened briefly in shock, but her general composure suggested she didn't find this admission shocking, just the vocal expression of it, maybe.

"You're sure of that?" she asked carefully. "Brantecore is one of our most distinguished and honored psychic physicians. His techniques are unparalleled, and the Wuckl lives he has saved can't be counted."

I looked hard at her. Viveu was saying these things, but not to convince me, or even convince herself. It came out like the scene in a murder mystery … where an accuser states what appears to be true before the aha reveal. Viveu didn't want me to be convinced. She was already convinced of something else.

I answered levelly: "He killed that other Wuckl, and then he tried to kill me."

"But your hands were all over that first Wuckl. To all eyes, it appeared as if you killed her … and violently." Viveu was sickened by that revelation, and that jibed with how I felt. Blood, gore, violence, sickening.

"He did that, he reached into my chest and …"

She stopped me. "Yes," she said in a whisper. "Yes. I could hardly bring myself to believe it. But I saw it, thought I saw it, a year ago. New arrivals tend to appear in the same place here, in this hex. Brantecore built his clinic here specifically to treat new arrivals … there's a belief that they sometimes come through the Well infected with some disease—the drone plague, he calls it. One that could wipe out the entire Wuckl population. But when I saw him alone one night, looming over a frightened Wuckl, and then felt him—"

"He's a madman."

She looked at me, confused.

"A mad … Wuckl?"

"I don't know," she said, dispirited. "But he claims to have treated, saved, hundreds of arrivals, cured them. According to my observations, he has never seen one live arrival. And the only ones who have ever lived are those he doesn't see—those who come through when he has business elsewhere."

"He's a serial killer?"

Viveu clapped her beaks, akin to a sigh or a sob. "I think so. And he's good. He has managed to find a way to kill that leaves no traces; he uses our psychic healing gifts to kill, disgusting. Not that the authorities would ever dare to try him. He's so popular, so admirable."

She paused.

"And me …?"

Viveu cluck sighed again. "It isn't so simple. He's clever, instinctually clever. When he heard me call out, he hastily arranged a scene … made it look like you killed that Wuckl savagely. That wouldn't go well for you, had you—lived, you know what I mean. No true Wuckl would ever commit such a heinous crime."

"True, meaning one born here, on this hex?"

"Yes."

"Brantecore did!" I hissed loudly.

"I know; that's his near miss," Viveu said. "He can't do this, keep killing and keep getting away with it; our very civilization won't allow it. This, you, was his worst mistake. He's bound to make more of them now, unsettled as he is, especially if he ever learns you're alive. And he'll fail now, I'll—we'll hit finally. We'll win!"

I sat defeated on the edge of the bed. "And Ortega said I would wind up on a hex where I could start over … . Well, being a target of a mad bird doctor doesn't seem like a good start!"

I looked up, finding Viveu's expression tender after a fashion but also inscrutable. "I—someone I knew long ago spoke to me about arrivals from out there—from outer space, the galaxies," she said. "'Not all the hexes are nice,' he said, but they can all be rewarding. They give people something they rarely get in their lives."

"What is that?"

"Another chance, a new chance …"

"Yeah?!" I said, almost shrieking. "Did that Wuckl that came through get a new chance? I suspect she was like me … just a passenger on that cruiser, or some other unfortunate soul, just wanting to get back to her nice home. To her comfortable life. I bet she didn't want a new chance. I sure didn't!"

"But here you are. And you're alive … Brantecore's near miss."

"Near miss, near miss! What does that mean?"

"Yes," Viveu said, "isn't that how we live all our lives? Near miss after near miss … fortune to misfortune, life to death, love to loneliness … it's near misses, isn't it? Avoiding that ruin, that loss, that death; sometimes the miss is so far off we hardly notice, sometimes we barely scrape by. Near misses, until suddenly it's not. Until suddenly you don't—"

Viveu stood up. "So no, it wasn't a near miss for that poor Wuckl, or—or all the other Wuckl who died at Brantecore's hand. But he missed you. That gives you something … something over Brantecore. Do you want to do something with it? Or do you want his next chance to be a hit? 'Cause if he gets you, then that Wuckl of yours … they will have died for nothing."

"You don't seem to talk much like a Wuckl," I said. I honestly didn't know, but it was all very aggressive.

Viveu did something like a smile, and through my Wuckl eyes, I could see it was forced. "I've met … Wuckl … from out there, an Entry, whom Brantecore missed, from where you were … maybe you just rub off on us a bit. It doesn't make what I said any less true."

I hated it, but Viveu wasn't wrong. And I didn't want to die … and I did want that white-headed monster to pay.

"This won't be easy, will it?"

"Easy," she said, with some venom this time. "What's easy …?!" Then she softened. "No, it won't be easy, but I'll prepare you. You can't stay in the Wuckl hex though. You have to get to another high-tech hex and petition for someone—someone I know—who will help you bring down Brantecore."

"Leave this hex," I said, panicked. "I barely know this one, and this one seems okay."

"It's too dangerous for you; Brantecore is well connected and well respected. And there's surveillance here. In a few days, he would suspect you here … and you're too naïve to go out to the city, say, and not make yourself noticeable. He would have you back. I would also have to explain the disappearance of your body. No, the only way you'll survive is to leave Wuckl."

I nodded, defeated. "Is there any way, any way at all, to find out who that Wuckl was that died?"

Viveu's beak opened in a weak smile. "I'll see what I can do."

VI

Viveu and I had a few days to get to know each other and to plan. Brantecore, being a famous Wuckl doctor, did get called away at times—and fortunately this was one of those times, so we had several days. She kept me in the basement of the clinic, across from the morgue. Viveu said the guards had increased since Brantecore's departure … she found it a worrying sign.

Just a few days in, I heard her arguing with a guard outside my door, who insisted on being let in to inspect the room. She stated that a drone plague body was being kept there, and possible re-infections could not be ruled out. The guard demurred, but when Viveu came in, I could see she was shaking.

"Are you all right?" I asked.

Her whole demeanor said no, but she gave the Wuckl equivalent of a nod. "But this can't go on. Wuckl aren't usually this thick, but even this guard will have to wonder how I can come into this room unprotected if there's a drone plague victim here."

"Can't I be moved somewhere else?" I asked helplessly.

"No," Viveu replied. "And it will be worse once Brantecore returns. We have to make plans to get you out now, over to the Ecundo hex. Only there can—"

I hissed *No!* almost too loudly. The plan Viveu proposed was just insanity; we spent a day not talking because I flatly refused it. But I had little choice. If anyone beyond Viveu discovered I was alive, I would be imprisoned, and they would never honor my pleas to keep Brantecore away. I might have this terrible—obviously fake—plague, after all! And he would kill me then, and no one would do anything about it. Funny thing about Wuckl medicine. The skill at it was so natural, so ingrained, the science that might underpin it was practically nonexistent. Forensics is not a very sophisticated discipline in the Wuckl hex.

I didn't see Viveu for a day, but she came back the morning of the third, and I relented.

"So what is this Ecundo hex?" I asked glumly as we planned.

"Wuckl," Viveu began dryly," is on an island made up of two hexes—with Ecundo being the other hex. We're very similar, but also different in our own ways; Wuckl is very temperate and forested, whereas Ecundo is flatter and much drier."

"Hexes can vary that differently?" I asked.

"Hexes can vary much more differently," Viveu added. "Frigid mountain hexes can turn into lush farmland right at the border. But that's the least problematic part."

Viveu reached into a big bag she always carried and pulled out some kind of pocket televisual device. "These are the Ecundo." I shuddered and refused this madness again. These Ecundo were like a rubber carving of a long-bodied scorpion … only with stingers sharp enough, and effective enough, to take seriously.

"They're nothing like the Yaxa," said Viveu, as if I should know what that meant. "But they are carnivorous, and relations presently between Wuckl and Ecundo are strained."

I sat bobbling … fearfully mute. "Also not great," she added. "Because while this clinic was built near the edge of the hex, it's at the midpoint of that edge … . And you need to travel from Ecundo to Rolga as quickly as possible."

"Then just take me there. Take me to the edge of …"

Viveu shook her head in the Wuckl way. I demurred.

"Realize, too," Viveu catechized, "that all the other adjacent hexes to Wuckl and Ecundo are water hexes, and many contain deep-sea citizens that don't mingle much with land dwellers … they could be even more inscrutable than those from the Northern hexes."

I asked what were the Northern hexes, but she didn't elaborate.

"A hexes tech level also matters," she said. "With the exception of the Rolga, all the adjacent hexes are non- or semitech hexes, like Ecundo hex. This is why you can't call for help from the Ecundo hex … nothing better than an old-fashioned gun or steam power will work there. The Rolga are a kind race, but as land and water races keep to themselves, they may or may not help you. You can transmit to other hexes for help from Rolga, though, such as the Zanti or as far as the Agitar."

"This is cloak-and-dagger nonsense," I said, frustrated. I made an instinctual move for the door, which generated real alarm in Viveu. "Why can't someone here; a friend you trust, help me?"

"No Wuckl here," she said with hostility that took me aback, "can help you directly; no one will help you. Brantecore is almost a celebrity. So … no. We need to find a trustworthy advocate beyond Wuckl first and have them examine you in a safe, high-tech hex. It's the only way."

On day four, deep into the evening, in a gesture that seemed like a peace offering, Viveu managed to get me out onto the grounds. I was thrilled to get out of that terrible cold room and marveled at the strange starscape of this place I would call home. The Well World could be on the other side of the Milky Way, or in Andromeda, or far off into the universe, and I wouldn't know, but the scene was a breathtaking aerie.

"Thank you for this," I whispered, "and thank you for teaching me so much about your—our—people."

She smiled in that Wuckl way, and I wondered as a human if I would have found it funny. "But what about you, Viveu? You don't talk much about yourself." She smiled again, differently, but said nothing. She was a nice, sweet creature, but there was something dark and hard at the core of her. She had an unwavering sense of justice, though.

I spoke a little bit about myself, which bored her a bit—I suppose my old life was boring—she kept asking me, "Yes, but what did you do?" to this or that. "I suppose my life was quite easy. You might have liked my friend Gerris; he had a more adventurous spirit than I …"

"Where is he?" she asked.

"He died," I said, and I spoke a bit about it. But I didn't want to remember that horrible day.

She grabbed my hand in hers and made a sound I knew now to be Wuckl crying. "I'm so sorry," she finally said, and we sat in silence under the stars.

The next morning, trapped again in that gloomy room, Viveu gave me a crash course on the land of the Wuckl (a peaceful, sophisticated place that, despite my one hideous problem, I thought I could live in) and the Well World (the Markovians, the strange philosophy of why this planet—artificial, covered in hexes, each supporting a discrete environment and different race—existed). She seemed cynical of it all.

Thinking of the Viveu of the night before, I asked how she could be so cold about the world now?

She smiled, enigmatically this time … a smile that I, as a new Wuckl, didn't quite register. "How can I be? Well, consider this. Life," she began abruptly, "is like skiing down a steep, endless mountain; you're frantic, terrified, nearly helpless, with your sole objective being to avoid all the rocks along the way—"

"Until you what, rest? Stop? Win?" I asked. She wasn't describing the life I knew … . I saw life as going down a slow sweet river, if anything.

"No, no," she replied. "You ski until you don't, until you crash, until you die … with every near miss along the way, the greatest success. If that's cynical, then life if cynical, cause that's what it is." But she demurred after that, asking more about the universe beyond the Well. I asked if the arrivals before me ever told her anything. She nodded slightly but added that the only Wuckl she knew *now* were all born on the Well World. Brantecore had evidently been thorough.

"But here," she added, to lighten the mood, "let me teach you something." She placed her hand on my chest and said. "I'm going to show you how we heal as we Wuckl do. It's going to remind you a little of Brantecore's actions, but it's *not what he does*"—she added this with real venom again that took me aback—"just be calm." I was shocked when her hand went into my chest, it was painless and gentle, but I all but screamed and leapt away. She calmed me and tried again, revealing to me techniques of the Wuckl healing gift.

"That should be sufficient to heal yourself if needed," Viveu said. "But it should also help you throw off the … hands … of another Wuckl." She taught me this technique with a good deal of seeming impatience, but I bore it up, as it seemed a useful skill to know.

How right I would be.

"Bennitt, Bennitt, you must awaken!" came the desperate whisper on my fifth night. It was Viveu. I rose swiftly, sensing her panic. "What? What is it?"

"Brantecore! He returns early from the capital! You must make your escape tonight!"

I rose and dressed quickly, not fully awake, which might have been for the best. Just getting out of the clinic was harrowing—guards were everywhere! Twice Viveu had to use her skills at cajoling and influence—once authoritatively as Brantecore's second, once seductively as a young available female Wuckl—to secure my flight.

We slipped sneakily onto the grounds, heading straight to the border fence. "I can't scale this," I hissed. "It's electrified."

"*I know!*" She hissed back, pulling out insulated cutters from a nearby hedge.

"Why didn't you cut this yourself?!"

"There are patrols! I couldn't risk it being found. I'll stand watch, get to cutting!"

It sounded all right, but I felt pushed and prodded in all directions, and I didn't like it.

"I wish Gerris were here," I moaned as I cut the final link. "I'm all alone in a strange new world."

Viveu cut me off with a shrill hiss, angered. "How can you think like that with such a gift given to you?"

"*Gift?!*" The guards were everywhere …

"Yes, you have a chance. And this friend of yours, Gerris, gave it to you. He sacrificed himself so you could live. That's the noblest gift anyone can give—or get! So honor it and stay alive! Be active; you've been too passive in your life!"

Viveu's tone scared me for a moment, but again, she wasn't wrong. I almost hated her for it, but I scrambled through the cut wire links to vaunted freedom. I liked it a thousand times less on the far side of that fence. Ecundo was a strange land, a hostile land, and I was on my own.

But I was free. That was a gift, I suppose.

I traveled through the night … . The Ecundo were like the Wuckl in several respects: active during the day, for one. It was a very flat hex, full of big pig-sized rodents that made travel challenging. It wasn't merely that they were in the way, but that if I were to plow through a massive herd of them—it would send out ripples in the herd, like water, that might be noticed.

By Electra, the hex was so flat. There was scrub, but it was short, and I, a "newly hatched" Wuckl, was not. I slept the first day, and then moved again gingerly through the second night. I had thought I'd seen some kind of Ecundo patrol, so I hid in the short, and very thorny, scrub and all but crawled for the rest of the night. Ever see a stork crawl? That's how silly I looked and exhausted I was when I all but collapsed on the third night.

I woke that morning to the face of a nightmare. Not Brantecore … but a big pink series of eyes flanked by two massive claws. I shrieked.

"*Shhhhh,*" said the Ecundo. "*Shhhhh.*"

"I pulled out the rod from my pouch and extended it. It was without power, but it was still a rod. I poked at it thoughtlessly.

"Ow, ow, *owwww,*" said the rubbery scorpion. "Ow! Could you, ow, stop that."

"Why, so you can—"

With lightning speed, one claw disarmed me, the other grabbed me by my delicate, too-easy-to-grab neck, and the terrible stinger, like the head of a snake, stared me down. I cried out once and waited for death.

"There? Good. Good? Good," said the Ecundo, being everything at that moment but the venomous, carnivorous monster I expected.

"Eh, eh?" it continued. "Scary, huh? Honestly, this scary thing is tiring … . Can I let you go? I'm Riet, pleased to meet you. Please don't run."

The menacing Ecundo let me go immediately. The whole experience was so baffling, I was still frozen in place. Scared and very confused.

"So … so you're not going to …?" I finally asked.

"What? Eat you?! No, why?" said Riet. "Why do Wuckl all think that?! There are acres of plump bunda all over. Why would I even bother with a scrawny, bloodless Wuckl? We're meat eaters here, not monsters."

I decided to … sit? I Sat. Sitting seemed less intimidating. Though in what way was I intimidating to a man-sized scorpion I couldn't fathom. Too many big bugs on the Well World. The Ecundo shifted over, too … it seemed to favor one side of its body over another, and I felt a dull radiation off of one of its legs.

"What are you doing here?" Riet asked. "You're not on the right side of your hex, you know? You know this."

"I—" I wasn't expected to encounter an Ecundo; Viveu and I didn't cover this. Much less talk to one, so what … directness?

"I'm-I'm Bennitt, and I'm—" Why not the truth? "I'm a new arrival here on … on the Well World." Just enough truth.

"Okay. Makes sense. Where are you from originally?" Riet's nonchalance was downright disarming. This took me back a bit … . What would a scorpion know about …?

"I'm from a—a place … far away, father than any hex—"

"What planet?" he goaded.

"I clapped my beak. "Torus Electra?" I answered. "The Confederation?"

"Yeah," said Riet, switching to standard Com dialect, though he clearly hadn't spoken it in some time. "I've heard of it. From Earth here myself …"

I squawked in delight. "Wow, another arrival! Thank Electra!"

"I've been here for a while," said Riet. "Makes sense that you're an arrival. Makes me the best thing you could have come across. My … peers wouldn't be so conversational."

"Oh," I said, feeling the blood drain from my head.

"They wouldn't eat you, either! By thunder! They would just be less neighborly while they put you back over the fence."

"I see," I said grimly. "Are you going to—?"

"Of course," said Riet. "You're on the wrong side here. And our folks are shooting lasers at each other, metaphorically speaking. You're not really safe here …"

And then Riet took a moment, seeming to read my body language. "And you're not safe over there either, are you?"

I paused, *very insightful*. "Do you know anything about what's been going on over in the Wuckl hex?" I asked, question for question.

"I might," Riet said warily. "Are you in trouble with the authorities? Are you sick?" Riet's tail swished briskly.

"I'm not sick!" I said loudly. "There is no plague!"

"I didn't say anything about a plague …"

"Why would you care about some sickness unless the Wuckl made a big deal about it," I said. "Diseases don't pass from races, Vi—a Wuckl friend told me so."

"True," Riet said. If it caught my flub, it didn't show that it had … . Damn, too many insightful bugs here. "True. But if there's no plague, what's killing all the Wuckl arrivals?"

"I—" my mind worked to answer this question right. The truth again? No, too direct. "I'm not sure," I dissembled. "But you know something. Why would you care what's killing arrivals in Wuckl? What does it have to do with you?"

Riet paused again … . Pausing arachnids are dangerous-looking arachnids … ugh. "I knew someone over there … a good person, when I knew them as a person. A colleague on my ship; I was a merchant originally. We felt fortunate to appear in the Well World so close to each other—you can find yourself halfway round the world from friends or loved ones." I thought briefly, painfully, about Gerris.

"We'd talk across the fence from time to time, my friend and I. They seemed to be making a good life for themselves over there … found a mate I think, was establishing themselves, then suddenly, they disappeared. Wuckl who overheard across the fence said some plague was making Wuckl crazy before killing them … coming from the arrivals, they said. Seemed like nonsense to me."

"It is nonsense!" I blurted.

"Maybe," Riet said thoughtfully. "You do know something, though. You're the first arrival I've seen in ages, and you're running from something."

"Or to something."

"Okay, friend," Riet said plainly. "You're in trouble somehow … so give me a reason to leave you alone rather than returning you over the fence, like I should."

"All right, but first, you've got a bit of a limp there … you're injured?"

"Got run over by a bunch of ornery bundas the other day … . They were delicious, but they did give me quite a tussle."

"Let me show you I'm … I'm not sick or crazy …"

The scorpion stopped; its tail rose briefly.

"Don't try anything funny," said Riet. "And it's not likely to change my mind on things."

So not like me … to offer help without getting something back, but I don't know. Riet became kind of a gift, a man from my world … maybe not a friend, but one with a shared history, one I could talk to. And for an incredibly menacing looking venomous monster, he was very convivial. And this psychic healing thing came very naturally … for a simple thing, like fixing a broken carapace or cleaning out an infection. I did it easily.

I took a chance, and it turned out all right. For all he said, my act of kindness did have the desired effect, especially when I pointed out I would just come over the fence again anyway. Riet not only turned out to be reasonable, but offered to take me as far as the Rolga hex. Acting as my guard—which I thought was generosity in excess—and in something of a low, flat, covered cart, made the trip go faster and smoother than the days previous.

It took us several days to cross the edge of the Ecundo/Wuckl border. I felt my heart pound hard enough to burst every time some Wuckl patrol approached the fence and nearly died that moment when two Wuckl guards called Riet over … . They asked casually about what was in his cart (I was covered in skins or Riet's bunda kills, itself deathly awful), but when he said it was his "fresh" bunda meals for the day, they demurred with a croak. We spoke a bit as we traveled; he told me about the homeworld of humans, Earth, a place I'd never known, and I told him about me—which, as with Viveu, seemed a topic of extreme disinterest. He even said to me at one point, when I spoke to him about a great meal I once had on New Jupiter. "That's your idea of fun? Where's the thrill in that? You've lived a dull life, my friend."

I changed the subject to my father's descent into selling sponge and my just discovering it. That drew more interest. Riet was sympathetic, but it was all so far away. I felt homesick for the first time, but something else, as well. Despite this problem with Brantecore, I felt more at ease than I ever did on Torus. Maybe Riet was right; there's a funny tension that comes with living a tensionless life. There's a weird pressure of seeming, of having to maintain appearances. It was terrifically pointless, for all of it. I wondered at times if Gerris chose my friendship for me or my money and position. Despite his lower status, he had … done … more than me. And that was it too—living on Torus was to live in permanent potential: One never did, one had things done.

"Riet," I asked, "what did you do, before coming here?"

"Worked in space, on a ship …"

"You would had to have, wouldn't you?"

"Heh. No Markovian gates on Earth, or, well, most Confederation planets."

His laugh was like a pop from an exhaust vent. "Captain? Janitor?"

"Heh, I was an engineer," he said. "Fixed high-end star drives and life support. Good work, though the Confederation folk were the worst. I hated the pomp and arrogance and corruption; I hoped to get away to the outer systems one day."

"Looks like you did," I said, a little abashed. Confederation Riet would have regarded Confederation Bennitt with contempt.

"I worked with a crew through the main system worlds for, oh, twenty years; freelance, we sometimes got work beyond the core. Good work … good people … ." The Ecundo's voice changed in a way notable only from its difference, but I would have sworn his voice caught in his throat.

"Very close, huh?"

"Very."

I said nothing else but considered Riet differently then. His stories suggested a contented Ecundo: he had a wife and nymphs galore. He hated the Com, but he gave up something to have this life. The Well's promise of a second life wasn't an uncomplicated bargain. Good or bad.

"And what about Brantecore?" I said. "How is he good for those new arrivals? Some of them may genuinely have come for a second chance, and all they got was death."

Riet remained still, looking like something fake or dead, but he raised his claws as he replied. "All this is the plan of the Markovians … . They did this as some great experiment, something to do with feeling they made a mistake and trying to figure out how to evolve again I guess, but do it right this time."

"What does this have to do with …"

"Experiments sometimes fail," added Riet. "They're most useful when they fail. They always tell you something. Brantecore might be—"

"A failed experiment? That sounds like an excuse to me," I said.

"Think about this, Bennitt," Riet said, his voice again sounding different than before. "Good people can do bad things for good reasons, even if the reasons are only good to them. Consider that when … well, give that some thought at least."

Riet's words confused me … . I didn't think he meant Brantecore. I wondered if the Ecundo was referring to my father, but I let that thought wither away into the dry night.

The beach before the Rolga hex was a ragged, shallow lagoon. I expected the line to be sharp as a line on a map.

"First time I've ever been to the shore," said Riet. "Ecundo and Rolga don't have much contact. My people aren't overly friendly …"

I nodded. I pulled out my communicator and turned it on … nothing.

"You're still in Ecundo land … walk out into the water a bit …"

I began to move, but Riet reached out with a claw … stopping me with surprising gentleness. "Hey, take this."

I grabbed a slender glass vial; it was shaped like an elongated Ecundo stinger, with a very sharp point.

"We sometimes keep extra—ammunition, in case we use up what we have naturally. Take it, just in case."

"Why?" I asked, now anxious. "I won't need it."

"Luck is 90 percent planning," he replied. "Won't hurt you to have it just in case." I took it, then did as Riet suggested. Keeping the communicator on, I walked into the water until suddenly the device began quietly beeping.

"Are you supposed to talk to someone?" he asked.

"Viveu said one of her allies from Rolga or Agitar would catch the signal and appear."

"That seems cryptic." Riet's tail swished.

"Yeah," I replied. "It's like being a spy in the tri-dees. Very shadowy."

"Yeah …" said Riet, equally cryptically.

It took less than an hour, but a ship came quickly up from the foggy sea to the beach. It looked like a big egg with a darkened windshield. I felt a great rush of relief upon seeing it … finally, to get to some safety.

"Bennitt," said Riet, who'd stayed with me, which seemed odd to me, but perhaps he missed company of his people from … before the Well. "Bennitt, I think you should run."

"Why?" I asked. Why would I do such a thing with the help I needed just moments away?

"You didn't notice … that ship came sharp from the right … directly from the Wuckl hex."

"No, you can't be ser—"

"Wuckl and Rolga are the only two high-tech hexes adjacent to each other here, and that's not a Rolga ship. I can't do this anymore. Go, Bennitt, run!"

I squawked. "That's a Wuckl ship?!"

The ship stopped just before the shore, their hatch opened, and a blue lance of light erupted from the dark and hit … the Ecundo!

He flew away like a scorpion hit by a shoe. "Riet," I screamed! He didn't fly too far but lay still where he fell.

I looked back at the ship, terrified, ready to run. Until two sights, one after the other, held me utterly paralyzed. The first was the creature that initially exited the craft: It was Viveu! And she was clearly carrying a long tubular device that could be nothing but a weapon. My mind raced. Was Riet an enemy? Did she save me from something …?

The second sight was petrifying. It was the white head of Dr. Brantecore. It took only an instant to take in the tableau for me to understand … Viveu was not my friend after all. She was on Brantecore's side. I'd been had.

"Very good, my able assistant," said Brantecore. Viveu trained her gun directly at me, her expression cold. "We can end this here, where there will be less to explain."

"Yes, Doctor," said Viveu, her eyes dead.

"Why?" was the only thing I could ask. "Why?"

"Good Viveu knows her place," said Brantecore smugly. "She has a career to consider, a future. What are you? Dross? An infection? Full of bad, toxic ideas, passions from worlds that the Markovians would have been better off wiping out … like they did in the past. They can't, though; they're not here … but I am. And I will keep the Wuckl people pure. They're good people, noble people. Healers …"

"Not you," I screeched. "You're a killer!"

"Those infections you can't cure, you must cut out." He moved toward me.

I made to run. Viveu moved swiftly, her gun trained on me. I noticed she kept looking over to the side … over to Riet.

"Oh yes, run. Viveu's weapon only stuns. It's very effective against those problematic … Ecundo, but it will fell you, too."

And then what? Just kill me. Or another scenario, make it appear that I killed Riet before using the Ecundo's poison on me … a simple act of self-defense against a crazed Wuckl …

Poison? I had the poison. Suddenly a surge of hope coursed through me. I couldn't let myself be stunned. Brantecore would want to kill me with his hands, with his powers. That's how crazy killers worked, right?

I couldn't run away … that wouldn't work.

Great Electra, this all only worked if I actually ran *toward* him. It's not what Viveu would expect … her eyes kept darting away. If I timed it right.

But I was paralyzed with fear. I couldn't move.

Then suddenly, everything moved rapidly, chaotically, around me. The tangled pile of segmented limbs and tail that was Riet snapped back into form and leapt at Brantecore. The act was sudden and left me stunned.

Not Brantecore, though. He dodged away from the Ecundo's tail and grabbed it … skillfully. He used his powers to pull the stinger right off—not with the skill and care of a Wuckl psychic surgeon. He did it to maximize pain.

I saw why. Viveu reacted perfectly, she reacted as someone unsurprised by all the surprises. Dammit, she meant for this to happen … she set this up. Riet's failure might not have been in the plan, though; but she turned her weapon on Brantecore all the same.

Viveu, for a second my enemy, now still my ally, was briskly disarmed by Brantecore.

"Amateurs!" he said, grabbing Viveu by the neck. "As if you could shoot straight, as if you could perform an act of violence against another. I knew your intentions all along! We Wuckl! We're healers, nonviolent healers. And you thought you were so clever … keeping your hate from me? I knew Viveu … I've always known. Ever since I purged that little cancerous creature that you'd developed feelings for all those months ago … he had to go; they all do!" Viveu suddenly screamed in pain, and I knew what Brantecore was doing.

Why?!" I screamed, again. Rushing to Brantecore, I reached into my pouch for the vial of poison … . I did it desperately.

But I was scared, tentative, and he was fast. With a strong chop, the vial flew from my hand and shattered on a rock. Brantecore dropped a senseless Viveu and grabbed me, one hand on the neck, the other on my chest.

"Nuisance!" the mad Wuckl shrieked. "I missed you the first time, but I won't again. We're here, in Ecundo, alone. These bugs won't care, even the Wuckl won't care. You're nothing. Better off gone."

Bugs, he said, *bugs* …

"You … too …" I hissed. "You … too …"

Brantecore paused, then opened his beaks in the shape of a Wuckl smile. "Did you figure it out then?" he said. "How I can be so strong? How I can take out two Wuckl and an Ecundo by myself? How can I be so at ease with killing … as a creature so opposed to it? No. I wasn't born here either. I used to be a man, and I used to be a soldier, a good one, one who did his duty, no matter how distasteful, one who followed orders. One who knew his enemy …

"Yet, I saw the Wuckl lived without enemies. Weak, friendly, so giving. But they did have enemies … . *I* would have conquered these Wuckl had the Well made me something else … had I been something other than them. But now I was them, and I knew who their enemies were … and like a good soldier, I did my part. I fought their wars … against all arrivals, those who would drive them mad. Challenge their healing ways. Viveu's companion … *you*! You would change them, corrupt them! You all had to go.

"So now you know," Brantecore said at last, pushing me to the ground. "It won't save you. You'll die now, parasite!"

Brantecore pushed his hand into me again, to terrific pain. I couldn't think; I was terrified. It wouldn't be a near miss now. I would die. I fell; the pain was terrible. Brantecore followed me down. "So weak, all you can do is fall? No fight in you; I'm doing this world a favor ..."

I hissed at Brantecore, my arms flailing ... he was so fast the last time he did this. But not now; he was prolonging the agony, savoring it.

My long, wiry arms flailed ... and I found it. A big ball, like a child's head ... with a long, thin nose ... tapered to a ...

No, not a head. Riet's stinger! In my desperation, I let instinct direct me. With a terrific scream, I buried the stinger deep into Brantecore's side. I hoped the pain of the strike would be enough of a distraction. But his reaction was electric ... my pain diminished as Brantecore flung himself off me.

"No no, how dare ...!" Again, my vision gray, my mind reacting to instinct, I grabbed Brantecore's arms and held them apart—he could possibly heal himself. He was strong, but that strength ebbed fast. "No, no ... I almost had you ... I never ..."

It didn't take a minute. Ecundo poison was wildly effective. I let Brantecore drop into the surf.

My chest burned with fire, but I could ease the pain a little with my own touch. And I did, when it was all over.

As for the others?

Riet looked like he was in shock, but his legs moved slightly, and I could sense a stable vibration; he would live. I healed the wound to his tail and moved to Viveu.

She was very weak ... there was a terrible bruise on her neck ... and she breathed raggedly ..." Let me help you." I moved my hands to her neck. "Let me heal you."

"No, you can't. You're too—" She coughed shrilly. "I'm sorry. He needed to pay ... . Riet was a friend, mutual friend of—" She gave a weak squawk of pain over the memory. "We planned this for so long ... . I'm sorry. Wuckl ... we're just not good at killing."

"No, but using? You used me."

Viveu, whose eyes even now started glazing over, shook her head. "Yes, sorry. So sudden, there was no other way ... you were a gift, but Brant ... ." Viveu coughed. "He had a plan, too. I was ... a danger ... to him—wasn't fooled by me. He saw a chance, too ... used you."

"He was right," I said finally. "New arrivals will ruin the Wuckl. Brantecore made you want to kill. So did your love. You were his near miss."

"Yours ... too."

"He'll have no more of those. He's gone." I began clucking in a gentle way ... Wuckl tears. "What can I do for you?"

"Live. Life is near misses ... enjoy them, while they ..."

I would have done more for Viveu, but I couldn't ... there were no more near misses for her.

Chapter Five:
LAMOTIEN: CLONE FIVE
Sam Knight

Clone Five dreamed of an open sky above her and a gentle, cool breeze tickling across her skin. A light snow was just beginning to fall. A forest of small, spindly trees whispered quietly at the edge of the clearing she all but floated in like a gentle, soft cloud drifting low over a bed of small, red-leafed plants. She didn't move, reveling in this rare, pain-free moment she had to herself between waking and sleep. The stimulation simulations would start again soon, and then she would be required to participate and respond, but meanwhile, for this one moment, she was her own.

Tiny plants with round leaves, colored rich reds, oranges, and yellows, spread away in all directions, a mosaic ground cover over the gentle hills. She couldn't remember ever seeing anything like it and contentedly wished the hazy dream to continue forever.

An unfamiliar sensation, like a mild electric vibration, rippled under her skin and spread throughout what was left of her body, and she felt an uncontrollable urge to stretch, her torso beginning the movement before she could stop herself.

Sadness crept into Clone Five. She had learned that not moving helped prolong these short, precious moments, but now, her tortured body ignored her wishes and began stretching. The blissful feeling was lost as the horrible knowledge that she no longer had arms or legs to stretch out returned to the forefront of her existence.

But her torso continued to contract anyway. Unfamiliar muscles began to contort, and she wondered if she had been given something to force her to exercise her remaining muscles, perhaps as a punishment for the increasingly frequent times she lingered at the edge of consciousness instead of waking quickly to do her stimulation routines.

It didn't matter. There was so little left they could do to her to make things worse.

Her body, of its own volition, continued to stretch, seemingly growing longer, somehow flatter, somehow becoming impossibly long—long enough a new kind of panic rose up inside her. Something strange was happening, something she'd never felt before.

The unfamiliar world still surrounded her, and she realized now that, ridiculously, she saw all of it, all around her, all at once. From the strange plants beneath her—which seemed to be pressed right up against her vision—up into the sky above, and out in all directions. Nothing in a sphere around her was denied to her sight. And it didn't look *right*. Most of it was hazy and out of focus, like a dream. Only the things she focused directly on seemed to resolve, and then only until she turned her direct attention elsewhere.

A poor-quality stimulation simulation, perhaps? But why alter her perception so? What were they doing to her now? Something to her brain? The one organ she had thought they couldn't take from her.

Was it already time? Had they sedated her to keep her calm and complacent, and she'd already lost the last three days of her life? Was this some new kind of neurostimulation to keep her brain active during the final surgery? Or some kind of one last horrid experiment on her?

The odd stretching sensation finally reached a peak, her body spread impossibly far and thin. She didn't understand what was happening, but she knew her body could push itself no further, that it had reached the end of its limits, becoming uncomfortable.

But it didn't hurt. Not like things normally did.

Was she dead? Perhaps she was already in surgery and this was her subconscious way of dealing with the horrible feeling of having all of her remaining organs removed from her body. Or maybe it was her brain that was being removed.

Either way, it was the last step of the process of taking and transplanting her body parts into the woman she'd been cloned from, ending Clone Five's life, and she knew it.

She had known it was coming for most, if not all, of her twenty years of life, but she wasn't ready. She should have had three more days until the surgery. They'd stolen her last three days.

It was bad enough they had created her as parts for someone else, that they'd stolen her body from her, piece by piece over the last two years, but she'd always known that was going to happen. She'd never known a life other than preparing for that. But now they had stolen her final three days, too. Her final chance to contemplate the nature of the soul, to reach out for a god to ask for help. Her final hours to … live.

Clone Five opened her mouth to cry out in fear, and rage, and anguish, to release overwhelming and unrelenting waves of terrible emotions, but no sound came out.

Panic overtook her. She was already gone. She couldn't draw a breath, couldn't feel her mouth or her throat. She couldn't scream. She'd been deprived of everything, including the chance to even lament her own death.

Clone Five's body slowly contracted, shrinking back in upon itself, the involuntary stretch, or, she thought, the illusion of it, finally ending. She continued to shrink, imagining she was curling herself into the fetal position, as she had done for years—until there hadn't been enough of her left to curl up.

Sobbing silently, internally, somehow, she felt her body shaking, though she knew it was only an imagined thing. She waited for the darkness to come and take her, as it had each time she'd undergone surgery, each time they'd taken another part of her body away from her. Except this time there would be no waking up to the horror of guessing what was missing, finding out they'd taken an eye, or an arm, or the other leg. This time, there was nothing else left to take. This time they were taking the last of her organs. They were taking her life. And, when the darkness came, it would not recede.

But the darkness did not come.

Though the ground under her occasionally shook (she imagined they were moving her body from sterile room to sterile room), the dream of the open sky above her, gray with the cover of thin clouds, continued on. The hush of the trees, the wind through their thin branches, rose and fell with the breeze. Light snow fell upon her truncated body. She could feel each snowflake as it landed upon her. And each one she focused on as it fell toward her seemed to fall right into her eye when it landed, even though they fell in different places.

Clone Five blinked, or tried to. Nothing changed in her vision. The strange anesthesia dream continued, still allowing her to see all around at once. She took in a deep breath, feeding oxygen to her distressed mind, but even that was not right. Instead of her chest rising and falling, she felt herself contract and swell, pulling fresh air into her body from all directions at once.

And the world around her continued. As did she.

Eventually Clone Five could wait no longer for the darkness to overtake her, for the dream to fade, so she sat up.

Her perspective of the world around her moved as she did, but it was all wrong somehow.

She looked down at herself, which was really just focusing her attention upon herself by ignoring the rest of the world around her, and she found her limbless torso was tightly wrapped in some sort of puffy, pulsating blanket. Some kind of nutrient pack, maybe? Something keeping her organs alive while they performed surgery? Or perhaps her organs were already gone, and they were keeping what was left of her alive for some reason.

The thought horrified Clone Five. This was worse than dying. They had somehow trapped her in life, denying even the escape of death. Anguish overwhelmed her again, and again, she tried to scream.

This time, something happened. This time she could see and feel the white covering swell as air was taken into her body, and as she tried to cry out, she could feel the air, from all over inside of her, coming together to form a pocket. A pocket that moved to where her mouth should be and then was expelled from her body like a burst of flatulence.

The sound, the only thing she'd heard other than the gentle breeze, was a shocking discordance in the peaceful red- and orange-hued clearing around her, and it stunned her into stillness.

Like her vision, her hearing also seemed to come from all directions as her very skin registered the vibrations in the air. She wondered at the world around her, straining to listen, to *feel* the sounds of the trees rustling.

After a while, it occurred to her that without arms to push up with or legs to counterbalance her weight, she shouldn't have been able to sit up. And yet, she was. Her body bent in the middle, allowed her to hold her head up higher, but … it was not her head. Not really.

It was just another part of her body that she could choose to focus out of, to have a slightly raised perspective. But she could as easily focus out of her other end. Her … . No. There were no legs attached there. It wasn't any more a lower part of her body than the other was an upper. It just was. She just was.

Nor did she have a front or a back. She was just as much facing down as she was up, or to either side. To all sides. She corrected her thoughts, marveling: there were no sides, not anymore.

Clone Five thought again of God, of her soul, and of an afterlife—all ideas, a hope, her favorite caretaker, a kindly woman with a gentle voice and calm temperament, had given her—and then had been executed for doing so.

Was this Heaven?

If so, Clone Five could only hope there was also a Hell, and for the first time in her life, she thought it possible there might be some kind of justice for her and her favorite caretaker after all. Perhaps there was such a place as Hell, with a space waiting for the Council Leader she'd been cloned from—something else the caretaker had illicitly told her about.

The Council Leader had never come to see Clone Five or, the caretaker had said, any of the previous four clones made to be harvested for parts and organs. They were nothing more than tools, experiments used in an attempt to overcome an imposed sponge addiction used to politically control the Council Leader, and the Council Leader had never thought of the clones as human beings, let alone her own flesh and blood, her family—another idea learned from the caretaker, the only person who had ever shown Clone Five any sort of compassion, concern, or … love.

Clone Five had barely let that thought settle when she came back to the idea of Heaven. If that is where she was, then maybe the caretaker was here, too! And maybe Clone Five would finally get to meet her four previous sisters, or, if there were any, subsequent ones.

The idea excited her so much she found herself gleefully running around in a circle like a child, a feeling she hadn't had in well over a de-cade. She laughed, but no sound came out. She didn't care. Everything was so wonderful! The soft plants beneath her feet—

Clone Five, stumbling to a stop, looked down at her feet, at her legs, and gasped. Or tried to; again, nothing came out.

But as before, she felt air moving inside her, coming together to form a bubble, should she choose to let it out, but by then, it was too late to be a gasp. Panic set in again. This was all wrong.

She could still see in all directions, though not as well from below anymore, which was indeed a lower part again. As she bent to look at her feet, she could somehow, though not well, see out from her feet as well, see her upper self, bending over to look. It was as though some impossible mirror toyed with her perception, as if one of her eyes was looking into the other. She focused, trying to look out from her feet, trying to see what was looking at her feet.

As the blank, oddly featureless face bending down came into focus, she was horrified to see, from the other vantage, rudimentary eyes forming on her feet, looking back into her face. She shifted her focus back to the strange face that looked like hers, but not. The more she realized what looked wrong about the face, the more the face changed and became right, became *her* face, the one she'd studied closely in the mirror so that if she ever met the Council Leader, she would recognize her.

Of course, Clone Five had always assumed that the Council Leader would be older and have cold, hard eyes, and probably a short, bobbed haircut like the caretakers and medical technicians had.

To her astonishment, as she pictured what she thought the Council Leader looked like, the face took that shape, gaining wrinkles and steely eyes. Even the short, black hair.

Clone Five shook her head and felt the hair move, brushing against her ears. It tickled and made her smile. Clone Five had been jealous of hair. Her head had always been shaved. Paying attention from her feet, she watched herself shake her head and enjoyed leaning forward and back to feel the sensation of the hair moving across her cheeks. She wished it were longer so that she could feel it everywhere—and then it was.

Draped over her face, the fine hair dragged across Clone Five's belly and legs and tickled as she rocked back and forth. She wished she still had hands so she could touch it. And then, she did.

She ran her fingers through the luxurious hair, enjoying the feel of the fine texture against her skin. Oddly, she realized, she could feel the texture of her fingers through her hair as well. Just as she could see and hear in all directions, she seemed to be able to feel in all directions.

Clone Five laughed with delight, the air bubble coming out of her when it should this time, though it didn't sound right. It was no matter. She spun around in joy again, feeling the wind move through each strand of hair, through each spread finger. The soft ground under her feet. The gentle, icy bite of snowflakes on her skin.

She *was* in Heaven.

When Clone Five first became hungry, it didn't bother her much. Mostly because she wasn't sure what the feeling was at first. Decentralized, it was an overall feeling of fatigue rather than an ache in her central gut— something she was now well aware she no longer had. But her hunger worsened as the snow changed from gentle flakes to whipping ice crystals, and the waning sun sank low in the sky. The temperature was dropping, and Clone Five began to suspect that, Heaven or not, this place was real.

She was real. Her new body—if you could call such a thing a body—was real. And it was naked to the world, suffering from the cold.

Huddling her arms together, she found she could shiver when she tried to, but it wasn't a real shiver, just as pushing air through a newly formed mouth-hole hadn't really been breathing. The faux shivers imitated the movement but they generated no warmth.

And it was getting colder, and darker, as the storm worsened.

The ground rumbled again. At first, she thought the reoccurring sounds had been the wind, but when one grew stronger and shook her human shaped feet out from under her, leaving her sprawled in the cold snow, new kinds of panic set in. Fears she had never thought of before began to plague her: thirst, hunger, cold, dark, shelter. She knew she needed to find shelter at the very least, but it would be better if she could find help. Someone to tell her where—and what—she was. Someone who could feed her, clothe her, protect her. Someone who could give her all the things she'd once had.

The thought shocked Clone Five out of her wretched contemplation and into focus. She couldn't believe she'd actually been wishing to go back to her old life of being a captive used for body parts. After years of dreaming and fantasizing about escaping and being free, she had been dissuaded within mere hours by a little discomfort, by having the ground move beneath her feet.

What would her caretaker think of her now? After all the secret whispers of escape to a better world? After the caretaker had given her life to try to provide Clone Five with even a small amount of hope that there was something more?

Shame burned hot inside of her, giving her the concentration needed to pull herself together, to move on and leave the clearing to seek shelter, be it in the scraggly woods or elsewhere—or even not at all. It was better to die out here, alone with her memories of the kind caretaker, knowing she was finally free, than at the hands of the monsters who had been carving her up bit by bit for their inhumane purposes.

Earlier experimentation had shown Clone Five that rolling as a ball in her new body was the easiest way to move around when heading downhill, but it was nearly worthless for anything else. Not to mention, that much contact with the snow was cold, and it was hard to focus on where she was going when her body, and thus the place she focused her attention from, was spinning. With practice, she thought she might be able to roll her point of focus in counter to the movement of her body, but for now, walking on four legs, she determined, was best for travel in general. It required less effort to balance than the two-legged stance she was used to, less concentration than three, or more, legs, and, when she really tried, running was much faster than any other motion she was able to think of. In addition, it got all but four small contact points out of the cold snow.

With newfound ease, and little more than just a thought, Clone Five shifted into a four-legged form: a dog she had once seen in a stimulation simulation. The new shape was comfortable, and she broke into a trot, heading the length of the clearing and into the setting sun, uneager to go into the trees just yet. If she accepted this world as real, then there were sure to be unknown dangers lurking there.

In places, some of the soft plants that had once filled the area with color seemed to be repelling the deepening snow, so she aimed for those. Having the islands of color as her goal helped the ground pass by quickly and quietly beneath her paws. By the time she reached the far side of the clearing, she was no longer cold.

Stopping to take in her surroundings, she allowed her focus to drift all directions at once and discovered snow had accumulated on her back. With a quick shake, as she had seen the dog do, it was off of her.

Looking into the thick copse of short, wiry trees, she couldn't see far and had no idea what was beyond or which way to go. She decided to climb a tree to see if she could spot something that might give her direction: roads or buildings perhaps, where people would be.

Clone Five hesitated at the tree trunk, trying to decide what form, which shape would work best to climb up into the thin branches. Standing up on her hind legs to reach the lower limbs, she morphed into her most familiar form with two legs, and reached up with hands that could grasp branches and pull her up, which they did, easily. The motion came smoothly, and while she did not feel overly powerful or strong, she marveled at how easily she lifted her own weight. She had always struggled to lift or pull herself with the arms of her previous body.

This body looked the same, when she wanted it to, but somehow didn't work the same way. Whatever muscles she flexed to pull herself up worked, but they were different. She didn't feel the same strain on her fingers, the same weakness in her wrists, and though when she looked, it appeared her biceps were flexing and straining to lift her as she expected them to, it didn't feel like those were the actual muscles doing the work.

Fascinated by her own movements, Clone Five was surprised to find she'd already reached the top of the tree, the thin branches swaying, bent under her mass. The movement didn't bother her, and she was not afraid of losing her balance or of falling. This body was a good one.

As the icy storm pelted her naked skin, she became chilled again and quickly focused on looking out from the top of the tree. The edge of the forest, if there were one, was lost in an approaching blizzard, but something else wasn't. Twice as tall as the other trees, a massive, rounder, and wider tree, thickly covered in gray stringy leaves, moved through the forest.

Clone Five gaped at the colossal thing. Her wonder turned to panic as it changed direction and came straight for her. She quickly climbed down, dropping from the lower branches, heedless of scratches. Frantically trying to decide where to go, she slipped in the snow twice. By then the thing was already upon her. She froze, shocked at the sight of a giant man leaning over the tree to look down at her.

"Glathrielian?" His voice filled the air around her as he frowned.

Clone Five didn't know what the word meant. Afraid to move, she continued staring up into the giant's face, cursing herself for not remembering she could have four legs and run very fast. It was too late now. He could smash her with one stomp of his foot before she got away.

"Are you a Glathrielian? You are so small. Is my translator working? Can you understand me?" he asked.

Years of forced obedience prevented Clone Five from not answering. "I understand you," she said, forcing pockets of air up through her mouth to make passable words, "but I don't know what a Glathrielian is." She stumbled over forming the unfamiliar word.

"You are Lamotien!" The man's face lost all expression and suddenly, horribly, he began to fall apart. Blobs, dozens of them, each the size of Clone Five herself, dripped from him, falling from his hands, his face, as though he were melting wax. Worse, as the man finished falling apart, as the white, shapeless drops hit the ground, they began rolling to converge upon Clone Five.

Not wasting time trying to scream, Clone Five morphed into the dog and raced as fast as she could, back into the clearing, away from the horror. Panicked, she all but flew over the snow, aiming again for the bare patches where she could get better traction even if for only a leap or two. The sounds of hundreds of feet hitting the snow filled her canine ears. Glancing over her shoulder, she found she was being chased by a pack of dogs, fifty at least, that all looked like her.

Unlike dogs, the pack did not bark, or growl, or make any sound other than that of their paws against the snow. Coming up quickly behind them were beasts of the same size, but shaped differently, with longer ears and broader feet that allowed them to stay on top of the snow and move even faster. As the newcomers overtook the dogs, the dogs, mid-stride, would morph into the shape of the new beasts and quicken their strides, matching pace.

Clone Five, losing ground, wished she could have that shape too, and then she did. Her wider feet dispersed her weight, and she stopped sinking into the snow. The pack of creatures stopped gaining on her, but she could not pull any farther away. In mere moments, the end of the clearing came into sight, and Clone Five ran out of room to run. She steeled herself to charge headlong into the forest, preparing to dodge through branches and brambles.

Something came unseen, swooping out of the turbulent snow flurry, and caught her up in ropes, lifting her from the ground, carrying her up into the sky. Not ropes, Clone Five realized as she fought to free herself. Tentacles. She was in the grasp of something resembling a giant butterfly with eight tentacles that wrapped around her and countered her every move to gain freedom. It quickly lifted her up over the trees, high enough to stop her from squirming for fear of being dropped should she break free.

As soon as she stopped resisting, she wished it had dropped her instead.

The tentacles didn't bore into Clone Five's body so much as melt into it, becoming one with her. Or, more accurately, melting her body, forcing her to become one with them. As she lost the sensation of her distorting body, she gained the feel of the giant wings pushing against the air to keep herself aloft. She saw the pack of beasts below—*arctic hares*—coming together, merging into one giant form, growing back into the ambulatory tree—*the colony*—waiting for her to land and join with them.

But these observations were not hers. The thoughts—the understanding—was not hers. It was ... theirs.

Ours.

The butterfly they imitated—*Yaxa*—the thoughts invading Clone Five were those of the Yaxa colony, not hers.

Clone Five had no thoughts. Or nearly none. She was no longer Clone Five, she was ... them.

Us.

The thought was not *hers*. Though it felt like it was. But some small part of her knew it was not. She was still herself, somewhere, barely, but they were taking it away from her, suppressing it, making *her* into *them*.

Us.

They were stealing her mind.

We are one, they told themselves, silencing the new addition to the colony, rendering it dormant, its function in the colony reduced to nothing more than mass, controlled and orchestrated through the whole. They reached into the part of them that was now little more than a new part of its mind, pulling the answers they needed from it.

The new addition to the colony was Lamotien, but somehow it didn't know that. It thought of itself as *human*, as *she*. They compared its memories of *human* with their collective memories. It was a match for Glathrielian, though those beings were nearly nonsentient after losing a war with the Ambrezans.

Examining the newcomer's memories revealed no knowledge of Well World and much that was strange and previously unheard of to any of the colony. They sifted memories and tried to understand the strange, alien, and terrible things found within. One idea, almost too far-fetched to be possible, came up repeatedly: a new Entry.

As they considered the possibility this Lamotien was truly alien, they delved deeper into its memories, digging into its strange feelings, into its fear of … being held captive … amputations … being nothing more than parts for use by another being …

Somewhere deep inside of them, a suppressed spark flickered with a terrible recognition.

Their thoughts became confused as *she* realized *she* was nothing more than parts again. As *they* realized *they* were nothing more than organs harvested to be used by someone else.

Individual memories flickered against the whole, mixing torrentially. *She/they* had escaped one hell only to be trapped in another, and in this new one, *she/they* had taken not only *her/their* bodies, but *her/their* minds as well.

Another flicker in the unity of their mind, and its grip on *her/they* loosened briefly.

Clone Five screamed with all she had left.

As they flapped their giant wings one last time, preparing to land, preparing to merge with the others on the ground, confusion and panic rippled throughout the Yaxa colony. Fear and horror of being nothing more than body parts spread through them like a virus. Individual thoughts and feelings, normally dormant when joined, broke through the thoughts of the whole in a tidal wave of panic, destroying the cohesive and controlling thoughts of the one which had been formed to hold them all together.

She? What is her*? There is only us. I am nothing but an organ donor! There is no I.*

Clone Five could feel her fear, her rage, the terrible memories of her violations echoed back at her from dozens of minds as they too cried out in horror.

And then the colony fell apart.

One moment they were a giant Yaxa butterfly, landing to merge with the rest of the colony, to continue the routine patrol of the border with the Godidal hex, and the next they were individual Lamotiens, nothing more than scared, small, white blobs, falling from the sky, landing in the snow, and rolling away in panic.

Taking advantage of the chaos, Clone Five imitated the others and rolled away frantically, but she did not do so aimlessly. She headed for the forest line.

As the sun finished setting and the night grew dim, Clone Five rolled on, and the trees of the forest went by in a blur. Working at assimilating the knowledge that had been forced into her brain while she was part of the colony, she paid no attention to her direction. The information had been broken and sporadically given only as the mind that had dug through hers explained things just enough and no more than needed to discover what they had wanted to know.

But she now knew those *things*, the white blobs that had dripped off the giant man's face, that had become a Yaxa, an *alien* butterfly, considered themselves—. She fumbled for a term that fit. Human is what she would have used, but it had been made clear to her that humans were *Glathriel*— just another kind of alien.

People was the term she settled upon as she broke through into a small clearing. Those things thought of themselves as people. A people called Lamotiens. And that's where she was: Lamotien. And worse, that's *what* she was, too.

She was one of those white, shapeless blobs, able to take any form she chose.

The revelation hadn't fully registered when the other being had been searching through her mind, despite the fact it/they had told her. It/they had been intentionally suppressing her thoughts, her ability to think, because she had been preventing the colony from acting as one. Endangering the colony. Putting the lives of all those ... people ... at risk.

How had this happened? How had she become a Lamotien? There was a clue, a hint of an answer in something they had called her: Entry.

She didn't understand how any of this was possible, but somehow they understood she used to be something else, from somewhere else, and now she was one of them.

Distant lights ahead caught her attention, and Clone Five slowed to a stop, only now realizing that, in her panic, she had stayed in ball form, and that she had managed to rotate her focus to counteract the motion of her body. Shifting to the wide-footed form, the arctic hare, she quietly moved closer to the lights until she recognized them as windows.

The buildings were blocky and stacked around and on top of each other. As the ground trembled under her feet again, Clone Five realized they were sturdily built against the constantly shifting earth. Through the lit windows she could see movement, and it didn't take long to recognize Lamotiens going about their business. Living their lives.

She thought again of the revelation that these things were *people*.

Before her fear had overcome the colony, passing from individual to individual like an electric shock, she had felt their minds there with her—no, they had been a part of her. All of them. The individuals making up the whole, collectively becoming the Yaxa, together had all comprised the one mind who made sure they all worked together perfectly. They weren't merely acting as one; they truly were one. And they had made her part of that one.

Despite her panic and fear, she had felt no hostility from them. Not as such. What she had really sensed was their feeling of unity, of belonging, of something Clone Five could find no word for other than *family*.

And Clone Five had destroyed it.

At first, it was not difficult for Clone Five to find her way back, following her own trail in the snow, but as the last of the twilight failed and more snow filled the track, it became harder to find. She was near giving up when a transport of some sort appeared in the distance, colored lights flashing against the night sky. As it sank too low to see, she assumed it had landed where she had abandoned the colony.

Lights came on in the distance, guiding her the rest of the way through the dark forest.

After a while, Clone Five stepped into the clearing in her human—Glathrielian—form, and hugged her naked self against the cold, the darkness, and her own fears. She didn't know what would become of her, but she had begun to understand what she had done to them—to these *people*—and that knowledge cut to her newfound soul. It had driven her back here, despite her fears, through the snow and the darkness, to face them.

In front of her, hundreds of Lamotiens were scattered about the clearing. Watching everything, Clone Five guessed she was witnessing a triage scene. Lamotiens were in many different forms and sizes. Some were more shapes than anything else, merging and separating, twisting and contorting themselves into whatever was immediately required until mechanical replacements were brought in: a ramp, a makeshift barrier, a table, a gurney, a tripod to hold another light. The flurry of activity was dizzying. At the center of it all, next to a small boxy construct she assumed was the transport she'd seen, and lit by the vehicle's floodlights, sat the tree-shaped creature the Lamotiens had first appeared as, though it now rested on the ground as a bush and was much reduced in size.

Some Lamotiens were working to help others who were obviously in distress, evidenced by their shapes constantly morphing uncontrollably. Others were penned inside temporary fencing, preventing them from running away again, and many seemed to be actively avoiding any kind of contact with others.

It soon became apparent that a few were actually guarding the tree colony, presumably preventing any infected Lamotiens from coming into contact with it.

Clone Five considered the word *infected* and realized it was correct. She had infected the colony with a terrible fear, a terrible idea that went against everything that they were, an idea that could, and probably would, ruin their lives. And maybe the lives of anyone they came into contact with. Clone Five had potentially doomed an entire people, because contact for these people was a literal sharing of minds, of thoughts, of ideas and experiences.

A spotlight fell upon her, startling her, and she fought the urge to turn back into a ball and roll away. Instead, Clone Five stood up straight and waited. She could not feel a heart pounding in her chest, though she felt it should have been. She lifted her chin, and for the first time, she understood something her favorite caretaker had said, shortly before Clone Five never saw her again: She had to do the right thing, or she would not be able to live with herself.

Clone Five had never had the chance to hurt someone before, she'd only been hurt. And she had hurt these people. Not intentionally, but she had nonetheless. And she didn't like it. Even in this world. Even with this new body. Clone Five could not, would not, leave others feeling the way she had spent the last few years of her life feeling. Not if she could help it.

An assorted collection of Lamotiens closed in on her. They all wore different shapes: a cat with arms, a four-legged bird, a squid-faced spider, and others, even more confusing. But they all had one thing in common: they all pointed a small device at her. Clone Five was sure it was a weapon, and she held perfectly still.

"Don't move," one of them commanded. Clone Five understood the language, though she didn't know how she was able to grasp the strange undulating pattern of sounds that reached her body.

"I won't," she answered, surprised when her own body rippled and sent out gentle waves of sound. This was how they spoke, she realized. And she had understood their language. And spoken it.

"You are not Glathrielian." It was an accusation.

"No." She finally identified which figure spoke. The one near the center, who looked like a giant mouse with elephant legs.

"What are you?"

"I am human. Or was. I believe I am now Lamotien. An Entry."

The leader took a step back. The other Lamotiens followed suit, and then they all stepped closer, touching shoulder to hip to tentacle. Clone Five could see their bodies merging, ever so slightly, at the points of contact.

"Lamotien has had no Entry in recorded memory," the voice spoke again. This time the cadence was different, and the sound waves that her body received felt different and came from more directions. Clone Five realized they had just formed a colony. Probably to communicate and to assess and make decisions. "We have no protocol. We do not understand what has happened."

"I do. This is my fault. I did not understand what it meant to be Lamotien. I did this to them."

"What did you do?" The weapons in the separate hands all came up as one.

Clone Five hesitated, not sure how to explain what she knew, what had happened when she had been forced to join the Yaxa colony. The act of the one mind, the colony mind, working for the good of the whole, had been condemned by Clone Five as invasive, abusive: a violation of her *self*. And the colony, once working as a whole, had fallen apart as individuals took on the shame and horror of what they had done to her—what was being done to *them* as individuals—by the colony.

Could Clone Five explain this to others well enough for them to understand? Was it possible that sharing that idea verbally could have the same disastrous effect?

She couldn't risk that.

"It is too complicated to explain with this form of communication," she said.

"You will not join with us. You will not spread this."

"Agreed. It is not worth the risk."

They stared at each other for an uncomfortable amount of time. Clone Five assumed they were debating what to do with her. Possibly considering eliminating her to prevent this from spreading any further.

An idea came to Clone Five. "I am already infected. I cannot be infected again. And I have recovered. Let me see if I can help them." She pointed to the Lamotiens in the temporary pen.

When the colony training the weapons on her did not reply, she shifted to what she thought was her Lamotien form, the amorphous shape she'd originally awoken in. She spoke again, her body vibrating the words out gently to convey she meant no harm. "What could I make worse? Give me a chance to help at least one of them."

The colony in front of her hesitated and then broke apart. Two stayed with weapons on Clone Five while the rest restructured fencing to isolate one Lamotien who was pressed into a corner trying to make itself look like a pile of snow. In its distress, the mimicry kept failing, causing it to flicker like a bad holo.

When it was separated from the others in the pen, the two with weapons waved Clone Five forward.

She rolled into the pen and waited, allowing them to shut it behind her, keenly aware that all of them focused upon her with weapons ready.

Moving slowly toward the cowering Lamotien, Clone Five stopped when it finally reacted to her presence.

"I am Clone Five," she said, her body vibrating very gently, remorsefully. "I was the one in the Yaxa colony."

Though there were no eyes, no face, no fixed form even, somehow Clone Five could tell the Lamotien had focused its attention on her, so she moved a little closer. "I understand how you feel. I am sorry I made you feel that way. I forgive you, and I would like to ask you to forgive me."

Fear rose up inside Clone Five at what she was about to do, but she shunted it away. So many terrible things had happened to her in her short life; there was nothing worse that could be done to her. And this was a choice she was making for herself.

She slowly extended a part of herself out toward the Lamotien. A part that she could focus out of, a part that, she knew, if the Lamotien accepted it, she could communicate through. A part that she could *join* through.

"Please forgive me."

The Lamotien reached back.

When they connected, beginning to merge, to join, their thoughts became as one. They became a new colony of two, with a single mind.

And Clone Five never could have imagined or asked for a greater feeling of unity and belonging. Of being made whole.

Her overwhelming feeling of elation became the other's feelings, as they were one and of the same mind now. And the other's feelings of guilt for having violated another, and the horror at having been violated, were cushioned by Clone Five's previous experiences and acceptances of them, of how she had coped with them, and of how grateful Clone Five was to now be sharing this experience of being made whole in ways she'd never imagined possible.

Information was freely exchanged within the single mind, and Clone Five began to understand the life of a Lamotien: the parts shared and the parts, as small as they were, kept private, or at least separate, for individuals. They were neither male nor female, nor terribly concerned with individuality, and through Clone Five's alien perspective, the Lamotien was awed by gaining such a clear understanding of the foreign ideas of self and sexes, and the way they interacted. Clone Five had many new things, new ideas, and new perspectives to share with the Lamotiens.

The Lamotien revealed the colony's surprise when they had first discovered such a small Glathrielian, let alone one with a semblance of intellect. Until then Clone Five hadn't realized how small in comparison Lamotiens were to many other species, and that the colonies were formed by many in order to perfectly match the sizes of others in mimicry, and the one mind they were together marveled at the conflicting ideas of feeling so small yet feeling normal sized.

As they decided it was time to break apart and try to help others, a new, terrible separation anxiety began to overwhelm the part of them that was Clone Five, but the rest of her, the other part that was about to separate, exuded understanding and confidence and love.

When Clone Five stood alone, an individual again, the people around her in the night, rolling around under the spotlights in all their strange forms and sizes, were no longer alien. They were family she wanted to be with, and she never could have imagined or asked for a bigger, more understanding, or more closely knit family.

Excited, Clone Five hurried to merge with, and help, her next family member in need.

Chapter Six:
OOLAKASH:
LOOKING BACK, I WOULDN'T
CHANGE A THING
Elektra Hammond

Angelita Marianna Luisa Fernandez determinedly stepped through the zone gate and was never heard from again.

Lita zipped through the Museum of the Well, a vast space she adored. She whizzed by the complex exhibits about the Markovians and the dioramas about the creation of the Well World. She'd been fascinated by the Markovians as a youngster, reading everything topical she could put her eidetic eyes on, so she'd pushed to expand the section on Markovian ruins in the part of the galaxy where the Confederacy held sway. Despite her current predicament, being here gave her a warm sense of satisfaction.

She shook off the reverie and kept moving.

She did regret all the improvements she'd made to the circulation through the museum. The main path was clear to everyone, not just those familiar with the exhibits, with gentle rose lighting marking either side.

The men? women? beings? chasing her were hampered both by their lack of knowledge of the museum's layout and their bulky environmental suits.

They moved as gracefully as bricks, ignoring marked boundaries. The entire staff would be busy with repairs for a very long time—it was easy to destroy what had taken so long to assemble.

Lita, zeroed in on *almost* escaping her pursuers, put the damage they were doing from her mind. It could be repaired later, when the current problem was taken care of. Compartmentalization was a skill earned at a high price on her homeworld—where she was often little more than a piece of meat. She pushed those distracting thoughts aside for later. Moving at speed, but with great care, she practically giggled as she ducked, dodged, teased, and shepherded them out of the museum toward a less populated area of the city complex. Even now, after several years in the hex, it was hard to hold back from the giddy, self-indulgent joy of speed. She slowed a tad to focus on the task at hand while trying to figure out who was chasing her. *Her sensors at the hex's edge had alerted her to a possible problem, and she went to the museum to figure things out, confident that she could handle whatever it was alone. She hadn't expected a major armed incursion.*

No.

She wasn't going to fall back into blaming herself for the actions of others. She let that go when she came to the Well World, when she got her second chance.

Even as she zoomed along, her past intruded. Again. She gave it a solid mental shove, but it re-emerged:

"Angelita Marianna Luisa Fernandez, stand still right this instant." Her mother stamped her foot, just the tiniest bit. "Dolores can't get your dress fitted properly if you keep squirming."

Angelita posed on a stool, trying desperately not to hop from one foot to the other, slightly dizzy. She had to obey her mother—after the foot stamp, dearest mother would start pulling her privileges if things didn't go well. She was covered in ridiculously expensive imported synthetic textiles, swaying as her mother and the designer argued about every miniscule detail of her new dress. It was to be in the very latest mode, smothering yet showing tantalizing hints of flesh in odd peekaboo windows like just below her belly button, sliding in and out of view under her skirts, while keeping most of her uncomfortably covered to the wrists and ankles. The open windows were everywhere—a feature of the electronics in the fabric—so her mother adored it, and Angelita's modesty didn't get a vote. It made her cringe to even think about it.

It was all the rage, so her mother adored it, and she would wear it.

The dress wasn't even completed, and she already hated it.

Angelita would be put on display. Every inch of her. Again. Simply an ornament to be pawed and grabbed. Her mother discretely watched, guarding her purity, waiting for someone with money or power, or better yet both, to offer a trade worthy of Angelita. The thought made her sick.

What had she done that her mother didn't trust her; thought she had to be guarded every single minute? Was her mother projecting her own desires onto Angelita?

Days later, her mother was a hostess at a high-level meeting, dragging her (wearing the hideous new dress) onto an interplanetary cruiser.

Angelita endured the pinches and grabs, listening without seeming to, as she realized her home planet was accepting an offer to join the Com. The leadership of her world had each been promised whatever they desired.

For one of them, that desire was her.

Had she somehow made the Viceroy think she was interested in him? Had she let her gaze fall on him while she worked out mathematical proofs in her head, fighting the sheer boredom? There was always some tantalizing new problem from her brother's studies for her to focus on, thanks to her eidetic memory and her bizarre habit (or so her mother called it) of reading textbooks.

When her mother glanced away, Angelita slid out of the room and wandered the ship until she found a dark corner in an unused emergency shelter near the engine room. There, she gave in to her despair, softly crying, horrid dress puddled around her, as she tried to synthesize a way out.

Time passed. Lita thought better about things and got up to return to her stateroom. She hadn't eaten all day, corseted into the hated dress. She was stopped by the sound of approaching people—people who clearly didn't care who heard them.

She crouched back down and listened as they wreaked destruction throughout the room, concentrating on the engine. Her dark hole, not part of anything important, was passed over. Frustrated, she again turned to tears.

Eventually, she gave up.

Later, in the darkness, there were sirens and jostling as more people joined her in the shelter. Then, noises and wrenching in the dark and somehow they were on another ship. Before they'd settled in, or anything, another emergency forced them all back into the shelter, and they somehow ended up on the Well World. Every story has a beginning.

Lita shook off the memory, years old and a lifetime ago, and pushed herself to even greater speed. She slipped through a discreet entrance and hid in the docents' shared office area, letting the intruders pass by.

Once they were safely past, she used the communications system to call for reinforcements. Then she waited, still hiding, like she had so long ago.

After Lita's secondary education in the hex was complete, her Guild Induction was both grand and glorious.

While she planned to continue her scientific studies as a hobby, she shocked her mentor in the Education Guild by joining the much less prestigious Political Guild. She was appointed deputy ambassador, a less important job than it sounded (akin in many ways to being vice president), since Oolakash weren't interested in other hexes all that much (even with translators, outsiders talked *so* slowly!).

It was like talking to people on a different planet in the same system, with the accompanying time lag. That frustration left the embassy in Zone empty nearly all the time.

Gradually, the ambassadorship had become a plum given to someone intellectually gifted who needed to slow down. They gained an impressive title and a private residence, rare among the Oolakash, with few official duties, which was even more rare. They advised the Ruling Council as much—or as little—as they chose, and they had to go to Zone if there was a dire emergency that required intervention from outside the hex.

Lita was technically at the beck and call of the ambassador, who barely spent any time at Zone, leaving her to manage her own schedule. And to focus on her unofficial duties.

She spent her off hours volunteering at the Museum of the Well, improving their exhibits, especially on the Markovian ruins elsewhere in the galaxy; brains the size of a planet, catering to your every desire, your every whim, by a simple thought.

She wondered what happened to the Markovians, who could lead lives of total hedonism or public service or pure research. In the end, did they all just get bored? Maybe she would figure it out here.

She reproduced all the reading she'd done before coming to the Well World, to share it with her new people. *Markovian Ruins: An Advanced Exploration* by Jared Markov and *Educated Guesses on What Makes a Markovian Gate Open: A Dissertation* by Eva Whitley were her favorites.

It seemed like last week that Lita had been assigned to a learning group, where she made her first Oolakash friends among the miniature sea dragonettes, and settled into the hex as home.

Lita had followed Dame Freeg, apprehensive, as they headed to the Gymnasium. She'd never been athletic—although her long and bony new body was certainly an agile swimmer and becoming more so every day. She hadn't inquired what the Dame's guild affiliation was and regretted it. The major importance of the guilds had been stressed during what orientation they'd cobbled together for her. The long bony heads and the tiny red eyes of her fellow Oolakash still spooked her—she flinched at reflective surfaces and was slow to learn the physical capabilities of her body, even as she exceled at the mental ones.

It was Dame Freeg who pushed her, who ran her through the simplest exercises a child would do over and over and over until she used her new body without thought.

Regardless, her hexmates were somewhat in awe of her, the first Entry here in more than three hundred years.

"Come along, little pipefish." Dame Freeg led the way along a smooth narrow orangish-ombre hallway. Everything here was worn coral-like corridors in an amazing rainbow of colors opening into even more colorful coral rooms, from study rooms to vast caverns. All was communal, and folk got along for the most part. She had everything she needed and had been encouraged to ask questions.

The hallway opened into a good-sized room full of ... tiny Oolakash at what looked like desks. It was a school. She'd mistranslated Gymnasium—or maybe it had multiple meanings. She was half thrilled and half horrified. She loved learning. But these tiny students were so young! Still, Lita resolved to learn quickly.

The glyphs of Oolakash were totally foreign to her, so she learned reading and writing with the youngest class of the sea-dwelling Oolakash, the sea dragonettes. So confusing that the place, the people, and the language all had the same identifier! Her classmates were confused to have someone so long in their group, but they were accepting. Her eidetic memory made learning quick. That, at least, had stayed with her when so much else had changed. They helped her learn, giggled at her silly mistakes, and adored playing chasing games with her during breaks. She became everyone's big sister, like Dame Freeg was everyone's aunt. That was common, she learned, with those in the Education Guild. The Dame continued to look in on her, mentoring her like family.

Once Lita could read Oolakash, everything accelerated. Free time was spent studying on her own. Here, that was encouraged and nurtured—in her other life (which receded further into the past as each day passed), she'd had to hide her scholarship.

Oolakashian water technology was far in advance of anything on her home planet, or anywhere in the Confederation—at least she thought it was. She didn't yet understand how salinity was being manipulated to create viewing screens, nor how the superfast water networks functioned—fast enough to keep even an Oolakash happy—but one day she would.

There was nuclear power involved, too, warming up the cool depths. While the Oolakash could tolerate the cold of the deepest sea, that didn't mean they couldn't appreciate a little warmth sometimes—and going up into the shallows was impossible. They needed the pressure of the lower depths to survive. Her orientation had been quite specific on that, and there were clearly visible warning signs if you strayed too high, heading into the lighter water of the Overdark Ocean.

The lack of pressure could kill you long before you ran into an irate Urifraud patrolling the shallows, determined to take out its anger on someone or something. Her life was a complete joy at this point. The housing guild had placed her into a sociable dorm convenient both to the school and an Education Guild cafeteria. She was too busy to figure out preparing her own food just yet, but students were entitled to government rations. She was trying each of the available options and finding every one of them delicious in her new body. She was apparently a foodie now.

Being happy will do that to you.

When her education was complete, she would choose one of the guilds—she hadn't decided which one yet—and become a functioning member of Oolakash society. The females ran things here, through the guild system, while the males (who were prized for their attractiveness—and even had the ability to change their coloration at will) took possession of the females' eggs, fertilized them, and carried them to term. After birth, they were the primary caregivers for the Oolakash young.

Some of the beautiful males worked, but not in the more demanding fields and never in leadership positions. Many of them worked in food preparation—they were often skilled manipulating their tentacles, making their food presentation top rate. As Apicus, an ancient of Old Earth, said, "You eat first with your eyes." He was right. Becoming an Oolakash hadn't changed that.

Lita had slowly made a corner of the space her own, with spare projects here and there, and the company of Tessie, her pet gooeyfish. Tessie's large clear dome gave slightly when it was stroked, and she preferred you to start at the outer edge and stroke gently toward the sensitive center. Visible through it were bright yellow radii that served some unknown biological function. Trailing under the dome were long dark tendrils that turned to bright pink halfway down, an unusual feature Tessie was often complimented on. Tessie was quite affectionate, keeping Lita company when she studied or she slept, and congenial with her dormmates.

Lita passed through the sea dragonettes, the pipefish, the dragonfish, testing on her own as much as possible, learning about her new home and the planet it was a part of ... the Well World. As much as she studied, there was always more information, despite the fact that Oolakash didn't visit other hexes.

Lita would never forget her arrival in the water hex:

Angelita Marianna Luisa Fernandez (now simply Lita) awoke with a start and looked around. The motion moved her entire body, sending her spinning through the ... water? She was underwater, but she seemed to be breathing just fine. That snake guy back in Zone had said some of the hexes were in water—this must be one of them.

When she slowed, she looked at her body. Bony, a bit rounded, and ... tentacles? Yes. Definitely tentacles. But they felt right. She used them to help explore the rest of her body. Armored bony plates covered the pouched belly her wealth of tentacles surrounded before it tapered to a ... tail? She had a tail now! She experimentally curled and uncurled her tail slowly, and the motion sent her smack into the passageway ceiling with a dull thud.

Lita gently felt her head with a tentacle, realizing she had no idea what it was supposed to feel like, but there were no sore spots. Her head was set on a long narrow neck, and she had those bony plates everywhere. She really wanted a mirror.

She swam along the corridor, building up speed as her confidence grew, trying to find someone, anyone who could direct her. *There must be some place for new arrivals to go, right?*

When Angelita saw the nightmare creature swimming toward her, those creepy red eyes in a bony horse-shaped head, she tried to backpedal and sent herself into another damn spin.

"Easy now, tadpole, I'm not going to hurt you. I'm Dame Tiffal." The nightmare creature waved its tentacles in a soothing pattern as it whistled the words at high speed.

It soothed her.

Looking at the creature, from top to the tapering tail, she realized she, too, looked like this.

Letting go of her old Confederacy fears, she tooted back, "I've only just arrived. I don't know where to go. Can you help me?"

"Of course. What's your name then, tadpole?"

She started to give her old name and realized that life was gone now. "Call me Lita."

"Now then Lita-tadpole, tell me where you traveled from."

"Zone. I think it was called Zone." She was getting more adept at the bugling sounds. Her new species spoke very quickly.

"An Entry!" The other *what-were-these-things-called* seemed quite excited. "I'll take you to the local Magistra. Come along, Lita-tadpole."

"What is this place called?"

"Welcome to Oolakash."

Once Lita got through primary school with those younger than her, it was time for her to do whatever *she* wanted. That had never been an option in her life pre-Oolakash, on that other planet, and she was nervous she'd choose poorly.

After much thought, she elected specialization in both chemistry and chemical engineering, fascinated by the basics behind the Oolakash's water tech. She looked forward to learning more about it.

The advanced education was part mechanized, part classwork, and she'd be expected to keep up with advances in her chosen fields once she became a Guild Member.

The routine of classwork, projects, grading, and teaching was almost relaxing—the required semesters passed in a blur of discovery.

In her spare time, she immersed herself in whatever information the Oolakash had on the Markovians. She combined it with what she'd read before she came to the Well World and upgraded the Markovian exhibits in the Museum of the Well, adding interactive learning modules and improving the overall flow.

The dead Markovian worlds in Confederacy space had *only* had a forty to forty-five kilometer thick crust made of Markovian brain, compared to the Well World, which was a huge Markovian brain covered with a thin planetary crust. Markovian worlds were thought to have allowed their residents to live like kings, yet the Markovians were all dead and gone, a true mystery. Where did they go?

Figuring it out was a passion project for her.

Working in the museum, often alone, was also sometimes useful.

Of course, Lita's job as Deputy Ambassador was a cover for her real assignment.

Her induction into the Spy Guild was small and secret, and most of the attendees were masked and unidentifiable. Lita's portfolio was to work within the government of the hex, building a web of connections. Her highest priority assignment was to combine her government contacts and her knowledge of water tech to discover who was trying to steal

Oolakash nuclear tech to reverse engineer it, rendering any Oolakash trade deals moot.

There had already been two attempted incursions that failed, possibly because they didn't realize how deep Oolakash's cities were. They'd likely be better prepared if they returned. Lita had set up a series of sensors along the borders of the hex to alert her to any activity there.

An alert from those sensors was why she was in the Museum of the Well before it opened.

Lita silently slipped out of concealment and darted past the intruders, daring them to catch her, only to lead them back the way they'd come. While they likely were unaware, she could sense the secret police in that direction (there were subtle vibration changes in the water, paired with high frequency notification blips), all in response to her signal.

From the intruders' gestures, it was clear they were running low on air, and she smiled fiendishly—messing with the Oolakash was a dangerous prospect, at best.

She whistled a warning that she was about to head past the brouhaha, with the strangers in pursuit, and swiveled around to watch the capture.

The Magistra of Defense for the entire hex was there, as she was one of the few Oolakash with a translator. Lita made a mental note to request a translator of her own—it would have made things easier. The Magistra asked why they were in Oolakash and waited for the inevitably slow reply. Other races were So. Very. Slow.

Lita could sort of understand their spokesman, who was speaking in Confederacy, which seemed like a language she'd known as a child. They *lied* and said they were paid to find an Entry. Lita knew they were after Oolakash water technology.

The Magistra acknowledged their response and continued the questioning for what seemed like days—it couldn't have been that long, really. It was just the slow speech of the would-be thieves. The Magistra ordered the guards to imprison them.

Perhaps their belongings would yield more answers.

Perhaps not.

They died slowly. The deep ocean is both unyielding and unforgiving.

Chapter Seven:
DUNH'GRAN:
A LIFE IN SHELLS
Davis Ashura

Jared Stencil paid little-to-no attention to the grass he was mowing. Instead, his mind was set on the past. His human past, which shouldn't be so important now. Not when he was a Dunh'gran, a kind of flightless bird, and living on a planet at the back end of the undiscoverable.

The transformation into this life had started when he'd uncovered a galaxy-sized Ponzi scheme founded by Carlito Messier, his employer at the time. Thousands of people had been hoodwinked, and when the illicit plan had been exposed, thousands more had lost everything they owned.

And Jared's reward for exposing this wretched scheme?

The joy of being run off his home planet where he'd headed off into deep space, one step ahead of the goons gunning for him. And after all that chasing and running, he'd somehow ended up here, in this place called Well World, to a hex called Calipolis, where he'd impossibly been transformed into this creature he'd never even heard of.

All because of some damn space pirates—rebels against the Com as they called themselves—and that misfit captain, Serge Ortega, who promised Jared would eventually grow used to his new body. But if so, when would that actually happen? Jared sometimes still missed being human.

He sighed, a warbling tone echoing from his raptorlike beak.

Then again, it wasn't all bad. At least here, he was safe. There was no chance Mr. Messier could ever discover him on Well World. From what Jared understood, only the desperate ever found their way to the planet. And if nothing else, he'd been desperate.

If only there was something to do, though.

For a person used to a nightlife full of dancing, drinking, and gambling, Calipolis was utterly dull. Worse, among the Dunh'gran, Jared had no useful skills. It turned out his new people loved one thing in life: racing. It didn't matter if it was running, flying, or hang gliding. They loved to race, especially on their old-style internal-combustion-driven motorcycles, even though they had electric vehicles for nearly every other aspect of life. *Getting into the wind* as they called it, rumbling along on motorcycles that sounded as loud as thunder rolling across the plains.

Jared had to admit, seeing a flight of Dunh'gran decked out in their leathers, roaring down a wide-open highway, was an awesome sight. He just wished he had some kind of talent for racing like the rest of his species. The wind rushing through his feathers, the feeling of flight, the thrill of chasing the sun …

But he had no talent as a racer. Not even a little. And in this regard, his human skills didn't help him either. They had been similar to his physical build: unimpressive. He'd been of average height and weight—one-hundred seventy-five cm and eighty kilos—with unremarkable brown hair and eyes. The only thing that set him apart from utter mediocrity had been his talent at finding patterns in numbers. It was what had earned him a junior partnership before thirty at the then-most-prestigious financial firm on his homeworld. It was that same ability that led him to learn what Mr. Messier had really been doing with all those investment funds.

Shady bastard.

And while the Dunh'gran had a fairly modern hex with exceptional engineering and technology, Jared's abilities in finance didn't really translate. His new people didn't care about economics. In this one regard, they were absolutely primitive. *Futures trading?* Nothing. *Derivatives?* Blank stares. *Leveraged exchange-traded funding?* Sheer confusion.

It was why Jared was forced to do something as basic and boring as mowing lawns. It was the only job at which the Dunh'gran government, which ruled Calipolis with a velvet-covered iron fist, thought he was competent. Riding around on an electric mower, trimming hedges, and all sorts of dismally dull kind of work.

He cheeped to himself at the boring nature of his duties.

Currently, he worked for Ouichopper Industries, a racing and industrial conglomerate. The company had a position available as a grounds-keeper at their corporate offices, one made available to Jared thanks to the government and his host family, the Santalines, particularly their son, Kars, who worked here too, as a custodial engineer—a janitor.

Speaking of …

Jared checked the sun. One of the advantages of being a Dunh'gran was always knowing the time by just peering skyward. His instincts were accurate to within two minutes. And in thirty-two minutes, it would be time to clock out.

Barely enough time to finish mowing the front lawn of this office complex that could have fit in without a second look on a dozen worlds in the Confederation—low-lying buildings, flat-roofed and with mirrored windows, set among a greenery of grass, shrubs, and the occasional thicket of trees. A faux forest setting. There was even a fake pond with a fountain spraying in the center.

Jared cocked his head, blinked, cocked his head to the other side, measuring … . There *was* barely enough time to finish mowing the front lawn, but if he raced … . A trill of excitement, and he gunned the accelerator. The lawn mower was slow, but it was fast enough, lurching forward. Jared cawed in pleasure, leaning into the wind as he imagined himself flying. Soon enough, the work was finished, but Jared never let off the accelerator even as he angled his mower over to the garage out back. With a screech of tires, he braked hard, slamming his ride into its proper place, his seat rocking before settling.

Then it was done. The racing was over.

Warbling a disconsolate sigh, Jared dismounted, plugging the lawn mower—the speediest vehicle he could drive—into an outlet before heading off. The lush smell of grass clippings filled the air along with the high-pitched electric whine of a dozen other mowers heading in. Not surprisingly, they had no riders since the rest of Jared's "flight" were a bunch of limited AIs.

Minutes later, Jared was walking along a narrow path leading away from the parking area to where Kars Santaline already awaited for him next to a dilapidated truck. Kars had purchased it a few cycles back off a group of visiting Slongorn. It was said that their vehicles could last a lifetime if maintained properly, but Jared didn't think Kars's truck had been well maintained. Rusty exterior parts matched a sun-damaged and cracked leather interior, and its electric motor sometimes caught and hiccuped, causing the vehicle to sputter and spark.

"How's my favorite Pharin?" Kars asked, beak open as he trilled a grin.

Jared stared at Kars, his tail-feathers flicking in a scowl. Before Well World, his surname had been Gnole, but on his arrival to Calipolis, he'd been given a new one. It was the surname given to any Dunh'gran who weren't native to the hex. "I'm fine," Jared said at last. "How's my favorite rooster?"

Kars bristled, his tail-feathers fanning. "That's a dirty word."

"So's Pharin."

"It's your last name."

"So? We both know what it really means."

Kars sighed a warble. "Foreigner who'll never be part of a flight."

"Then maybe you should stop saying it to me like it's a joke." Jared stared the other cob down, a ritual among the Dunh'gran to demonstrate dominance. It helped that he was taller and thicker than Kars. More handsome, too, at least based on his brighter plumage—the blue and brown feathers along his back that merged with iridescent reds, greens, and bronze on his wings and tail. Then there was the gold crown atop his otherwise bare head. "Pleasingly-patterned" was how Jared would have been described; a higher status among the Dunh'gran, except for the fact that he was a Pharin.

Kars's hazel eyes—a feature shared by most of their people—flickered, and he seemed to deflate. "Let's go home. Seraph says we're having sanflower and nanjer seeds and meat for dinner."

"Seeds and meat." Jared smirked. "How delicious."

"Just be glad you weren't reborn as a worm or a fish," Kars said. "The Well World computer could have turned you into something like that. Who knows what you'd be eating then."

Jared extended his wings in a shudder at the thought.

Through the magic of the AI who ran Well World, it hadn't taken him long to get used to his new form. He appreciated it now, the clever, bony terminal phalanges that served as fingers at the ends of his vestigial wings; his lovely plumage; and his deadly clawed feet and raptorlike beak meant for tearing. In fact, while he remembered his life as a human, those recollections had become strangely distant, like a dream … everything but how he had ended up here.

Mr. Messier. *Bastard.*

Jared shoved aside his anger—easier now six months on from his arrival to Well World—before settling into the truck, strapping in tight.

And as soon as he had his restraints in place, Kars launched them homeward, driving like a bat out of hell. He took every turn as hard as he could, rarely let off the accelerator, and raced anything that moved. Same as the other drivers, everyone centimeters from disaster. The entire time, Jared cawed and hollered, grinning. *Going fast was the only way to go.*

Even still, he distantly wondered how there weren't multiple vehicular deaths every day. After all, it wasn't like Fraught was a small town. This was a moderate sized city of half a million, and there was definitely traffic. Maybe the Dunh'gran managed because their reflexes were so much better than those of humans.

Whatever the case, half an hour later, their drive ended as they pulled into a quiet neighborhood close to the country, in front of the Santaline family home. Although the house rested on the ground, it was more properly called an aerie or a nest, and it looked like one too, given its rounded walls and bowl-shaped roof.

"Oh. I found something you might like." Kars reached into a small compartment, withdrawing a thin stack of papers.

Jared glanced them over. They looked like financial documents. "Where did you get these?"

Kars trilled a nervous grin. "In a garbage receptacle. It had all these numbers and stuff. I figured you might find them interesting." He trilled louder, chuckling now. "I don't understand the math, but I know you enjoy that stuff."

"Numbers and math define how everything works," Jared said in distraction. "Without them, nothing makes sense."

"Didn't you say numbers got you in trouble in your life above?" Kars didn't give him a chance to answer. "But maybe you're right. Who knows? Maybe you'll use these papers to learn Mr. Liliana's secrets and become rich like him."

Jared let loose a high-pitched trill, chuckling. "Wouldn't that be something." He pecked at the papers, perusing them, his golden crown feathers flaring into a frown. There was something oddly familiar here. A pattern he recognized …

The papers were snatched from his hands. "Come on," Kars said. "The family's waiting. It's time to share a meal."

The Santaline family home belonged to Amia and Dorn Santaline, Kars' parents. They'd been married for decades, which wasn't a surprise since Dunh'gran mated for life. Strangely enough though, the females sometimes found a different male than their mate to father their children.

Odd perhaps, but the society worked.

What wasn't odd, however, was Kars's sister, Seraph Santaline. Born of the same clutch as Kars—most Dunh'gran females only clutched once or twice in their lives—she was lovely, charismatic, and caring. The one happy star in Jared's existence.

Currently, she was bowling out their meals, a mix of fried seeds—sanflower and nanjer—and the raw meat of a gannat, an herbivore akin to a goat. Wide-eyed and dull, the creatures were tasty whether eaten raw or cooked.

"Wash up," Seraph ordered as soon as Jared and Kars entered the aerie. "Amia and Dorn aren't home yet." She named her parents, which was her right as an adult. Until *Caraster*, the yearlong celebration all Dunh'gran experienced after their twenty-fourth cycle, she had been a minor. But afterward, she had been considered an adult and had all the privileges of one.

Kars also had those rights, but given how little he'd achieved in life—a janitor wasn't much in the eyes of most Dunh'gran—he generally didn't call his parents by their first names. Seraph, on the other hand, a newly minted detective in the Corruption Services Bureau of the Dunh'gran Ministry of Justice, held a much higher standing.

Which was also a far higher standing than Jared's own as a groundskeeper.

The situation reinforced Jared's desire to make something of himself. To become a person of importance, just like he had back in the galaxy—the real universe. He couldn't see himself mowing grass and cutting shrubs for the rest of his life. He was meant for more.

But how?

Financial services work wasn't an option. Neither was working in racing, a highly sought after and respectable profession. Even engineering would be difficult. While Jared was good at math, competition to get into an engineering school was impossibly fierce, especially for a Pharin.

"What are you looking at?" Seraph asked.

Jared started, squawking when he realized he'd been staring at Seraph. Then again, she was easy to stare at. Seraph was several centimeters shorter than him, with a perfectly shaped beak, fierce eyes, and a light brown plumage with blue highlights at the tips of her wings and tail. But it was her silver crown, a rare bright color among hens, that highlighted her beauty.

"Well?" Seraph pressed.

Jared blinked, latching onto an easy lie when he recognized he was still staring. "I was thinking about some papers Kars showed me."

Seraph's interest went to her brother. "What kind of papers?"

Kars bounced from one clawed foot to the next in nervousness. "Nothing important."

Seraph's tail feathers fanned out. "Kars."

He warbled a sigh. "There were some papers in the trash. They looked interesting. Lots of numbers and stuff. I thought Jared might like them." He tilted his head side to side in a shrug. "You know how he's always talking about math."

"Let me see them," Seraph ordered, moving in a Dunh'gran's darting motion to her brother's side.

He reluctantly passed her the papers. "They're just numbers."

Jared peered over Seraph's shoulder. "They aren't just numbers," he said. "They're ciphers. An easy one, too." Not thinking about it, he pulled the papers from Seraph's hands. "See what I mean." He explained the simple substitution cipher and how it changed some of the formulas. Same with the verbiage. But there was more to it than just that.

But whatever else he might have said was interrupted when the front door opened and in walked Amia and Dorn. Both were in their early sixties—middle-aged—and it showed in how slowly they moved compared to their children. Of course, it didn't mean they really were old. Amia and Dorn had at least five or six decades of living ahead of them.

"What an exhausting day," Amia declared.

"Hard as always," Dorn agreed, inhaling a deep breath. "I'm hungry."

The two of them washed up, dipping their beaks into the water bath. Same with their wing tips, which they flapped dry. As soon as they were done, everyone gathered at the table, pecking at the food and discussing the day.

Jared kept quiet and out of the way, however. While he lived among the Santalines and would stay with them until he could afford to care for himself, he wasn't really part of the family. He was an outsider—a Pharin—no matter how much the Santalines, especially Seraph, tried to make him feel welcome. Truthfully, she'd never treated him like a Pharin. She'd treated him well.

"When are you going to mate?" Amia asked Seraph. It was the most common question she asked of her daughter. Never of her son, though. Little was expected of Kars at this point.

"I'll mate at the same age that you did."

"Why would you do that to me?" Amia squawked, wings flapping in agitation. "Why would you follow in my clawsteps. Learn from my mistakes. If you wait too long, you'll only have a chance to clutch once in your life."

Seraph shrugged, tilting her head back and forth. "Once is enough."

While they argued, Dorn—apparently tired of their conversation—flipped through the news in the daily broadsheet paper—most of it given over to weather, wind, and racing—while inaccurately answering the questions on some quiz show on the holovision.

"This species is the only one to have lost their home hex."

Dorn's reply: "What are turtles?"

The answer was humanity.

"The speed of light in a vacuum is a known constant."

Dorn answered: "What is one hundred thousand kilometers per second squared."

Jared wanted to roll his eyes. He could see where Kars got his lack of intellect, which was a shame. Kars and Dorn were good people.

Jared's attention shifted away from Dorn when Amia whistled in agitation. "Mating isn't something you should put off until it's too late," she was saying, still stuck on the earlier conversation with her daughter.

Jared stopped listening again, returning his attention to the papers Kars had brought home.

Minutes later, he had a vague understanding of what they entailed. The names mentioned weren't spelled out, but based on the accounting, several decades ago, someone had inherited a fortune upon the death of his employer. Even after the heavy death taxes, the beneficiary had proven fairly well off and had used his inheritance to build a racing team and industrial conglomerate. There was also a large, recurring payment made to a group of Murithel. Six of them. Something about a transference.

Jared glanced up from the papers. "What's a Murithel?"

Seraph explained. "A species of mammal on Well World. Non-tech but excellent at psionics. Rumor has it that they can transfer souls."

Jared's eyes widened. Was that actually possible? Given everything he'd been through getting to Well World, he supposed so, which meant the documents suddenly made sense. But what about this final line? This promise of proof?

A knock on the front door interrupted his assessment, and while Kars went to answer, Jared continued his study of the papers, vaguely noting muffled conversation from the entrance.

He glanced up when Kars hopped away from whoever was at the door, fright evident on his face. Pressing forward after him were two large cobs, looking mean and ready to inflict some pain.

The cobs were each larger than Jared, and he wasn't a small Dunh'gran. They also had a menace to them, scarred knuckles on their keratinized terminal phalanges and sour frowns to their beaks and postures. They filled the room with their sense of threat.

Jared set the papers on the counter behind him, bouncing from one foot to the other in abrupt nervousness.

"We don't mean to interrupt your meal," one of the cobs said. "But our employer insisted we speak to those who might have taken what didn't belong to them."

"Who are you?" Seraph said. She stepped forward, in front of her parents, shielding them. "Who do you represent? And what do you seek?"

The other cob gestured to Kars. "He knows what we want. He was caught on camera pilfering from our employer."

Kars straightened, wings flapping his outrage as he squawked loudly. "I never stole anything from anyone."

"The camera says otherwise."

"You still haven't said who you represent or what you seek," Seraph said, her voice commanding. "Think clearly on how you answer. I'm a detective in the Ministry of Justice."

Now it was the cobs who shuffled their feet.

While they figured on how to answer Seraph's demand, Jared twisted his gaze from one intruder to the other. What could Kars have stolen? Was it the papers? It seemed unlikely. Kars had said he'd pulled them out of a waste bin—unless he'd lied. Regardless, the papers had seemed important based on Jared's brief examination of them. And now their importance seemed even greater.

"We have our orders," one of the cobs said at last.

"I've heard enough," Seraph said. From a hidden holster under a wing, she pulled a pistol on the cobs, one meant to stun, not kill. "Call headquarters," she said to her parents, eyes never leaving the cobs. "Tell them to send a couple of units."

Upon her words, the front door opened and shut again, and a soft clacking tread introduced another Dunh'gran into their aerie, also a cob. This one wasn't much older than Jared, and he was also every bit as pleasingly patterned. "There will be no need for that."

Jared squinted, head tilted. He knew this Dunh'gran. It was Kinth Felina, secretary to Carabis Liliana, the owner of Ouichopper Industries. Jared had only met the handsome cob once, and it had left him with the same oily-sick feeling as when he'd met Mr. Messier's fixers, the ones sent to kill him for exposing their boss.

Which meant this intrusion *was* about the papers. They remained on the counter, and Jared surreptitiously eased over toward them, a niggling suspicion forming.

"I think there is a need," Seraph said, disagreeing with Mr. Felina, aiming her pistol at him.

Mr. Felina smiled, gesturing. The other two cobs pulled pistols of their own, and theirs *were* meant to kill. "I think not."

Seraph's defiance melted while Kars hopped up and down in alarm. Amia and Dorn folded their wings and huddled close, fear evident in their eyes.

That same fear touched Jared, and his mouth filled with saliva as he coughed in terror, bouncing slightly. He wanted to do nothing but run and hide somewhere, but he couldn't. He'd seen this kind of play before, back when he'd exposed Mr. Messier. It told him a terrifying truth. None of them might leave the house alive if Mr. Felina didn't get what he wanted … *or* if he felt his employer's secrets had been compromised.

What to do?

An instant later, the nugget of a plan formed. *The house phone.* It was behind him. Heart racing, Jared eased over to the phone, back to it, trying to hide his motions as he brought it to life by feel and dialed the emergency contact number. The authorities would hopefully be listening.

Leaving the phone alive, he stepped away from it, retrieving the papers Kars had taken. "Is this what you're looking for?" he asked, holding them out.

Mr. Felina hissed in pleasure. "Our stolen property. Give it to me."

Jared held onto them. "It's strange you want them so badly. A lot of work and threats over a bunch of nonsense and math."

Mr. Felina smirked. "Nonsense that has caused more problems than you know."

"Sure. But then we both know these papers don't represent nonsense."

"You've studied them?" Suspicion tinged Mr. Felina's voice. "I thought you were just a groundskeeper."

"I am, but I also like puzzles. And these papers have one."

"You talk too much, boy." Mr. Felina held out a wing, phalanges extended. "Hand over the papers."

Jared smiled, certain now of what the documents indicated. "Mr. Liliana inherited his wealth after the death of Pran Quelianin, his former employer, a wealthy industrialist. An odd beneficiary, no?"

"Nothing odd about it. They were as close as a father and a son."

"Except that on the day Mr. Quelianin died, he and Mr. Liliana were racing, and afterward your employer became the sole inheritor of his estate."

Mr. Felina offered a low-throated trill of mockery. "Let me guess. You think Mr. Liliana murdered his patron. Is that the puzzle you think you put together?"

"Why would I think that? He never had any reason to murder Mr. Quelianin, did he?"

"I've heard enough." Mr. Felina gestured, and Jared found the other two cobs pointing their guns his way.

He managed to keep himself from hopping in fear, doing his best to project confidence. "So, according to these numbers, Mr. Liliana used his inheritance to build Ouichopper Industries … but only after paying off a group of Murithel, specifically six of them. We all know what some of them can do in groups of six."

Mr. Felina's face went vacant, the repose of someone figuring on whether or not to commit murder. "Your stupid friend"—he indicated Kars— "wasn't meant to find those papers. They were meant for someone else."

The final piece of the puzzle clicked into place. "You were blackmailing Mr. Liliana."

Mr. Felina trilled low. "You're clever for a groundskeeper."

"More clever than you know." Jared carefully stepped aside, letting Mr. Felina see the phone. "The authorities are listening."

"Authorities can be purchased." Mr. Felina's phalange went to the trigger of his pistol.

Jared hopped in place, terrified. He had to do something.

With a sudden motion, Kars grasped the pot of food on the table and flung it at Mr. Felina and his cobs. They reacted with alarm and outraged shouts, wings shielding their eyes.

"Run!" Seraph shouted, rushing for the front door.

Jared got there first, bowling over Mr. Felina, with Seraph and Kars right behind him. A series of shots rang out. Jared ducked low and kept running. He threw open the door to Kars's truck, starting it up. An instant later, Seraph and Kars bowled inside as well.

More shots blistered the air, slamming with dull thuds into the bed gate.

"Go! Go! Go!" Seraph yelled.

Jared squealed the truck into motion, mashing the accelerator.

Jared swung the truck into traffic, which wasn't heavy in their lightly populated part of the city. But worse for them, they were heading out into the country, and since it was well past sunset, most Dunh'gran were already home. There were a scant few vehicles on the road, and less vehicles meant there wouldn't be any way to lose Mr. Liliana's enforcers by miring them in traffic.

And those enforcers came. A gray vehicle, nondescript but clearly expensive, trailed after them, closing fast. Jared had spotted it outside the

Santaline aerie. It had to be Mr. Liliana's thugs, and there was no chance of turning the truck around and getting past them.

Jared cursed under his breath when, a mile later, the light posts lining the road faded away to nothing. Now there were no other cars about. No witnesses either.

Nevertheless, he kept the truck aimed out of town, into the darkening countryside.

"Can't you go faster?" Seraph demanded.

"I've already got the accelerator hitting the floor," Jared answered. More worrisome, the truck's electric engine was whining like a drill hitting metal.

"My truck was built for durability," Kars added. "Not speed."

Seraph patted herself down, chirping in annoyance. "Does anyone have a phone?"

Jared shook his head. Same with Kars.

Seraph chirped again. "Shit. We're in trouble."

Jared glanced in the rear-view mirror. Coming up fast was the gray vehicle.

Kars worried his wings. "Do you think they hurt our parents?"

"I don't know," Seraph replied, sounding just as worried.

Jared shared their concern. Amia and Dorn had taken him in and had done their best to make him feel welcome even though he was a Pharin. He owed them much. Just as important, good people didn't deserve to die in the cross fire of a corrupt industrialist.

"What do those men want?" Kars asked.

"The papers," Jared said. "Someone screwed up by leaving them out like they did."

"You mean that story you were telling us back home was real?" Kars demanded.

Seraph bobbed her head. "It's common knowledge. How Carabis Liliana was the sole inheritor of Pran Quelianin's fortune."

"It wasn't common knowledge to me," Kars said.

"What about the Murithel?" Seraph asked Jared. "Did you know what you were implying?"

It had all been a guess on Jared's part, and he trilled a manic grin. "You saw their reaction. What do you think?"

"I think this is a lot more complicated than a newly minted detective should have to face."

Jared glanced at Kars. "How'd you get the papers anyway? They weren't just lying in a waste bin."

Kars fluttered his wings in sorrow. "They were in a folder lying on Mr. Liliana's filing cabinet. There was a note on top about wanting to get paid or something bad would happen. I just saw the numbers and thought they'd make you happy."

Jared made to reply, but just then the gray vehicle surged forward. His eyes widened as it filled his rear-view mirror. It swung over to the other lane. Jared cut them off. Again, the other vehicle swung over, and again, Jared cut them off.

"Faster. Faster. Go faster," Kars urged.

A sign indicated a left-hand turn coming up. The gray vehicle shifted over. This time, Jared didn't block.

"What are you doing?" Seraph screamed.

The gray vehicle accelerated, pulling up alongside them. Jared knew what the other driver intended. His heart pounded into his gizzard. But he did what was necessary, tugging on the steering wheel, timing it so the truck and the gray vehicle slammed together at the same time. A crash and crunch of metal ensued.

Despite the terror, Jared cawed out his joy. The driver's side window was down, and a breeze filled the cabin. He had gotten into the wind.

Kars cawed with him. "You lunatic!" Among the Dunh'gran, it was a high compliment.

The left-hand turn.

Jared stomped the brake. Tires squealed. Rubber burned, stinking the air. He hauled the truck around. It slid, tipped slightly, slammed down, aimed in the correct direction. Jared mashed the accelerator again. Tires spun, caught, and the truck surged down a narrow lane.

Fields of sanflower and nanjer flashed by in the darkness.

The gray vehicle had raced past. They'd have to come around to catch up.

"What now?" Seraph asked. "We haven't lost them yet."

Jared had the bare bones of an idea, but he never had a chance to voice it. Here came the gray vehicle, entering the road. It spit gravel as it surged forward. Jared's gaze locked on the rear-view mirror. His gizzard dropped. The gray vehicle would be on them in moments.

"Turn!" Seraph shouted.

Jared's attention went back to the road. Just in time, he hauled the truck into a tight right-hand turn. Tires squealed. They straightened and bolted down the lane. The other vehicle took the turn more smoothly, racing after them.

"Strap in," Jared shouted, checking his own restraints.

Seraph and Kars got themselves locked into place.

Just in time. The gray vehicle rammed the back end of the truck, launching it forward.

Jared grunted, his phalanges nearly leaving the steering wheel. The truck lurched right, then left. He fought, barely keeping the vehicle under control and on the road.

Gaze flicking to the rear-view mirror, Jared finally had the truck straightened out just as the gray vehicle smashed into them again.

Kars shrieked, and Seraph was thrown forward, hauled back by her restraints.

Another slam from the gray vehicle, to their left rear quarter panel this time.

The truck twisted, threatening to go sideways and roll. Jared struggled to keep it straight, sawing on the steering wheel. A few harrowing turns, and the truck shot straight ahead.

"When did you learn to drive so well?" Kars shouted, sounding both frantic and impressed.

Jared had no idea. He was working off instinct, the instinct of a Dunh'gran, maybe.

Here came the gray vehicle again.

The truck hiccuped just then, the engine whining even louder, sounding like a teakettle about to go off.

It gave Jared an idea. He viewed the charging vehicle, waiting for the right moment.

"Hold on!" he shouted.

A slam of the brakes caused the tires to squeal anew. The cob driving the other vehicle had no chance to slow. The nose of his vehicle crumpled as it slammed into the back of the truck.

One of Mr. Liliana's enforcers was flung through the front windscreen into the bed of Kars's truck, his terrified face burned into Jared's memory …

And then chaos.

Jared's phalanges left the steering wheel, the impact too great to maintain control. The truck lurched, left tires lifting, slamming back down. They spun, caught the edge of a gully. Screams filled the cabin as the truck flipped. Time dilated. More screams. Seconds seemed to last forever as the truck rolled, slowing eventually. At last, it came to rest with a final whine and crunch of metal, rocking softly.

Silence.

Jared wanted to vomit. His entire body ached, and his thoughts didn't work right. Had he lost consciousness? Probably. And what was this soft stuff all around him?

"Is anyone hurt?" Seraph asked, breaking the quiet.

Jared tried to answer but could only manage a groan. His mind was coming back to life but only in fits and starts. He blinked, trying to clear his vision, but the soft stuff .... He pushed on it, finally realizing it was a protective foam that had exploded into the truck's cabin, keeping them safe. But surely he must have broken something. His bones were hollow, easily fractured, a Dunh'gran's most frequent injury. But when he felt for damage, shock and relief filled him at the lack of any obvious breaks.

"Kars? Jared?" Seraph pressed.

"Give me a minute," Kars replied.

"We don't have a minute," Seraph said.

She was right. They had to get moving before Mr. Liliana's men found them. Jared's muffled thinking finally cleared, and he tried to restart the truck. Instead of whining to life, though, a fire sparked from the engine bay. *Oh, no.*

"We have to go," Seraph urged.

Jared struggled with his restraints, freeing himself at the same time as Kars. He grabbed the papers, the source of all their problems, and an instant later, the three of them fell out of the truck, gaining distance as the engine fire grew. Seraph led them into the tall fields.

They hunched low, and Jared's attention went to the broad line of flattened crops leading to the road. No one was coming from there, and he recalled those final moments before the truck spun out. The gray vehicle had crumpled, and at least one of its occupants had been thrown clear.

Minutes passed, and another flame flared to life. The other vehicle's electric batteries must have caught fire.

More minutes. But still no one.

"Maybe they're all dead," Kars suggested, his tone hopeful. He had a wing tucked close to his side, likely broken, but he didn't squawk or complain. *Tough cob.*

"Come on," Seraph said. "We need to see what happened."

Jared didn't want to do anything of the kind, but he also didn't want to look like a coward in front of Seraph. Instead, he paced directly behind her as she led them back to the road, none of them speaking.

They reached the road, and the fire from the gray vehicle displayed what Jared had hoped to see. Mr. Liliana's goons were dead. The two large cobs had been thrown clear, and the secretary, Mr. Felina, had died inside the vehicle, crushed when it had crumpled.

Jared stood in silence, staring at the scene. Once again, he could have died. He should have, just like when he'd fled from Mr. Messier's men.

But he hadn't. Perhaps some god was looking out for him, maybe even the last Markovian that Captain Ortega had mentioned in passing. A cheerful thought. "We better get walking," he said, ending the tableau.

The next few weeks passed in a blur. Once Jared, Seraph, and Kars made their way back to civilization, the Ministry of Justice quickly found them. Shortly thereafter, Jared had explained to high-ranked officials what he'd discovered in the papers Kars had stolen.

From there, it hadn't taken long to untangle Carabis Liliana's web of deceit. And to say the news had shocked the hex would have been an understatement. Jared's employer *was* Carabis Liliana, but prior to that, he had been Pran Quelianin. And even earlier, Gerandil Pharin, someone from the Com and not native to Well World.

After achieving great wealth, Gerandil had hired a group of Murithel, and using a combination of their skills and Dunh'gran technology, he'd transferred his mind into the body of Pran Quelianin. Later on, he did it again, this time into Carabis Liliana. Each time, the transfer had been into the body of a friendless orphan.

An ingenious plan, with Gerandil's final hope to remain alive long enough to see himself freed from Well World. He'd apparently been counting on a myth known to the Murithels, in which the mythical last Markovian could send a person from Well World back into the known universe if he so chose.

It was a dream that might have once held appeal for Jared, but not anymore. His role in unmasking Gerandil's scheme had brought him fame above what he'd ever expected, and everyone now saw him in a different light.

Everyone but Seraph. It didn't matter if other females threw themselves his way or great opportunities were offered to him, including admission to a prestigious engineering school. Seraph still treated him the same. For that, he was grateful.

Which brought him to tonight's meeting.

He knocked on Seraph's door, a broad strip of woven wood, and she answered, smiling with a fluff of her tail feathers. "I was hoping you'd stop by."

Jared's heart raced faster. "Oh. Why's that?"

"You're moving out tomorrow, into the dorms of the engineering aerie, aren't you?"

Jared preened, unable to hide his pleasure as his golden crown flared. At twenty-seven, he'd be the oldest hatchling in attendance, but he had no worries on that account. He wanted to make his way in the world, and the school would be the first step.

"You should be proud," Seraph said. "But I'll miss you. It's been nice having you live with us."

"What about you?" Jared asked. "Will you stay here, too?"

"For now," Seraph said, trilling a chuckle. "Someone has to watch out for the family. They're all still pretty shaken up by everything that happened."

Jared trilled a wry response, glad her parents hadn't been injured and that Kars's broken wing was healing well. "You're right. They won't always have me around to keep them safe."

Their conversation momentarily fell quiet.

Jared spoke up. "I don't necessarily *have* to move to the engineering aerie. The school is close by. I could stay here until I graduate."

"Do you really want to do that?"

"Only if you think it's a good idea."

Seraph cocked her head, speaking bluntly. "Why don't you just say what's on your mind? There are so many stories about people from beyond Well World. Few of them find happiness in their new bodies, and nearly all end up like your former employer, Mr. Liliana. Bitter and wanting a way off planet to rejoin the larger universe."

She wasn't wrong. Jared also longed for the wide-open galaxy beyond this one vast world. He wanted the dreams he'd worked and nearly died for. But was that still his only truth?

Seraph rustled her wings, gaining his attention. "How do you see your future?"

His future … . Jared peered past her, gazing into her room but seeing elsewhere. After a few moments of deliberation, his gaze settled on her. "I want contentment."

"And you think you can find it here? In Calipolis?"

"Maybe. I think so. I want so. I want to find contentment in this place. In this home."

"And if you're ever granted a way off planet?"

His heart raced, and his beak went dry. "I wouldn't leave." He reached for her phalanges, twining them with his own. It felt like the bravest thing he'd ever done. "I've finally gotten my wind."

Chapter Eight:
BETARED:
THE FIRST GATE
Marsheila Rockwell

"The kingdom of God is just behind the darkness of closed eyes, and the first gate that opens to it is your peace." ~ Paramahansa Yogananda

The first thing Elida Silduun registered when she opened her eyes was the cold.

It was like nothing she'd ever felt before, like some ravenous creature had sliced through her flesh and was even now gnawing at her bones, lusting for their very marrow.

She'd been warm once, she remembered.

On a rescue freighter, with Kyana, heading back to their homeworld, after their transport had been attacked by anti-Com pirates.

No, she thought, as a pain worse than the cold lanced through her. *Not with Kyana. Not anymore. Not ever again.*

But there *had* been others with her. Strangers, filled with confusion and panic as the ship encountered some sort of space anomaly. Entered it.

Then there had been only blackness.

As there was only blackness again now, the snow and ice and hungry chill fading away into a cold that was deeper still …

The next time Elida awoke, the cold had abated, replaced by warm furs and a nearby crackling fire. She appeared to be in some sort of cave, its roof lost in darkness far above her. Had the freighter crash-landed on some unknown ice planet?

If so, where were the other survivors? She was alone in the cave, but someone had to have brought her here, out of the cold, had to have lit the fire and covered her with blankets.

Someone had saved her life.

As she herself had been unable to save Kyana's.

That's why Elida had been on that doomed transport in the first place. Which she sourly supposed was fitting, given that her own cause had been equally doomed.

Elida didn't know why she'd ever thought she could take on the sponge syndicate by herself. But her fury and grief after Kyana's death had needed an outlet, a target. The people who had addicted her daughter to that vile substance and then refused to provide the antidote seemed like the obvious choice.

Unfortunately, those people also held most of the Com worlds under their sway, including Elida's own. She hadn't gotten anywhere close to the drug lord whose product had poisoned her child, but she had tracked down the dealer that Kyana had gotten her first dose from, though whether the girl knew that's what had been happening at the time was up for debate. The dealer hadn't been forthcoming on the subject. Granted, it was hard to speak without a tongue.

Or without a head, for that matter.

The dealer had been in arrears with the drug lord, so the syndicate chose to overlook his murder and Elida's role in it. But they also warned her in no uncertain terms that if they ever saw her face anywhere in their system again, she'd die a death that was magnitudes worse than the one her daughter had suffered.

Elida might still have continued her crusade—it wasn't as if she had much reason to live, after all. She'd already lost her daughter, the only person she loved, the only one she'd had left. But she simply couldn't get close to the real culprits. Elida was just one woman, with few resources and no allies. The syndicate ruled the entire galaxy, with all its riches at their disposal.

And so Elida had found herself first on the transport, and then on the rescue freighter, not even sure where she was headed, because it hadn't really mattered. Kyana wasn't with her and wouldn't be there to greet her wherever she wound up, so one forgotten corner of the universe was just as good as any other.

When the space anomaly had appeared outside her window and threatened the ship with an unfathomable void of endless black, she had not panicked. She had welcomed it and the release it promised.

She had never been more disappointed in her life to open her eyes again, here in this cave. But the stubborn fact remained that she had, whether she wanted to or not, so she might as well find her rescuers, assess the situation, and learn how she had wound up here, wherever "here" might be.

As she sat up, Elida realized that she was not covered in fur blankets, as she had at first assumed, but in actual fur. She pawed at the coarse brown hair with hands that were now clumsy clawed mitts, trying to find the closures to the ridiculous suit, wondering if this was someone's idea of a cruel joke.

She gradually realized that it was not a suit she wore, and while it might well be sadistic, this was no jest. As best she could determine without a mirror, Elida had been turned into some sort of bear.

No sooner had she reached this conclusion than a trio of other bears entered the cave through an opening she hadn't noticed. When they saw she was awake, one of them came over to her while the others continued deeper into the cavern. He walked upright instead of on all fours.

"Finally," the bear said as he approached. His fur, like hers, was a rich loamy brown, and he had a plump stomach and round face that made Elida think of a child's toy. But when he spoke, his voice gruff and low, she could see long fangs jutting from his jaws like the stalagmites and stalactites that riddled what she now thought of as a den rather than just a cave. Whatever else this bear might be, he was not a harmless bedtime companion. He was dangerous. "Thought you'd never wake up."

"Who are you? Where am I?" Elida asked, surprised at the deepness of her own voice. "*What* am I?"

"Well World, Betared hex. Betared. Female, in case you were wondering."

She hadn't been. It hadn't even occurred to her that she might be anything else.

"I don't understand."

"You Entries never do at first," the bear—Betared—said, his sigh coming out like the sound of boulders tumbling down a mountainside. "It'll come back to you after your brains unscramble a bit. Suffice to say, you must have come through a gate, and the Well of Souls in its infinite wisdom, processed you through as a Betared. Lucky us."

He didn't sound like he thought it had been *good* luck.

But as he spoke, his words jogged Elida's memory, and she did in fact vaguely remember a sort of orientation with her fellow passengers once they'd passed through the black space anomaly that was apparently a roving gate. Such anomalies were often triggered by despair or desperation; Elida recalled wondering if she had been what attracted the Well's attention, but she hadn't cared enough to ask at the orientation—or whatever it was—and she didn't care now. One planet was as good as any another, and the body she inhabited didn't matter, unless it could somehow resurrect Kyana. A Betared body, she knew instinctively, could not.

"Why am I here?"

The other Betared shrugged.

"The Well thought you'd be a good fit for us, I suppose. Remains to be seen. You have to survive before you can fit in."

"Survive what?" Elida asked, trying to frown and realizing her new mouth was not equipped for anything other than a snarl. She settled for that.

The male Betared jabbed his muzzle toward the opening he and his companions had come through, a surprisingly human gesture.

"Outside."

"Outside" turned out to be an arctic hell, with ice-imprisoned trees, snow-shrouded mountains, drifts twice as tall as she was, and a wind that bit deeper than grief.

The male Betared—Faven—had told her that the Well having sent her here did not suffice. She would have to survive three days and nights out in this nightmare landscape on her own to prove to the rest of the Betared that she was worthy to be one of them.

She'd almost laughed in his face at that, although she wasn't entirely sure she *could* laugh in this form. Why did Faven think she cared about his or any of the other bipedal bears' approbation? Or that she cared about surviving at all?

Kyana was gone. Dead. Elida had not been able to prevent her daughter's addiction. Nor had she been able to keep her only child from an agonizing death at the mercy of that addiction.

Elida had been living solely for vengeance since then, but what little of that she had managed to attain had proven bitter and hollow. She couldn't reach the real villains, couldn't stop them from plying their evil trade, couldn't keep other mothers from losing their children, from drowning in the sea of endless pain that now engulfed her.

She had nothing left to live for, and the thought of lying down in the snow and letting the cold take her was not the deterrent Faven assumed it was. All she needed to do was find the right place.

Back on their homeworld, when Kyana was a small child, she had loved to go to the forest preserves and climb the crimson-crowned trees there. She said they were redheads like her. She'd scamper up their slick silver bark as if she'd been born to do so, then get lost in the foliage in a matter of moments. And she would stay up there for hours, having always preferred the company of those animals that made their homes in the leaf-cocooned quiet to those that made their homes in the steel-cocooned cities. She'd liked to say that because they didn't use words, they were more honest. Elida supposed her daughter had been right. It was hard to lie without language.

So Elida wanted to find a place with trees, if she could. Not the scattered ones here and there near the den entrance, but a copse at least, preferably a forest like the ones Kyana had loved. It wouldn't be the same, but it was as close to her daughter as she was ever going to be able to get, now.

Elida wasn't sure how long she walked—the harsh wind never let up, blowing snow into her snout and obscuring much of her vision. Not that seeing would have helped. The sky remained a dismal gray, with no sun or moon ever breaking through the thick cloud cover to light her way.

That was both good and bad, she supposed. Good, because sunlight— or even moonlight—reflecting off so much snow would effectively blind her. Bad, because she had no way to mark time other than by the growling of her stomach and the weariness in her limbs, and they were as easy to ignore in this form as they had been in her previous one. Hunger and rest meant little when you didn't care whether you lived or died.

She *did* care if Faven and the other Betared found her before she could join her daughter, though. She had only three days to do so, and no way to tell when that time was up aside from bodily cues despair had long made impossible to decipher.

Elida also hoped to come across a river. Sticking her nose into drifts and munching on snow was a poor substitute for actual hydration, for all that it was presumably comprised of the same substance. And trees would be more likely to grow in abundance near water, one of the many arboreal facts Kyana had recited to her so often at bedtime that it was as seared into Elida's brain as her daughter's voice itself was.

Of course, where there was water, there were often animals, and people—or, here, creatures that were both—none of which Elida particularly wanted to encounter. But the longer she walked without finding what she was looking for, the more acceptable that risk seemed.

In the end, this choice, like so many other things, was taken from her.

The wind began to lessen around her, and Elida realized she'd wandered blindly into a valley, with mountains stretching tall on every side and the only outlet the narrow opening she'd come in through.

It would be as good a place to die as any, except for its distinct lack of trees.

Elida paused to consider. Paradoxically, now that she was out of the wind, she started to feel the cold again, as if her senses had shut down in the face of the buffeting arctic blasts and only came back online now that the freezing gusts had let up.

There was no point in going back the way she had come; she already knew she wouldn't find what she was looking for there. So, the only way forward was … forward.

Elida eyed the ring of mountains critically. There seemed to be lights glimmering far up in the higher slopes, maybe ice reflecting a sun invisible here beneath the cloud cover. But the twinkling lights seemed to be spaced too evenly for that, and Elida suspected they might actually be fires from a Betared community, perhaps marking the entrances to dens like the one she had awoken in.

But even if they betokened fire rather than ice, they were too high for Elida to reach in her exhausted condition. And Faven had made it clear that her scent glands had been altered in such a way that any other Betared she came across during her timed trial would know to withhold aid, so trying to make the climb would likely be pointless, in any event.

Deciding that some of the nearer slopes were small enough to warrant only the title of more easily scalable hills, she made for those instead. The snow was still falling here in the valley, crunching under her clawed feet as she strode purposefully toward her goal, and she reasoned that if the snow could get in, she could get out.

Part of her brain understood that she was probably delirious from hypothermia, hunger, and lack of sleep, that the thoughts she was having were not rational. But then, they hadn't been for a long time before she came to Well World, had they? And yet they'd gotten her this far. She trusted them to see her through to the end.

Which very nearly came more quickly than she had bargained for, because no sooner had she wearily topped the lowest of the encircling hills and paused, bent over for several gasping breaths, than a deep rumbling sounded above her.

She didn't pay it much mind at first, assuming it was her stomach complaining over the sound of her wheezing. But as her breath quieted and the sound only increased, she finally peered upward into the storm-veiled heights of the mountain for which this lowly hill acted as a mere shoulder.

And saw a wave of snow, boulders, and uprooted ice trees barreling down at her at an almost incomprehensible speed.

It took precious seconds to process what she was seeing through her sluggish brain—far too long. She'd barely turned, falling to all fours, intending to lope away down the path she'd just broken through the knee-high snow, when she was hit broadside by a root-festooned stump, its rings ironically as crimson as the leaves on the trees Kyana had adored.

The impact knocked her over, and she became just another piece of debris in the avalanche as it roared its way down the mountainside, screeching its arrogant indignance to anyone unfortunate enough to be caught within hearing range. She tumbled along, buffeted by branches, jagged hunks of rock, and the ground itself, sometimes on top of the dingy white wave and sometimes so far beneath its surface she was sure she would suffocate before it had exhausted its inhuman fury. Her flesh was pummeled by stone and wood and huge chunks of ice, her head struck more times than she could count.

She wasn't sure how long or how far the snow carried her, but it eventually quieted and slowed, with her near enough to the top that she only had to clamber a few feet to reach air.

Elida lay amidst the avalanche's aftermath, panting and battered. A sound gradually worked its way through her ringing ears to her brain and for a moment she tensed for another snowslide, knowing she'd be unlikely to survive a second round. But then she recognized the roaring not of surging snow, but of the ocean.

The smell of salt was the last thing she registered before consciousness faded and her eyes shuttered once more, the scarlet tree root that she'd somehow managed to grab and hold onto in the midst of the snowy torrent slipping silently from her now-limp grasp.

Elida groaned as her eyes fluttered opened and she was, for a second time, filled with ineffable disappointment.

She looked around her blearily as she struggled to rise from the snow that had delivered her here. She was on a muddy, barren beach. Not far from her, frothy waves crashed against black rocks that promised destruction for any ship foolish enough to try to find berth there.

But there *was* a ship. Or a boat; Elida couldn't see clearly. One of her eyes was swollen almost shut and the vision in the other was blurry, likely due to one of the many head injuries she'd sustained on her trip down the mountainside.

Yes, it was a boat. She could make out some details as it came closer to the deadly barrier of sable stone. She wondered if its captain also had a death wish. But the boat maneuvered skillfully through some gap Elida could not see, and to her surprise, a giant beaver hopped out of the craft into the water, attaching some sort of harness to its flat, hairless tail before pulling the boat to shore.

Another giant beaver and five humans disembarked. It took her a moment to realize that the humans—three young women and two men—were chained together in a line.

One of the women had long red hair that fell in natural ringlets to the middle of her back.

Kyana.

Part of Elida's brain knew that wasn't possible.

A much larger part didn't care.

With a strength born of equal parts adrenaline, grief, and Betared rage, Elida lurched up onto all fours and charged toward the beavers and their captives. Toward the woman who could be her daughter. Who could give her a reason to live again.

She took the first oversized dam-builder by surprise, leaping onto its back and using her claws and fangs to tear through its fur and into the tender flesh beneath. The beaver let out a shrill scream and fell forward. Elida wasn't a giant, but bears prepared for a hibernation that never came were at their heaviest, and she outweighed the creature twice over. The sound of ribs cracking beneath her could be heard even over the breaking surf.

The other beaver—the word *Ambrezan* flashed through her mind, but she didn't understand the thought or know where it came from—was not so easily dispatched. It pulled some sort of gun from the belt at its waist and fired at her.

There was no way it could miss at this range. Elida closed her eyes.

At last.

But the expected shock and blossom of pain did not come. Resigned this time, Elida opened her eyes once more to see that the chained humans—*Glathrielites*—had worked together to rush the beaver while its attention had been on Elida. They had tackled it to the mud, and one

140

of the women wrestled its gun away. She didn't seem to understand how to use the weapon, though, so instead of firing it, she used it as a club, swinging the butt end down against the beaver's head with enough force to smash its skull, covering herself and the other humans in a pink and gray spray. It took Elida a moment to realize that the woman was Kyana.

One of the men knelt and rummaged through the various pouches on the beaver's belt until he found a knife and what must be a key. He handed the knife to Kyana and quickly unlocked their shackles.

Then they turned as one toward Elida.

She couldn't hear what they were saying over the sound of the waves—soothing now, not harsh or violent as she had first thought. Like a mother's lullaby, coaxing her to rest. Her heartbeat had slowed, almost as if in response to the ocean's song, but Elida knew it was because her body was giving out. Days without food or sleep followed by being caught in an avalanche were finally taking their just due.

Along with a gunshot wound to her gut that she hadn't immediately registered, the overstressed pain centers in her brain having finally been taxed to the point of randomly returning messages unread. She touched a hesitant paw to a spot where she could sense seeping wetness, and it came away dark with blood and viscera.

Meanwhile, the humans seemed to have come to some decision. Kyana tossed the gun aside and stalked over to Elida's side, dropping to her knees in the blood-soaked sand. Elida watched helplessly as the woman examined the wound, shaking her head and muttering.

Then she looked up at Elida and for a moment, the two locked gazes, bear and human, Betared and Glathrielite.

Mother and daughter.

It seemed to Elida that Kyana's eyes were sad, but the set of her mouth was firm. Good. She had tried to teach her daughter to be strong and to fight for what was right. She just hadn't anticipated that the enemy Kyana would wind up facing would be one even the mightiest could not withstand.

"I love you," Elida said, or tried to say, but her jaw wouldn't work right, and her throat was raw, and the only noise that came out sounded like a growl. Still, Kyana seemed to understand. She gave a slight nod as she ran her empty hand over Elida's chest until she found the spot she was looking for.

Kyana raised the knife, its silvery blade glinting purposefully in the dimming light. Then she brought it down, straight into Elida's heart, stopping it mid-pump, giving her mother the gift she herself had never received—*peace*.

And this time, when Elida closed her eyes, she knew it was for good.

141

Chapter Nine:
AGITAR:
NO MATTER THE SHAPE
Jennifer Brozek and Samantha Chalker

Randolf sat on the ottoman watching Conrad's sleeping face. It was so different than before. Instead of pale skin and pale hair, he now had the dark blue skin and hair of the Agitar race along with a triangular-shaped face, pointed ears, and short sharp horns that peeked out from the mass of curled hair. He didn't even want to think about the oddness of hooves versus feet or the clawed hands.

Still, no matter what he looked like, Randolf would have known Conrad anywhere. It was in the way he held his mouth and the set of his shoulders—relaxed or tensed. It was also in the way the man … Conrad … (he was no longer a man though he was still male) looked at the world around him in that wary way.

It didn't matter that their current world was a private suite of rooms in a high-tech tower with what felt like luxurious furnishings. Two bedrooms, the living room they were in now—Conrad napping on the couch, him sitting on the ottoman next to the large comfortable chair—kitchen, office, bathroom, and a balcony that seemed too high off the ground for comfort. Though, he had to admit, the view of the city was spectacular. Tall towers stood among winding streets and raised tunnels that seemed filled with transit of some kind. It was quiet up this high.

Only the wind and the muted sounds of life around. It could have almost been a human city if it weren't for the unfamiliar gaits of the tiny Agitar people far below.

Still, the apartment was, in reality, a well-appointed kennel. All their needs were met: clothing, food, mild entertainment. There had even been small, robotic cleaning machines that came and went, doing their jobs with near soundless efficiency before disappearing back into their places somewhere within the walls. But it had several locked doors that they could not open.

He and Conrad had been whisked here to this prison of padded bliss as soon as they had arrived to the Agitar hex. They had not been allowed to leave. It had been phrased as a request, but the locked door to their apartment told both of them that it was a command. Apparently, they were a special kind of special in this hex.

Turning to look at himself in the nearby mirror, Randolf saw the same basic shape as Conrad's and flexed his own clawed hands. They felt natural despite the drastic change in his form. That was the strangest thing about their new reality: Conrad had always been bipedal. Randolf had not. It was this difference that had allowed Conrad to carry him through the gate in order to ensure that the Well World kept them together.

He remembered thinking as hard and as fiercely as he could with his augmented intelligence that he would not—NOT—leave his ward and, no matter the strength of the alien technology, he would do all he needed to do to remain with Conrad. Otherwise, he would tear down every wall in his path to get to him.

It seemed the Well World listened.

Conrad shifted and smiled, his eyes still sleepy. "Still getting used to all this?"

Shrugging, Randolf shook his head. "We've always been able to talk. But seeing you eye to eye without effort takes a little getting used to. Do you miss not looking like you were born?"

"No. It seems natural. Like I was always this way." Conrad stood and walked over to where Randolf sat. He started to put his hand on Randolf's head, paused, hovered it above his shoulder, then stopped, looking between his hand and Randolf's face. "Do you miss it? Not being as *you* were born?"

Randolf reached up a gentle hand to move Conrad's hand to his head. "No. But I miss you being comfortable with me. I'm still Randolf, your shield. I'm still here to support you as I was meant to do. It doesn't matter what you or I look like now."

Petting Randolf's hair, Conrad didn't say anything for a long time. Then he stopped. "I miss knowing your boundaries. When you were in your other form, we knew how to interact."

Chuckling, Randolf glanced up at him. "I can still run around you barking and jumping. I can still press my head to your chest, though, a bit more carefully. And if you'd like, I'll still lick your face. I mean, we might get weird looks now, but when have we ever cared about that?"

"When have *you* ever cared about that?" Conrad corrected. "Me? I'm ... still unsure about the world. Even more so."

"Doesn't matter. I'm still here for you. Instead of putting my head on you," Randolf stood up, "I can do this." He first placed his palm on Conrad's chest. "Or this." He moved his hand to Conrad's shoulder and squeezed. "Or this ... ." He pulled Conrad into a gentle hug. "And say, as I have always said, it will be all right. Everything will be all right."

Conrad melted into Randolf's arms. "Thank you. I'm glad you're here. I need you. Though, I have to admit, I prefer this voice to the carefully modulated speech box you once had." He pulled back from his support companion, spine straighter and shoulders squared. "I *do* need you. Especially with this upcoming meeting."

"I will be here."

"I don't know what they want from me."

Randolf shook his head. "Doesn't matter. You, we, will figure it out."

The door chimed. It was a polite warning that Dioney, "the administrator" and their singular contact with the outside world for the last two days, had arrived. Dioney did not wait for anyone to answer before he opened the door and entered the apartment. Nor was he alone. Serge Ortega, the walrus-snake hybrid custodian who had met them as they'd come off the emergency shelter, was with him.

Conrad stood with his arms crossed at his lower back in the living room in a semiconscious "parade rest" stance he took whenever meeting important people. He breathed out a slow breath as the two denizens came in, trying to keep his shoulders relaxed. Randolf stood back and to the left of him, his head cocked in watchful readiness.

Dioney nodded to them both. "Good afternoon. I'm glad to see you both up and well."

Attempting to smile, Conrad loosened his posture more. "Thank you. I know this isn't a casual visit ..." he nodded to Ortega, "so, please sit. Tell me what you need." He gestured to the lounge and couch, taking the chair for himself. Randolf moved with him in a familiar (but also unfamiliar) way.

His companion took a seat on the ottoman, not quite in front of Conrad but putting himself between Conrad and their visitors.

Dioney sat on the couch while Ortega settled himself in front of the lounge. "Not one to beat around the bush, eh. Good. I'm not going to lie, we do need you. Or, rather, the Well needs you. I was informed as soon as you arrived. A Gedemondas I'm friendly with sent me a message, and when one of them gives you a portent, you listen."

Conrad blinked. "The Well … needs me? For what, and why?"

"When you and the rest of the others from Brazil's ship stepped through the corridor, the Well made a determination on where best you should arrive and to what species," said Ortega. "I'm repeating myself here precisely because it's also this process that's in trouble."

Conrad's curiosity turned to confusion. If the Well was in good enough shape to house so many species and civilizations in these hexes, then surely it could fix itself. Especially if it was self-aware.

Ortega seemed to notice his growing confusion. "We have a hacker who is trying to take control of that part of the Well's functionality: determining which hex new arrivals should be assigned to. We don't know why, but it can't be good. This has never happened before even though some of the species on Well World evolved to have limited control of the Well in some sort of magic, religious, or technological way."

Conrad nodded even though so much of what Ortega said flew right over his head. Nervousness grew alongside his confusion. What could *he* do about it?

"When the Markovians built the Well World, they had guards in place to enforce the rigid and stable environment across all of the hexes." Ortega grimaced. "This is in danger."

"But nothing is ever 100 percent secure, and it was only a matter of time." Conrad paused, wondering how the hacker would've managed to get intimate access to the system. Would they have tricked Ortega by using his status? Or could there be a species somewhere in the Well that could use any ability they have and somehow come into contact with that computer?

"I suppose," Ortega said. He watched Conrad for a long few moments, letting the silence grow.

Clearing his throat, Dioney interrupted Ortega and Conrad. "Perhaps we should move this to the office, where Conrad can see the problem in real time."

Thrown off but not willing to be a bother, Conrad stood. "Of course. If … if that would be better for you."

Dioney nodded. "I think it would. We need to know sooner rather than later whether or not you can deal with this issue."

"I … ." Conrad stopped himself from babbling and nodded again. He didn't want to explain to this person that he'd barely begun to think on the issue, that he needed more time. Randolf stood as Dioney passed them, headed to the office. He glanced at Conrad, who could see the concern in his eyes. "It's fine," he murmured, reassuring Randolf. "Let's see."

Conrad gestured for Ortega to follow Dioney, but he shook his head. "I'll bring up the rear. More comfortable that way."

Dioney was already at the computer, typing away at it. He pulled up an unfamiliar program. It seemed to be a window that was titled "Maintenance Operations" and displayed what seemed like dozens of individual buttons you could click on with an ancient mouse. The program featured an assortment of graphs, charts, and dizzying amounts of information on the current state of the Well, the number of people in each hex, the weather … everything needed to make sure the Well World kept working. Dioney pushed back from the computer and relinquished the chair to Conrad. "This computer is connected to an intranet only for the ambassadors of Well World in this Zone. It has real-time monitoring of some of the Well's functions. It is a very restricted, specialized, and valuable resource—and it's all yours."

Sitting down at the computer, Conrad noticed a button on the program labeled "Defensive Field Status," decided it was part of an overall Firewall System, and clicked it. Interestingly, as he gazed over the functionality, he noticed that the Well exposed what seemed like an intentional flaw located in pieces of technology in high-tech worlds, a spell in any that might seem magical, or something inherent in the species that would trick someone into trying various ways to "break into" the Well computer. The Well would learn what would be done and simply protect itself like an immune system learning to make antibodies from a virus. As he studied the screen, Conrad was very aware of the way Dioney stood over his left shoulder. It reminded him too much of his former teacher, one Oscar Hardy, who had been a vicious taskmaster—merciless with his critiques and his tongue.

Just thinking of the professor made Conrad's hands sweat. The man had been a sadist in public and private but worse in public. He delighted in terrorizing his students in the name of "doing good work under pressure." In truth, the man just wanted his victims to suffer, and suffer Conrad had.

Until Randolf had had enough and bit the horrible man.

"You see the problem?" Dioney asked.

It was hard for Conrad to not see the question as a trap. The computer screen in front of him swam for a moment before it came back into focus. At first glance, everything was both familiar and unfamiliar. Computer programming had an inherent logic to it. It was the interface that often stymied new programmers.

While he had an idea of what the program was and how it worked, he didn't know the nuances of it … nor could he know, given how little time he'd had to look at the screen … much less the code. He stared at the Maintenance Operations window, trying to make sense of the incredible amount of data he was seeing, but Dioney loomed over his shoulder watching, waiting for him to mess up. He could already hear the mockery in the other Agitar's voice. Could hear it in Professor Hardy's reedy tone. Moments ticked by like the pounding of a nail on a coffin.

Then Randolf was there, pushing his way between Dioney and Conrad. "Excuse me. I'd like to see as well." He didn't give the administrator an opportunity to refuse. Randolf put his hand on Conrad's shoulder and leaned forward as if looking at the screen. He murmured, "It's fine. You're safe."

But it wasn't fine. He wasn't safe. Conrad was trapped in a new world, in a new life and body, and was expected to perform intricate calculations and deep thought on a problem he was not fully aware of, using tools he was not familiar with. There was no way he could solve this problem, and the administrator knew it. It was a trap. It was *all* a trap. Conrad's heart sped up, and his hands trembled.

"Is something wrong?" Dioney asked.

It seemed like an innocent question, but it wasn't. It was the beginning of the opening salvo. This was how it always began. First faux innocent questions followed by mocking observations that ended in a humiliating tongue-lashing couched in genteel words.

"I don't think we've given him enough time …" Ortega began then stopped as Conrad's breath hitched in his throat, and he looked at Dioney and Ortega with wide, fear-filled eyes.

Randolf whirled on the two of them. "You need to leave. Leave now."

Dioney had the gall to look confused. "What? But we've just begun."

"Leave!" Randolf barked, puffing up, balling his hands into fists. "Leave. You don't know what you've done. Leave now! Now!"

Ortega, ever the survivor, grabbed Dioney's arm and pulled him out the door. He added just before he shut the door, "We're sorry. We forgot about your—Conrad's—circumstances. I will contact you in a day or two. Or you can contact me. If you want a new administrator, let me know."

Even with the door closed, the damage had been done. Randolf turned back to Conrad, who had a hand to his chest and gulped for air. Dropping to his knees next to the chair, Randolf wrapped his arms around Conrad's trembling body and squeezed tight, whispering, "It's okay. It's okay. You're safe. I'm here. You're safe."

They stayed that way for a long time.

While Conrad slept, Randolf used the holographic communication device to contact Serge Ortega. He did not believe most denizens of the Well World had access to this technology, but as the Well needed Conrad and what Conrad could do while not under duress, Ortega made certain "special" lines of communication open to them.

Randolf put the cube on the table before him and pressed the button to activate it. Opening like a flower, light beamed from its corners to coalesce into a pulsing ball of orange light. He eyed it with some suspicion before asking, "Would you contact Serge Ortega, please?"

The device pulsed from orange to yellow. A few seconds later the holographic head of Ortega appeared. His white mustache bristled around his mouth. "Ah, Randolf. I was expecting to hear from Conrad. Is he all right?"

"He is sleeping. As his support companion, I need to talk to you."

"Go ahead."

Randolf paused. Everything was so different now. He'd never been able to advocate for Conrad so directly. That didn't matter. He had the ability to do so and the ear of the man … being … who could help. "You understand that Conrad has had a tough life. Privilege doesn't mean easy. I need you to know you and Dioney cannot do what you did to him again. I won't allow you to do that."

Ortega's floating head seemed to contemplate him. After several long moments of silence, he nodded. "I will do my best not to, but please explain exactly what we did wrong."

"You presented Conrad with a problem to solve without allowing him time to study it or to get used to the programming language and framework you, the Well, uses. You shoved him into the spotlight and asked him to recite a monologue without allowing him time to do more than look at the script's front cover."

"That's rather poetic of you. How did you become Conrad's support companion?"

Tilting his head, Randolf looked for an insult in the question and found none. From the look on Ortega's face, he really wanted to know. "Well, as far as I remember, I was deemed the most intelligent of my litter and most compatible for the enhancement protocol. After it proved successful, I was fitted with a voice modulator to augment my ability to provide for Conrad. It took a while for me to understand that I was not the usual sort of support companion and not to speak in front of strangers. That's what I was. This is what I am now." He paused. "Do you understand what I said about what you did to Conrad?"

"Yes. Yes, I do. Does Dioney need to be replaced? He was quite contrite that he upset your ward. I'll explain it to him, if you prefer."

"If he can respect the boundaries, he can stay. But I want him to wait until we let him into our territory when he visits. Alert us, and *we* will let him in when we are ready."

Ortega's face took on an unreadable expression. "I understand. Anything else?"

"Give us time. Give Conrad time. Unless there is an emergency, he needs to focus. You've explained what you, the Well, needs. Now give him the opportunity to do it."

"Agreed."

Conrad stared at the program screens before him. Once the pressure of having to suddenly perform for an audience was gone, he'd been able to look at the program for what it was ... and see the problem the Agitar monitoring framework had been able to highlight.

The physical interface to the Well computer resembled an old computer from Old Earth, with a fairly large and bulky monitor, a loud, clackity keyboard, and a computer mouse that used a ball toward the area where the thumb is in order to move the mouse that was on the screen. Conrad had learned about these old computers in the Old Earth history classes he took, but had never interacted with one before in his life. It was difficult to even use the keyboard with the clawed fingers he had. Conrad idly began to have small thoughts on whether someone brought in this computer from somewhere and installed it to the main Well computer, before he snapped himself out of the distraction.

"Randolf, I think I know how they managed to get a foothold into the whole thing." Conrad's mind bounced between keeping track of several little details at once in context with the huge amount of information presented. It was far beyond any supercomputer he'd been used to.

"Oh? How did they do that?" Randolf asked, dutifully sitting in a chair nearby.

Conrad let out a little sigh. "My initial hunch was right, and this hacker managed to trick someone with a lot more ... authority ... into doing what they wanted. They wouldn't have much success without taking advantage of that."

Randolf nodded. "How would they have pulled *that* off?"

"I don't know. That authority figure might have been duped into responding to a crisis that shouldn't even exist." Conrad's foot started impatiently tapping, and the outer edges of frustration began to set in. There was too much data, and all of it had to be examined. He went through a laundry list of responsibilities that the Well owned, right from what was programmed in the Markovian brain to every facet and every nook and every cranny.

The room stood silent for a few minutes before Randolf asked, "Who would have been tricked?"

"I don't know. There's usually—" Conrad cut himself off as an idea suddenly came to him. "The Well is a computer, but it's like a brain; a main Expert System that tells every other program that it interfaces with what to do. As such, that 'brain' can remember events in the short term and long term. It can remember who has a greater 'authority' to tamper with things—fix things—and what they have the power to do. This means we can see who has been corrupting the data and under what credentials. It also remembers who was the last person to interact with its core functionalities."

At first, Randolf looked as if he was following, then he frowned in confusion. "What does 'interact with core functionalities' mean?"

He had to remember that however much Randolf could communicate with him and calm him down, Randolf didn't know anything about technology. "Oh … oh, I'm starting to not make sense again," Conrad smiled. "However, I'm excited because now I have a path forward."

Randolf also smiled, happy that at least being someone Conrad could explain his ideas to—*rubber ducky decoding*—would mean he would remain happy and calm.

"The Markovians, when they constructed the Well World, had to have known that they'd inevitably screw up something and would need to keep track of what mistakes they made." Conrad clicked through the various programs. "There would have to be something of an equivalent of what programmers call a 'log' around here; something that would record every action those authority figures would do—found it!"

He clicked through the log, viewing what seemed like a mountain of text on a screen, tediously viewing each line, but stopped halfway through. "Damn it!"

"What happened?" Randolf sat straighter, more alert, watching him.

"There's a missing chunk of it. A full twenty-minute period."

Conrad could feel another PTSD episode coming on but was still determined to try and figure this out. The Well trusted him to get this task done, but the question he had on his mind was, what next?

Randolf suddenly yelped and jumped to his feet, looking around, surprised.

Conrad turned to his companion and glanced around the room, also looking for the danger. "Are you all right? What happened?"

"Ah … yes, I'm fine. It was a shock, but it didn't hurt like it did when I was a corgi," Randolf said, taking stock of his Agitar body and looking at his hands. He let out a quick surprised gasp when an electrical charge appeared in both palms.

Conrad stood up, eyeing the bouncing tiny Tesla coil–like sparks of blue electricity in both of Randolf's palms.

As Randolf closed those hands, the electrical charge went away, but he saw he could make the charge reappear at will.

"That's so cool!" Conrad looked at his own hands then back at Randolf.

"I don't understand it. Is this what Agitar can do?"

"I think so. Yes." Conrad opened his hands and concentrated. He forced energy into his hands until little sparks began forming, followed by the same Tesla coil–like dance of electricity in his own palms. Suddenly, Conrad had another idea up his sleeve.

"I think I know why the Well made us Agitar. Electricity. When computers perform mathematical calculations, they rely on electricity to do it. Those calculations take a wide range of power consumption, either a little or a lot in every incredibly small time frame. Not just one constant stream of it. There must be a program in the Well that also monitors it."

Conrad dove back to the computer, typing fast, bringing up what looked like something that visualized the electrical draw of the Well. The horizontal line danced around in odd ways, extending left to right with random bounces up and down. "If Agitar can command electricity, we can also feel it. I've just isolated it to a few key areas, and if I'm right, I can narrow it down."

He set his hands on the monitor, hearing and feeling faint buzziness all around him as the monitor began flickering rapidly. There it was. He felt what seemed like a heartbeat and closed his eyes, then focused deeper into it to see if there were any patterns. To him, it was like he could hear how the hacker was corrupting the system inputs to the Well's brain.

He moved his focus to the transition point between what he believed was the compromised system and the Expert System … then saw he had been so very wrong.

What had been a torrent of data from the Agitar's framework was barely a drop of water in an ocean of information. He could not see it, but he could sense it. What he had thought was the Markovian Well had been nothing more than a mask, a shadow of its enormity. The computer in this room was connected to the floor of computers on the level below … the whole floor was made up of computers just to *connect* with the Well's brain. It was like looking into the face of a god and understanding he was seeing only an eyelash.

It was so much, and he had been so naïve. How could he have thought he could help the Well, let alone fix it? Conrad's breath hitched in his throat, and he tried to make his hands move from the monitor. They wouldn't budge. He was trapped, a fly in a web. It was going to burn him out. He couldn't—

Warm hands on his shoulders. Warmth and electrical power flowed into him. From the top of a chasm far away, he heard Randolf say, "I'm here. You're safe. It will be okay. I'm here." More electrical power pulsed into him, giving him the mental strength to change his focus. To step back from that awesome presence, one too big to contemplate.

Turning his focus back to the Agitar framework, suddenly so much less terrifying in its scope, he honed in on the Firewall System and its much more manageable Honey Pot program. The Firewall was connected to the Expert System. If he could teach it to recognize the infiltrator, he could let it teach itself how to spot the corrupted credentials and deny the call, despite its authorizing permissions.

He sighed with relief and considered the parameters of what he needed to accomplish. Seeing the hacker's pattern in the electronic pulses, he followed them back to the systems called and the data corruption. It was possible to affect the Well's brain without having to access it directly, much less look at it.

"Are you okay?" Randolf asked after about thirty seconds.

"Yes. I am now." Conrad smiled a reassuring smile. "All I need to do is write a program to home in on what the hacker is doing, then, using the Firewall's Protection Protocols, deny them."

Over the next few hours, Conrad wrote a program on the old computer. He was thankful that it knew anything he could throw at it and that the hacker didn't know about his plan.

Running the program, a pop-up box with the words "Intake Distribution" appeared, for what he assumed to be the more complex name for how the Well assigns species and hex to a person. This was the program that had been taken advantage of by the hacker. Now he just needed to cut off the hacker's access. He had to show the Honey Pot program within the Firewall System what to do.

Typing, he activated safeguards that would isolate the Intake Distribution program. All seemed well, until he noticed that those same safeguards slowly became ineffective.

Dammit, thought Conrad. Whoever this person was noticed he was doing something. He began to look for what might be an infected program and traced it all the way to a small maintenance program that would power magic in the relevant hexes that had it. When that, too, slowly became ineffective, he noticed that all of these actions stemmed from a single source.

Deducing that the Well would enforce technological zones, Conrad narrowed it down to a zone with a high level of technology. At first, Conrad was able to identify the hacker's handle, Sophus. After Conrad deactivated their access, the hacker next tried to fool Conrad by naming themselves Artemis and reconnecting. Conrad had been monitoring any avenue the hacker could connect to, and he deactivated Artemis as well. Finally, tracing the hacker's connection, taking clues from where the connection originated, he traced it all the way back to the Parmiter hex. Now, he just had to remember to relay that to Ortega. The custodian could take it from there.

"Just need to do one last thing," Conrad muttered as he furiously clicked around on the computer. "Cut the head off the snake. Reset their whole access, forcefully log them out … ." Then, he would load the whole thing up to the Firewall System, which would interface with the Well, then they would see if it could learn like he thought it could.

After watching the safeguards hold solid for an hour, Conrad leaned back and sighed. "It's over."

If the hacker tricked someone into giving them access again, the Firewall's Protection Protocols would bump that person out of the system for good. That might be a problem in the future, but it would be a problem for someone else. Or for Conrad in the future. At least then he would know where to start.

The two of them sat in the living room again, waiting for Dioney to arrive. Ortega had already called and thanked Conrad for his work. He asked if Conrad would be available for future projects for the Well, if needed. As expected, Conrad had agreed. He had succeeded with a complex task using old and new skills. It was a good feeling.

"How did you know to feed me your energy?" Conrad asked. "Especially when I needed it most?"

Randolf shrugged. "I did what I always do. Touch and reassurance. It's different in this body, but no matter the shape of it, my support is the same. I relied on instinct and experience. When I felt the electricity in you pull at me, it was like your emotions. I threw you a rope the only way I knew how. When I was four-legged, it was a whine, a bark, a tug with gentle teeth. Now, it is a hug, a word, and shared energy. I don't understand how it works. I don't think I need to. Do I?"

"No. I don't think so. I just marvel that you always seem to do exactly the right thing when I need it."

"Training and instinct. Experience and need." Randolf looked toward the large window for a long moment before he turned back and asked, "What do you think Ortega meant by us being finally able to go through the "normal orientation" for Agitar?"

Conrad shook his head, then shrugged. "I don't know for sure. I suspect it's a bit more *"welcome to your new home, here's how things work"* instead of *"here's an impossible problem to deal with because we don't know how."* I suspect we will be moved to new apartments as well. I don't mind that. I'd like us to have a bit more choice in our housing if we could."

"We'll still be together, right?"

Conrad chuckled and gave him a knowing look. "Of course. I don't think there's any force in the Well that could separate us."

"At least *that* one thing won't change."

Both of them looked up as the door chimed. Randolf stood but waited a moment. When the front door remained closed, he smiled. "It looks like some other things do change." He walked to the door and opened it, knowing while a whole new world waited for them, he and Conrad would remain the same.

Chapter Ten:
ALESTOL:
THE DREAMING
Arlen Feldman

There were sights, though he could not see.

There were sounds, though he could not hear.

Calum Brach had walked through the gate in Zone, confident that he could blend in anywhere, like he had a hundred times before. The trick was to start moving and never stop.

But he couldn't move.

That's odd.

The world faded to black.

He awoke abruptly.

The world around him was awash with electromagnetic energy. He had no eyes or ears, but he could sense the world in every direction in a hundred gradations of gray. It took Calum a moment to realize that this didn't seem odd at all—like his brain had always been able to handle seeing in all directions, but he'd been horribly limited by only having two eyes.

There was thick vegetation all around him, hundreds of different insects, small lizards, and other creatures running through the underbrush. Nothing was sharp, but he could sense movement clearly. And temperature—the slight differences between the creatures and their surroundings. He concentrated on a flying insect and could make out the vague blur of its wings and the vibrations of the air, almost as if he could hear the individual beats.

The insect flew away from him, and as it got farther away, the details faded until the insect vanished from his senses.

Six meters, he thought to himself. I can only "see" about six meters. Although, with the thickness of the plants around him, he could only see a fraction of that in most directions.

Why aren't I freaking out? he wondered. Something about whatever transformation he'd gone through had also made him accept that transformation, like all the drones his father and associates had genetically engineered and then drugged into believing they were happy with whatever role they'd been shoved into.

Calum tried to get angry about whatever the Markovian brain had done to him, but it just wouldn't happen. *Whatever I am, perhaps I can't get angry? Can I be sad, happy, anything?*

He didn't know. But, at the very least, he definitely felt the *need* to be angry, which was a start.

And he still couldn't move. He tried, but there was nothing *to* move—no arms, no legs. Well, there was *something*. He concentrated. There was an odd sensation in his gut, and he saw a dozen dark-gray tentacles shoot from him, stretching out about a meter. He could wiggle them slightly, but that was about it. The only major thing he could do was retract them.

Brilliant. He had tentacles, and he couldn't even use them for anything.

A movement a couple of meters away caught his attention. One of the little lizards had come too close to a stubby, barrel-shaped plant. A burst of gas came from the plant, enveloping the small creature. It took a step … two … then dropped.

Calum could see a fuzzy pulse racing in the creature's neck, see the terror in its eyes, the heat rising from its body.

And then tentacles shot out of the barrel-shaped plant and dragged the still-living lizard inside.

It took Calum only a moment to make the connection. Whatever that plant-looking thing was, *he* was one as well.

But he couldn't possibly be a plant, could he? They'd not said anything about thinking plants as a possibility at the Zone gate. At least not that he remembered. They must just be some sort of species that *looked* like plants.

He examined the other creature. It really *did* look like a plant, rooted firmly in the soil. It was about a meter-tall, a thickish barrel shape that domed at the top. There were no branches or flowers that he could see. He could make out a series of divots at the base of the creature where the gas had come out, but he couldn't quite tell where the tentacles came from.

If he were one of these things, then he'd presumably have those same divots? He wanted to examine himself, but his senses only seemed to shoot outward. If he *were* one of these things, though, could he shoot gas like that?

He concentrated on the idea of *gas*. There was an odd sensation deep inside, and suddenly a gray cloud surrounded him.

Shit. I'm a plant.

He let himself fall back into unconsciousness.

Calum woke to the sensation of scurrying. Another one of those lizards. It was less than a meter from him, chasing a flying insect. Without consciously thinking about it, Calum emitted a cloud of gas, then *his* tentacles shot out and grabbed the creature. It struggled for a moment, then went slack.

He could feel it inside of him, already starting to dissolve in some chemical bath filling whatever counted for his stomach.

It felt good.

He hadn't realized how hungry he'd been. It took a few moments for his mind to catch up—he was eating a still living creature. He wanted to be disgusted but it seemed, well, *normal*.

This is what I am now. An intelligent plant. Apparently, the planet-brain that chose his form had a sense of humor. And a mean streak.

Calum had run from school and family out of disgust. Disgust for his father and his self-righteous colleagues, who were sure that they knew best for the entire human race. And, of course, *they* would not be held to the same set of rules as everyone else. The hypocrisy of it was what got him. It wasn't that they were smarter or more virtuous—they just happened to be the ones with the power and the money when the music stopped. They only ended up being smarter by deliberately engineering everyone else to be stupider. He remembered the arguments he'd had with his father over this, and the contempt the old bastard had shown him. *You'll understand when you're older. When you're in charge.*

Part of what had made him run was the fear that his father was right—that if he stayed, he would start to believe all that crap. It wasn't just that, though. Calum had also run because he loved being on the move, loved interacting with other people, falling into a new life for a while, then moving on again.

And now he couldn't move. Couldn't even have a conversation.

But, if he were intelligent, then presumably the other plant so close to him was as well. Could he talk to him? Her? It?

Calum wondered if he was still a He. It seemed unlikely. Did plants have genders? Ah well, not a big deal either way, but he decided to keep thinking of himself as a He until he had a reason not to.

He looked at the other plant again, and then tried to yell at the top of his voice.

Nothing.

But … it *felt* like he was talking, that he could talk in some manner, just as he could "see" and "hear" in some manner. Was it just some residual feeling from what he had been? Or was there some way for him to communicate that he just hadn't figured out yet?

The gray shades of the sky were changing, and the temperature was dropping. He didn't feel cold, but he could sense the change in the electromatic waves that were hitting him. Was he *sensing* ultraviolet and infra-red? Didn't plants detect light using photoreceptors? At some level, it was something else that didn't matter—his brain was now interpreting everything as *seeing* and *hearing*, so he might as well stop trying to invent a new vocabulary to understand it. Not that vocabulary was particularly useful to him with no one and nothing to talk to.

If he'd had to imagine a living hell, it would be one where he was entirely cut off, unable to communicate. He remembered feeling that way when he was at university. He couldn't relate to his playboy peers, whom he despised. And the faculty and staff were afraid of him because of his father, so he couldn't really communicate with them either.

But he'd been a fool—at this moment he would relish a conversation with the most arrogant classmate or the most sycophantic servant.

Again, he tried to summon rage, but it wouldn't come. He was just numb. Probably part of the conversion process to stop him from completely flipping out. Maybe these plant creatures were able to live without interacting with anyone, but he still *thought* like a human. It was just a matter of time until he went completely insane.

At least he seemed to be able to sleep. Or go unconscious, shut off his mind, whatever. *Sleep* was as good a word as any. The last few times it had just happened automatically, but surely if he concentrated, he could do it …

During the night, he woke twice. The first time was when a lizard ran just a little too close. He had gassed and grabbed it before he'd even been aware of it, then had gone back to sleep.

The second time, he had an itch in his mind, like something was scraping across his synapses. He opened up his senses, which worked pretty much as well at night as during the day. But there was nothing out of the ordinary—different insects now, something long and thin slithering off into the underbrush. And, of course, his silent neighbor. Looking around him more carefully, he realized that there were more of the barrel plants around him of various different sizes and shades of gray, each partially hidden by the undergrowth. There might be any number of others out there too that he couldn't see at all. Not that it mattered—he couldn't communicate with any of them.

He let himself sink back into sleep again, wondering if he could just spend the rest of his life unconscious.

Calum woke feeling refreshed and surprisingly chipper, which just made him angry. The world-brain had changed him enough that he was able to accept being what he now was, and he absolutely didn't want to.

Happy and then angry. Faint emotions, but emotions.

But it *was* a beautiful day—UV radiation was soaking into him, giving him energy. He could practically feel the nutrients flowing into him through his root systems.

He had a root system!

And Calum was fairly sure the roots had *grown* from the previous day, spreading down into the soil and further out. It was a cool, pleasant sensation.

He ate twice that day. Another lizard and some sort of snakelike creature—although the gas hadn't worked quite as well on that. The thing had almost managed to wriggle away, and had fought when Calum had grabbed it, sinking fangs into one of his tentacles. Calum hadn't even felt it. It had provided some variety in his diet at least, even if there was no actual flavor or taste. Something else lost. The rest of the day, he mostly just daydreamed and slipped in and out of consciousness.

Another night passed. And another.

His father would have been happy, he supposed, now that he couldn't run away. He pictured his father planting Calum in a pot outside his office and lecturing him daily about his responsibilities as a sentient plant, which made him laugh—or think about laughing, which was the closest he could get. At least he hadn't lost his sense of humor. At some basic level, he was still *him*.

During the next night, Calum heard talking. He looked around, but there was no one there. He couldn't make out the words, but it sounded like singing. He concentrated, but it kept fading in and out. He tried talking, then yelling, over and over, desperate for any sort of connection. It was almost worse than when he thought he was completely cut off—to know that there was something going on, but be completely excluded from it.

If it had been someone there to chop him down, he would have welcomed it, so long as they talked while they were doing it.

Then it was gone.

He stayed conscious the rest of the night, but he didn't hear anything else.

Light. Color!

He wasn't awake, so this must be a dream? But he'd not dreamed before—not since he'd got here.

Streaks of color shot past in all directions. Blues and greens and reds and yellows. Vivid neon colors. Behind the streaks, he could make out indistinct floating shapes. The shapes were regular—pyramids and cubes and octahedrons and much more exotic structures in a hundred different colors. They looked like escapees from a geometry class.

He could hear a deep, rumbling hum that made his whole body vibrate. Calum suddenly realized that he was moving—floating like all those other shapes. With the barest thought, he sped up, started flitting at high speed through and around the other shapes, intoxicated by his returned independence.

I can move!

But then the brightly colored world started to fade into grays, the floating shapes going fuzzy, then disappearing.

He was back in his small clearing. Calum could sense the world around him with perfect clarity. It was full of life, but it felt dead. And he was back to being fixed in place.

He would have cried. If he'd had eyes.

The next day, Calum couldn't decide if he'd had an incredibly vivid dream or if it had been real. He finally decided it must have been real for no other reason than that he couldn't bear it if it weren't. He captured and ate one small lizard, but a second one managed to get away, its momentum carrying it beyond the range of his tentacles. After an hour or so the little creature shivered, got to its feet, and ran—only to be captured by his neighboring plant. There was definitely a lesson about life in there somewhere.

Finally, the day came to a close, and Calum let himself sink into unconsciousness.

The sound came before sight. That same deep, vibrating hum. Then the vivid colors and shapes. Calum had the vague impression of being in a desert under an azure sky. But it could just as easily be a geometric yellow plane below and a blue plane above.

He didn't have limbs or roots. He had facets and edges and vertices. It felt entirely natural.

Calum started to race off like he had the night before, but something was tugging at him. He fought against it, but it was like fighting a black hole. Calum found himself spinning toward a mass of floating shapes. As he watched, they started merging, creating ever more complex polytopes in increasing numbers of dimensions—more dimensions than he should be able to perceive.

And he was being sucked into it. He was terrified that, once he touched it, he'd be destroyed. Or never be able to get back out. But he didn't have any choice. He felt one of his vertices join with the mass, then he was transforming and spinning and reflecting through shapes and dimensions without conscious volition. The movement slowed, and his vertices and edges slid into place with his neighbors' until he was a small part of a giant six-dimensional hexeract. Calum was amazed to discover that he still had his own identity even as he became part of this massive construct. Was amazed that he could recognize all these extra dimensions and even knew what these fantastic shapes were called.

His facets were vibrating in time with the hum, which was now so deep that he almost couldn't hear it. He realized that he was humming as well.

And then it stopped just being a hum. He was pierced by the simultaneous thoughts of all the creatures in the massive structure. For a second it was agony, then it was blissful. It was more than just words, but deep understanding and feelings shared between them all.

Joy. Sadness. Hope. Anxiety. Pride. Guilt. Compassion.

How could he have thought that his new form couldn't hold emotions? He'd never felt such strong emotions in his life. It was like he was part of some giant mirror. And he wasn't just feeling others' emotions—they were *his* emotions as well. His own memories of each of those emotions mixed in with all of his new siblings'. They understood his own emotions, had stripped bare any attempt by him to hide them, even as he understood their own raw feelings.

They were the Alestol. *He was* Alestol. *They took pride in being what they were, felt joy in coming together like this, in The Dreaming. But some were no longer there—had disappeared from The Dreaming without warning. The sadness was at the loss, the anxiety that they would lose more, the compassion for those who had lost close friends. And compassion for* him. *For his suffering*

161

with his father. For having to run. For having to change. For going so long without connecting.

Calum's dream-self could weep. Brilliant diamonds flew out of him, whirled up and outward in complex patterns. The others were startled at first, then he felt them gather around him mentally, supporting him, all focused on him until he almost couldn't bear it. He felt them pull back, giving him space. He could tell they didn't understand the need, but there was no judgement.

The giant shape started breaking up, reversing the process of combination, splitting up into tetracombs and hypercubes and then back into platonic solids and a hundred more exotic shapes.

And then Calum was back rooted to the ground and to three simple dimensions. He wasn't sure which was more constraining.

He faded into exhaustion-driven sleep.

Calum slept for two straight days, although he was vaguely aware of semi-waking to eat. It was a good thing that he did that automatically. That *Alestol* did that automatically. It was surprising how much better he felt just knowing what species he was.

It was already getting harder to remember his previous life. He still resented being *literally* tied down, but he didn't feel so cut off anymore. The Dreaming made up for a lot.

He only vaguely remembered his mother but assumed he'd shared emotions with her. She'd died when he was a small child, and that must have been the last time until last night that anyone had cared enough to try.

How much of his unwillingness to connect was to avoid being found out, and how much of it was just an unwillingness to share emotions? Was that something he'd learned from his father? The only emotion he'd ever observed from the man was anger. As far as Calum had run from him, had he carried that lesson with him?

He spent hours worrying about this—something he wouldn't have been able to do in his original shape. Was his father right? If Calum hadn't fallen through the Markovian gate, would he eventually have grown up into him? He'd already worked hard to avoid getting emotionally attached to anyone.

For the first time, he wondered what his father had been like when he'd been younger. Just like Calum, he'd grown up in the elite bubble of his planet's oligarchs. Had the old man hidden his own emotions for so long that they'd atrophied? It was hard to imagine the butchering bastard as young, let alone as someone who laughed and loved and cared about anything.

If he *had*, it was almost worse. If he'd once been that way, *knew* what Calum was going through, but didn't make even the slightest effort to reach out to his son.

The second time Calum joined The Dreaming it was just as strange, but more solid. *He* was more solid.

He hadn't noticed the first time, but the others didn't just rush to create the joined shape. They spun through different patterns and tilings, sometimes shooting back and forth between different dimensions to create complex and beautiful polytopes, experimenting with ever more intricate mappings.

They were playing! It was amazing to watch, and even more amazing to get caught up. He let himself change shape and color, and others changed and merged and reflected around his own different shapes, choosing complementary colors. He couldn't help but laugh.

Calum could clearly feel the vertices and facets of his final octahedral shape, even as they unfolded to became part of the hexeract. But as the shape formed, he realized there was something wrong. The hexeract was incomplete, missing edges and faces.

They all shifted, creating a different shape, runcinated in six dimensions, making use of the vertices that were present.

Sadness. Satisfaction. Worry. Joy.

How could he have thought it was better to keep the world at arm's length? It was *exactly* what his father did, and as far as he'd run, he'd just done the same thing. But this joining, sharing, feeling—Calum had shut himself off from the human equivalent only to discover what he'd missed when he was no longer human. Not that he had any idea how any of it worked.

We are joined by our roots. We talk with the help of the mycorrhizal fungi that clings to us and passes on thoughts. We are sad because more of us have disappeared. We have satisfaction that you have a stronger connection to us. We are worried because we don't know where the lost ones have gone. But we have joy in being alive and in The Dreaming and the connections between us.

Have any of us disappeared before? Calum was surprised that he could ask a question so clearly.

We all grew together. One was killed when we were very young. It was lost from The Dreaming. You are the only one to join The Dreaming since we were seedlings. We had no parents as you did. Regret. Regret for not having the experience. Regret for your own pain.

163

Gratitude. Joy. He was grateful for their regret. He was joyful for finding a family now.

It took less time for Calum to recover than after the last Dreaming. His mind was pleasantly blank as he digested a particularly large lizard. As much as he appreciated The Dreaming, and not being alone, it was something of a relief to be back in his own head. He wondered if that was because of his former life, or if the other Alestol felt it too.

How strange to not have parents. He supposed that biologically there must be some form of progenitor. Perhaps the current generation of Alestol had grown from seeds spread by the previous generation? Odd, though, that none of the older generation was around. Perhaps the process of creating seeds killed them? If so, was that perhaps where the missing Alestolians had gone? They'd seeded and died?

That was a depressing thought. How long did they live before that happened? How old was *he* for that matter? Calum hadn't entirely reconciled himself to the idea of being motionless for half his life and part of a complex mathematical gestalt the other half. But he definitely wasn't ready to die either. Did the Markovian planet-brain really have it in for him? Somehow that didn't seem right.

If he hadn't gone through that damned gateway, what would he be doing? Moving on, finding another place to blend in for a while, careful not to leave any trace.

But he'd always thought there would be a future. A family, maybe. Doing *something* that would make a difference. Perhaps overthrowing his father and his friends—although, he admitted to himself that would require more of a commitment to something than he'd ever been able to muster. Besides, in the power vacuum that followed, it would be easy for something far worse to take over.

In the silence of his own brain, he wondered if he might have ended up stuck in charge after all. Might make the same or worse decisions than his father had made.

The upside now was that he wouldn't have a chance to make any such mistakes.

His neighboring Alestol was gone.

Calum hadn't noticed anything, had no idea when it had happened. He strained his senses to try and get any extra details. There was a slight dip in the ground where it'd been, but that was it. No seeds, nothing. Although perhaps they were too small to see?

He hadn't even known its name. If it even *had* a name. In The Dreaming, it hadn't seemed relevant. Now not knowing seemed really sad. If he could have, he would have wept for his unnamed friend.

The shapes in The Dreaming evolved as more and more Alestolians disappeared. Calum was not the only one to be shocked when they couldn't go beyond five dimensions. But when they were limited to four, no one seemed surprised.

The next Dreaming started out pessimistically. The humming and sharing of emotions were just as powerful, just as cathartic, but the theories were of predators, of invaders from other hexes, of disease.

Loss. Remembrance. Joy. Hope.

They were sad to have lost their friends, but remembered them, and felt joy to have known them. They hoped their siblings had moved on to a better place. Calum wasn't so sure he believed that, and he could tell that he was not alone.

How old were the ones that disappeared?

Mostly they were the eldest. But some were younger.

If they'd been animals rather than plants, then the oldest and the youngest would be the weakest—the easiest targets. But plants got bigger and stronger as they grew—at least to a point.

The Dreaming happened less and less frequently. Calum ate when he could, but otherwise let himself sleep most of the time. He felt hungry and tired all the time.

Several times, he thought he glimpsed movement. His first irritational thought was that some of the others had returned, which made no sense. His second thought was that there was some predator out there—a predator so fast and deadly that it could take an Alestol without being noticed.

Interesting change in perspective. In his previous life he wouldn't have thought of something that ate plants as a *predator*. It would be crazy if they were being destroyed by some sort of local equivalent of a cow.

On the other hand—tentacle—it would have to be an awfully quick cow, and one that was immune to their gas.

The old Calum would have run away at this point. Not so much of an option now.

It was weird, but Calum was fairly sure that he wouldn't run now, even if he could. He cared too much. He had turned over a new leaf. Hah.

There were only a couple dozen of them left. Not enough to pass beyond three dimensions now. There was the tug to merge, but it was a weak thing. Most of them, Calum included, just orbited each other morosely.

Since he wasn't really from here, he wondered if he'd be left when all the others were gone. He'd just be sitting all day by himself, then in a Dreaming made up of his own single, simple shape.

Very briefly he wondered if this was all some sort of elaborate punishment his father had arranged. But even *he* wasn't that powerful.

Calum wondered if he deserved to be punished. He'd not done much with his life, but he didn't *think* he'd done anything to deserve this. Perhaps it was all of the things he *hadn't* done.

Besides, it wasn't just him. He was spending all his time feeling sorry for himself, but all the others around him were going through the same thing. They'd spent their whole lives here and were losing people who they'd interacted with for *years*.

And they'd all helped him when he really needed it. Was there something, *anything* he could do to help them?

First, though, he needed to bring them together. He cycled through a few different shapes until he found something that seemed appropriate, then concentrated on his goal—a combined shape that would work with the few of them that were left. Eventually the others picked up on his thought and started transforming into triangles and pentagrams, linking and joining until they formed a shape he *knew* was called a dual-inverted snub icosidodecahedra, although he was sure he'd not known the term before.

Happiness. Surprise. Humor.

It was a new shape. One they wouldn't have made if there had been more of them, and it was beautiful.

Grief. Depression. Fear.

NO. It took Calum a moment to realize that the thought had come from him. It thundered around the shape.

Remembrance. Understanding. Hope.

But we don't understand.

Where do we go? Perhaps this is just our natural span? When there had been hundreds of voices in The Dreaming, that would have been too literal a thing to ask. It had all been about emotions and memory. Now, though, he felt the whole group concentrating on the questions.

We don't feel old. We don't feel sick.

Calum didn't either. In fact, every day he'd felt better than the day before.

How do you feel? He pushed the thought out into the hum. It shot around.

Sad. Strong. Restless.

Restless. The same thing that he had been feeling since he'd got here. Since he'd been a child, really.

The Dreaming broke up. It hadn't answered anything, but it seemed to lift everyone's spirits.

The next day even more of the Alestolians were gone. He'd only been able to see so many from the spot where he was rooted, but now he could only see the outline of one other. He wondered where they'd been in the fantastic complex transformations of the night before.

Transformation. The word floated around in his head. There were lots of different types of transformations, even in the real world. And one type …

Could it be that simple? If he'd had a mouth, it would be hanging open.

Would the Markovians have bothered to create sentient creatures that couldn't move? The Dreaming was incredible, sure, but the species was incredibly vulnerable if it couldn't escape from any serious predator or natural disaster.

Of course, it might be *exactly* the sort of thing that the Markovians would do—he had no clue how they thought. But what if The Dreaming was a starting point? A way to learn how to think and be? If the shallow assholes he'd grown up with had started their life with something like that, perhaps they'd not turn into the closed-off controlling monsters of his father's generation.

But you couldn't stay still forever. You'd eventually have to take what you'd learned out into the world and do something with it.

You'd have to grow up.

Which meant leaving a place of safety, perhaps, but having a chance to move and grow.

His father had been right about that, if wrong about everything else.

Calum was *sure* he was right. His friends hadn't died—they'd moved on, *grown up.* And the only reason they wouldn't come back to tell the others was because they *couldn't.* No adult could properly explain adulthood to a child.

He could barely wait for nightfall. When it finally came, he tried to join The Dreaming.

It was hard. Harder than it had been since that first time, like the connection was weaker. Because there were so few of them left? He could feel his roots, and they didn't seem to have as firm a grasp as they'd had.

Finally, he found himself on the great yellow plane. There were only a dozen of them there, and the pull was almost nonexistent. But, rather than the morose behavior from last time, they swam and folded and reflected around one another, swapping colors so often that it was almost blinding.

Eventually they merged into a simple shape, a rhombicosidodecahedron with sixty vertices.

Sadness. Acceptance. Joy.

We are sad to be fading, but we accept what cannot be fought. We have joy for this last Dreaming and for this life.

For a long moment, Calum was unable to speak. He could feel the compassion of the others, wrapping around him. He felt the sadness. Felt the joy. But he wasn't ready for acceptance.

Hope. Understanding.

What if we aren't dying? What if we are changing? Maybe we are transforming from one form to another, just as we do here?

Possible, came the thought from the group. *It cannot be proven or disproven. But it is a good thought.*

Instead of just breaking up, the shape began to rise, looking like a massive multicolored ball. It started to spin, going faster and faster until smaller, simpler shapes shot off it in all directions. It was scary and exhilarating all at once. Calum heard the sound of laughter at the sheer exuberant pleasure of the movement. He was laughing too as his mind slid back into his rooted form.

He could be completely wrong about the transformation, but he was glad he'd told them his theory, glad he'd provided some hope and some joy.

And he was sure he wasn't wrong. Instead of dreading being left, or dreading being taken, he was now looking forward to moving on, growing up. Whatever that meant.

He swore to himself that as an adult, he would not forget this. He would remember that life was as much about joy and love as about responsibility and sadness. He wondered if his father had made a similar pledge before growing older. It didn't matter. He could only control his own thoughts and actions. His father had never believed that.

Calum felt his roots begin to retract.

Chapter Eleven:
BOIDON:
THE PACIFIST WAR
Catherine Asaro

She opened her eyes—and what?

Sitting with her paws curled under her body, she pondered … nothing. Her mind was a blank slate. No memories. Nada. And yet, a sense of urgency tugged her. She had to—*really* had to—to—

To what?

Well, I have to do something, she thought. *I can't just sit here.*

She looked around.

Pretty. Fields rolled everywhere, carpeted with grass and wildflowers in red, yellow, and pink. Fliers with gauzy wings drifted among the blossoms, looking suitably artistic. Nearby hills rolled in gentle slopes until in the distance they met a blue sky where puffs of clouds hung out with each other.

"Huh," she said, ever the soul of articulate discourse. As pleasing as it looked, the landscape offered no answers as to why her brain had gone on hold. She felt comfortable, though, sitting in the grass.

Sitting?

She *wasn't* sitting. She was—well, she didn't know exactly what she was doing. She had paws curled under her body, honking big paws, thank you very much. She craned her head around to look along her body.

"Hey," she yelled, so startled that the words burst out before she had a chance to think. "I'm a *cat*."

No one answered. Nothing changed either. She remained a cat. A *big* cat. She stood up, and her body moved with smooth, muscular grace. It occurred to her that as a cat, she shouldn't be able to speak like a human.

Human. Okay, progress. She was a human being. Except, apparently, she wasn't.

"Hello? Anyone here?" She turned in a circle and saw nothing on the lovely green hills except a few trees. Such bucolic tranquility. That didn't feel right, not at all.

"Dinorama," she said. Okay. Dinorama. It was her name.

"Seriously?" she muttered. Who named their kid Dinorama?

"Dina," she said. Now *that* felt right. "Dina Ramos." She was a human, or more accurately a lion, named Dina Ramos.

Except … Dina still didn't feel right. And that situation felt *safe*. For some reason, she needed to keep that safety at all costs, even if it meant using the wrong name.

A creature twitched in her side vision. Startled, she turned toward it. The creature tried to evade notice, retreating to the edge of her vision even as she turned. She *pounced* and—blast it! The critter whisked away as fast as she moved. She kept chasing, and it kept fleeing, always just out of reach, leading her to run in a circle around and around, *ho* this was fun, around and around, never any closer to that tufted demon; how did it keep going at exactly her same speed—

"What a minute." Dina stopped. The creature stopped too. It gave a last twitch and lay there, inert. Oh yeah, now she recognized the maddening little beast.

"Really?" Dina asked the universe, which had no sympathy for her today. "I'm chasing my tail?"

A chuckle came from behind her. With a start, Dina whipped around, growling low in her throat. She instinctively unsheathed her claws, letting them dig into the field.

Two big cats waited a distance away in the rippling grasses. They sat on their haunches with their paws in front of them, a young male and female. Each had a human face, or almost human, though a trace of fur showed on their skin and their ears looked tufted. Their faces blended into their cat bodies at their necks. They otherwise looked like lions, with fur the color of a desert basking in sunlight. Their appearance so flustered Dina that she forgot to keep growling.

Nothing to do about it, they'd seen her idiotically chasing her tail. Somewhere in the back of her mind she had the oddest sense, as if a woman kept shouting at her, telling her this was impossible, that this change in her body formed the fabric of nightmares.

Sphinx, Dina thought.

Yes. Sphinx. That described these cats. A few of her memories were returning.

"Who are you?" she asked the newcomers, more to distract herself from her sphinx body than because she thought they could tell her. Even if they spoke, she had no way to know their language.

Counter to her expectations, the male sphinx said, "I'm Anhur."

The female said, "I'm Mehyt." She considered Dina. "You're new here, aren't you?"

Okay, she understood them—but that made even *less* sense. They weren't speaking Spanish—

Spanish. Hah! She knew Spanish, and some other language too, what was it … Confederate! Yes, she also spoke Confederate.

These big cats used a different language, neither Spanish nor Confederate, yet she understood them. The memory of why it worked that way balanced on the edge of her cat-mind, but it insisted on eluding her. At least the human part in her mind that considered this a nightmare had calmed down. It felt as if her neural processes were rewiring her new brain to accept her new body.

Neural processes? That didn't seem a very sphinxlike phrase.

"Are you all right?" Mehyt asked.

Ah, blast it, she was just staring at them. Mortified, she said, "I'm Dina." The fake, safe name. She didn't dare reveal any weakness, especially about her lost memories. If they knew how baffled she felt, the danger could—could—

Could what? She saw no danger aside from her fearsome tail.

Oh, what the hell. Maybe these sphinx-people could help.

"I have no idea where I come from," Dina admitted. "Or who I am. I just, uh, woke up here." Wow, that sounded even wonkier out loud than it did in her mind.

The sphinxes didn't look particularly worried, just curious, as if she presented them with a riddle to solve. They walked forward, lean and graceful. Dina backed away and bared her claws, which she hadn't even realized she'd retracted. Damn! She had to be more careful.

Careful about what?

An attack, Dina thought. Before she came here, she'd hidden during a covert maneuver. Hidden from whom? The obvious choice fell to these sphinxes who continued to advance on her. Yeah, they seemed friendly, but they were lions, huge ones. She had no doubt they could tear a human apart and barely work up a sweat in that gorgeous fur.

Dina growled, low and deep. Both Anhur and Mehyt stopped and settled in that "sitting on haunches" posture, watching her. They seemed more baffled than hostile.

It could be a trick, Dina thought.

"You have no idea about your identity?" Anhur asked.

Dina gave a low roar. Ho! That sounded impressive. She did it again, this time more to appreciate the deep rumble than because it seemed necessary.

The sphinxes watched her with thoughtful expressions. "I think she's an Entry," Mehyt said.

Anhur turned his head to Mehyt, revealing an impressive mane of hair, golden and tawny. It fell down his neck to his lion shoulders. "That would make sense."

"What are you talking about?" Dina asked.

"I wish you could talk to Bob," Mehyt told her.

"Who the fuck is Bob?" Dina asked.

"Quite some language," Anhur rumbled. Then he added, "Bob is the only other Entry who's come here in decades, maybe longer. He died years ago, though."

"Entry?" Dina asked.

"Someone from outside our world," Mehyt said, as if that were a perfectly natural statement.

"Outside Boidon, at least," Anhur amended. "This hex, where we live."

Dina snorted. "Oh, well, in that case."

"It's true," Anhur told her. "He said he came from the Confederacy. He died before my birth, so I don't know much more."

Confederacy. That meant she wasn't the only one. She had to remember what that meant, and yet—a part of her also wanted to forget it all, forever.

No. She couldn't forget. She couldn't do that to people she had loved.

The memories began to return.

They didn't come in a flood, but as a trickle, easing into her conscious mind while it adjusted, giving her time to accept the truth. Yes, she remembered the pain and defiance, the grief and fury. Her world had fallen to the Com. She'd lost everything, including everyone she loved. The Com turned them into automatons, absorbing them into a hive mentality until, in the end, they barely recognized her. Yes, she remembered. She wished she didn't, that she could go back to that blissful time just a few moments ago when she knew only the sun, hills, and flowers. In agony, she recalled every detail of that desperate moment when she and her followers took their final stand in the star-liner, hoping to stop yet another world falling to the Com by kidnapping the official headed to finish the process. It had all gone wrong, ending in disaster.

Dina backed away from the sphinxes, then turned and took off, running through the fields. She couldn't face these memories with anyone watching her. More bubbled into her conscious mind, especially the meeting with Ortega, the way he'd described how this world would alter her. Dina wondered that she didn't go insane with these changes. Maybe she truly had lost her metaphorical marbles.

She ran hard. Her new body loved the speed, the energy of her youthful muscles. Hills and trees flashed by, and the blue sky stretched above her. She felt driven to attack someone, anyone, *anything* to stop the urgency that drove her. She had to fight, to battle for her world, for the Confederacy, for humanity.

Except she'd stopped being human.

So, she ran, trying to cope.

Unfortunately, for all its power, her lion body couldn't keep up that grueling pace for long. As she tired, she slowed down until she was walking through grassy meadows that swayed with her passing. Anhur and Mehyt had stayed with her, one on either side, keeping a respectful distance.

Finally, she stopped and sat on her haunches. Mehyt and Anhur came over and sat as well, facing her. *I'm not Dina,* she realized. Dina was an alias she'd used on the *Euphrates.* Her given name had been Alejandra Garcia, but that life had vanished forever. She would be Dina here, a new name for a new life.

"I have to get out of this place," Dina told them. Ortega claimed it was impossible, that she could never leave this world, but she couldn't, *wouldn't* accept that. She hated being trapped, no longer human. She felt good in this body, powerful, intelligent, healthy instead of suffering from all the injuries she'd sustained while fighting the Com, but it didn't matter. It wasn't *her.*

Mehyt spoke gently. "You can never leave."

"A way must exist." Dina willed them to understand her urgency. "I'm fighting a war. I must get back."

"I'm sorry." Anhur sounded like he meant it. "But you can't."

"No." Dina didn't want to hear him. "You're wrong."

Mehyt spoke with compassion. "Come with us. Meet our people. Let us help."

Dina didn't want to go anywhere with them. She wasn't ready to accept that she had become part of their existence. She spoke stiffly, putting them off. "What, you have nothing else to do?"

"Not really." Mehyt looked embarrassed. "We were searching for some cows that graze here."

"We hoped they'd give us some milk." Anhur looked ready to lick his lips. "It's delicious."

Milk. Seriously? These cats, for all their ferocious appearance, hardly seemed a threat. Even so. She needed to run again.

And what will you gain by dashing about like a maniac? She needed information, not speed.

Dina let out a rumbling breath. "All right. I'll come with you." She paused. "For now."

The groaning came from beyond the ridge.

Dina listened with a sensitivity beyond anything human ears could manage. Yep, there it came again, groans on the other side of the low hill to her left. The sound went on for several moments, then stopped. She, Anhur, and Mehyt had traveled parallel to this sweet ridge for a while now, sometimes running, other times ambling in the streaming sunshine. The tall grasses that grew here resembled bulrushes with velvety brown heads shaped like cigars. They swayed in the gentle breezes.

She recalled now where she'd heard the names Mehyt and Anhur. They were a goddess and a god in the pantheon worshiped by the ancient Egyptians on Earth. It fit with what Ortega told her, that when beings of one hex left to settle a planet, sometimes a few from a different hex slipped through with them. She didn't know a lot about sphinxes, just random facts she'd learned as a schoolgirl. A place in Giza, Egypt, had a famous statue of a great sphinx sitting with his paws extended in front of him. The only other factoid she recalled was that a female sphinx with wings had posed a riddle to someone named Oedipus: *What goes on four legs in the morning, two legs in the afternoon, and three legs in the evening?* Dina couldn't remember the answer. Regardless, given that the Egyptians had worshipped cats and immortalized one of their pharaohs as a sphinx, it suggested they hadn't considered these creatures noxious.

Ho! There it came again, a chorus of moans beyond the ridge, discordant and loud. Dina stopped, unsettled.

Anhur looked around and halted, followed by Mehyt. They walked back to Dina.

"What's wrong?" Anhur asked.

"Don't you hear it?" Dina flicked her tail at the ridge. "That wailing."

"Ah." Mehyt settled onto her haunches, then stood up again as if she wanted to run. "It's the Teliagin camp."

"Say what?" Dina asked. The groans shivered through the air, making the fur along her back stand up. She slashed her tail, and it swept across the ground.

Anhur spoke with urgency. "We should leave." He and Mehyt spun around and took off, using their powerful legs to propel them forward, accelerating to their fastest speed in seconds. Dina sprinted after them, amazed at how easily she caught up. Her rushing adrenaline drove her to go fast, fast, *faster*.

The cries they'd heard exploded into an infuriated roar. Three creatures crested the ridge, running alongside them. They looked nearly two meters tall, built like humans but much bigger, with bulging shoulder muscles and massive physiques. In her heightened state, Dina saw them in disjointed flashes, a glimpse of matted blue-black hair that fell down their backs, two vicious horns on their heads, red skin the color of blood. A terrifying face—huge, flaring nostrils—a mouth with fangs like daggers. Most of all, she saw their eye, one gigantic *eye* that dominated their forehead, making them look like enraged cyclopes. They galloped on massive legs that ended in hooves, freaking *hooves,* not like horses, more like elephants, huge and flat, destroying the grasses as they relentlessly gained on their prey.

Even as Dina realized she could never outrun their pursuers, a cyclops reached Anhur. With a shout of triumph, it tackled the sphinx, and they both tumbled to the ground. As they fought, bellowing and roaring, another cyclops went after Mehyt—

A force smashed into Dina and hurled her into the air. With a yowl of rage, she twisted around, coming down on her massive paws. She launched herself at the cyclops that had attacked, her claws extended. It was much larger than her, but right now she didn't care. Its huge biceps flexed as Dina raked her claws down its torso, which was bare except for some straps that held knives. The skin of the cyclops shredded under her attack, and her attacker howled with fury.

In her side vision, Dina glimpsed Mehyt and Anhur battling two other cyclopes. The giant facing her roared, and a small corner of Dina's mind recognized the patterns of language. In the same moment she jumped at the cyclops, it hurtled a spear. As she dodged out of its path, a realization shot through her battle-pumped brain; these one-eyed monsters carried *hunting* gear. The cyclops came after her again, brandishing a sword she could never have carried, because now she had these blasted paws instead of hands. She didn't need knives, though. Her claws were bigger than the daggers on its chest strap.

As the cyclops lunged at her, she leapt to the side—and discovered she had more than enough speed to outmaneuver its lumbering charge. Good! She whirled and caught it across the legs with another swipe of her claws. Her attacker screamed in protest as it crumpled to the ground.

"Dina, *run,*" Anhur shouted. "*RUN!*"

Dina ran.

They left the cyclopes behind, the monsters roaring in pain and protest, the sounds of their fury fading with distance. Dina doubted her group had done serious damage to the creatures, but at least the cyclopes had taken enough injuries that they either couldn't or didn't want to follow their prey.

"What the hell was that?" Dina gasped as she raced alongside Mehyt and Anhur.

"Teliagin," Mehyt answered, never slowing her pace.

Dina had no idea what that meant, but she saved her energy for running.

They slowed as they climbed a hill carpeted in long grasses and blue flowers. At the top, they all sat on their haunches, catching their breath while they gazed at the valley below them. A town spread out in the fields. It looked like a cat's dream of paradise, with climbing structures everywhere, shelves, walls, towers, even spiral staircases that went nowhere, all with platforms, rooms with open windows, and other inviting places where you could curl up and nap. The structures were supersized, built to accommodate lions rather than domestic kitties. Inviting trees with ample branches and sturdy trunks also stood around the town, offering yet more places to climb and lie. Other open areas had lawns that looked exceedingly comfortable, especially for the sphinxes dozing there in the sunshine.

"Oh, my," Dina said. They'd found heaven. She'd love to pad down there, fetch some milk to lap up, and then climb into one of the houses to sleep. She didn't dare risk it, though. Even if she'd trusted the lions in that inviting place—which she had no reason to do—she had wounds to tend, gouges where the cyclops had raked her skin and fur.

"Home," Mehyt said.

"You live there?" Dina asked. "Aren't you worried the cyclopes will attack?"

Anhur growled. "Before today, no. They mostly stayed in their camp."

"You called them Teliagins," Dina said. "What does that mean?"

Mehyt tilted her head toward the way they'd come. "The Teliagin hex borders ours to the north. It's similar to ours, but the climate is colder, and they have less game." She paused. "At least, I've assumed they have less game. They come here to hunt for food."

"For smaller prey," Anhur said. "This is the first time they've attacked any of us."

"You just let them come here and kill stuff?" Dina asked. Sure, she was starving for a tasty bite of meat. But still. That didn't mean she'd invade a neighboring hex and attack its people. Or its cats.

"We should talk to the Council," Mehyt said.

Dina couldn't decide if that sounded promising. The Confederacy had a reasonable but overly bureaucratic Council, and also a military that mostly acted in the best interests of its member worlds. The Com had subverted all that, creating a repressive regime that suppressed individuality and forced cultures to fit their mold.

Who knew what she'd encounter here.

Sphinxes filled the wood-paneled hall. The first thing Dina noticed, as she entered with Anhur and Mehyt, were the *fliers*. Some sphinxes had wings! Their feathered glories stretched wide, especially when they unfurled those great pinions. Even with that large size, though, she didn't see how the wings could lift such powerful animals off the ground.

Then again, who knew what went into their creation. It reminded her of an ancient saying from the writer Arthur C. Clark: *Any sufficiently advanced technology is indistinguishable from magic.* The sphinxes lived in a low-tech hex, but their designers could have given them all sorts of marvels, "magic," courtesy of the Markovians.

Rumbles filled the room. After a moment, Dina realized all that noise came from speechifying lions. Apparently verbose politicking wasn't confined to *Homo sapiens.* It quieted as she walked with Mehyt and Anhur to the front of the room. An exceptionally large sphinx stood on a dais there, a winged lioness with traces of gray in her tawny hair. When Anhur gave her a sign, the lioness nodded and withdrew, motioning Mehyt and Anhur forward. The dais had no chairs, only pads where they both settled on their haunches and looked suitably regal. Dina stayed back, trying to draw as little notice as possible.

Mehyt and Anhur rumbled at the gathered sphinxes, describing their fight with the cyclopes, evoking roars from their listeners.

"We barely escaped alive," Mehyt finished.

A winged sphinx spoke from the assembly. "They're invading our hex."

"What invasion?" That came from the powerful sphinx who'd offered the dais to them. She ruffled her wings in a challenge as she returned to where they sat.

Anhur spoke with respect. "We relinquish the dais to Elder Bast."

Bast inclined her head to him, then settled on her haunches like a goddess and spoke to the crowd. "One attack isn't an invasion. Other than today, they've only hunted small game."

"Send an emissary to their camp," a wingless cat called out. "Ask why they attacked."

Yeah, right, Dina thought. Someone tries to kill you, so you knock on their door and say *excuse me, what was that about?* It didn't take a genius to figure out their disagreeable neighbors had decided sphinx meat offered a better banquet than small game. Today, three delectable cats happened to stroll by while the cyclopes were moaning, probably about their lack of tasty treats.

Anhur squinted at the gathering. "Uh—they didn't seem inclined to chat."

A huge lion spoke. "What did you do to threaten them?" His wings rustled open, sending the other lions around him backing away with throaty growls.

"Nothing!" Mehyt protested. "We were just walking along, minding our own business."

A lioness spoke, her human face lined with age, her wings folded above her body. "Perhaps you youngsters stumbled on some sacred ground of theirs."

"It's our ground and hex," Anhur said. "Besides, it's the same place we always go."

"You must have done *something*," another lion said.

"For fuck's sake." Dina stalked over to join Anhur and Mehyt. "Those asshole cyclopes *attacked* us. They wanted to make us dinner."

Bast looked her over, a slow and disapproving appraisal. "Who are you?"

"Um, yes, well, we forgot to mention that," Anhur said. "We think she's a new Entry."

Bast's magnificent tail slashed back and forth. "An *Entry?* Are you serious?"

Growls through the crowd. Damn. It sounded to Dina like a magnified version of a trait common to every cat she'd ever known. They did *not* like intruders in their territory.

Dina spoke in what—she hoped—came across as a resonant voice. If nothing else, she was at least loud. "These cyclopes are in *your* hex. They invaded *your* territory. Doesn't that bother you?"

"How would you know?" Bast asked. "You've been here how long? A whole day?"

"Well, actually only a few hours," Dina admitted.

Bast answered with a disdain worthy of a goddess speaking to an insect. "And in that extraordinary amount of time, you've become an expert on our neighbors?"

"No. I realize that." Dina spoke with respect. "Before I came here, though, I led a rebellion against tyranny." The Com would never consider themselves tyrants, but tough. In her book, any government that massacred human individuality qualified. "I know aggression when I see it. Those cyclopes were hunting us."

She expected Bast to scoff. Instead, the sphinx regarded her with that unfathomable gaze cats had perfected in some long-ago age, that time when they decided humans would be better off if felines took over the universe. Not that many humans realized they'd been subjugated, given that their new masters slept most of the time. Right now, though, this sphinx bunch seemed wide awake.

A giant lion at the edge of the dais spread his wings into their full glory, a span of golden feathers several meters wide. Ho! Until now he'd only listened to the debate, focusing on each speaker with an intensity Dina recognized, the same method she'd used during rebel meetings where she let others talk while she evaluated. Now he paced across the dais and joined them, surveying their group with a golden imperial face that would have done an Egyptian pharaoh proud. Sun-god cat.

Bast and the guy sphinx rubbed heads while he rumbled *Bast* and she rumbled *Ra*. Then Ra sat back, majestic on his haunches, and spoke to the gathering. "Has anyone seen the Teliagins do anything here besides set up a border camp and try a bit of hunting?"

A wingless lion spoke. "They seem to hunt a lot more now."

"Not just on the border, either," a lioness added. "They're coming farther into our territory."

"They're after my milk-cows!" a lion said.

Another lioness spoke. "Mine, also." With a rumble of amusement, she added, "Only the smell keeps them away. They don't like cow patties." Her tone darkened. "Even with that, though, I've had to protect my herd. The Teliagins kill anything they can catch."

Ra spoke in his resonant voice. "I've seen more of them recently. I found a place where I can watch the border, the perfect place for mentation. Soft grass and rabbits." He gave what sounded like a purr. A *loud* purr. "Too many rabbits, really. Their population needs culling."

An approving growl rolled through the assembly.

"I don't believe this," Dina muttered. Cyclopes weren't the only ones hunting for their next fast-food fix. She spoke to Mehyt in a low voice. "What does he mean, mentation?" Maybe it was a technique for catching those poor bunnies.

"Thinking, of course," Mehyt said. "He ponders riddles." With respect, she added, "He's trying to prove the Riemann hypothesis."

"Ree what?" Dina stared at her blankly. "Is that some sort of battle strategy?"

"Perhaps you've heard it called the Riemann conjecture," Anhur offered, keeping his voice low while Bast and Ra continued to talk with the assembly. "No one has yet proved it's true."

"Conjecture?" Dina still didn't get it.

"Math. It's what we do." Mehyt spoke shyly. "Ra and Bast do pure math, the highest form. I only solve differential equations."

"That's what sphinxes do all day?" Dina couldn't believe it. "Fucking *math?*"

Mehyt gave an annoyed growl. "I assure you, my equations have no reproductive abilities."

"Isn't this a low-tech hex?" Dina asked. "How can you solve equations?"

Anhur squinted at her. "What does math have to do with tech?"

Dina would have laughed if she hadn't been so agitated. It was the age-old argument. Whose work ranked first, the theorists who figured out how the equations of science worked or the experimentalists who put that knowledge to practical use? She scowled at them. "While you're all solving puzzles and sleeping, these cyclopes are going to 'cull your population' to their hungry hearts' content."

"I hate to admit it," Bast said. "But this loud, cussing Entry has a point."

Dina turned with a start. The sphinxes had stopped talking and everyone was listening to her. Embarrassed, she sat back on her haunches.

Ra considered them, then spoke to the assembly. "Today I saw something new. The Teliagins are making weapons. Swords, spears, maces."

Growls rolled through the assembly, hisses too, not the baby sounds made by little house cats, but huge whooshes of air. An older lion spoke. "When you put it all together, it does look like an invasion."

"You see what I mean!" Dina jumped up, then froze when both Bast and Ra glowered at her. She shut her mouth and sat down.

"They have their own hex," a lioness protested, one with a young face and no wings.

"Ours is nicer," a lion answered, young and tawny, also without wings.

"It's age," Dina murmured to Anhur. "You get wings when you get old."

"Of course," Anhur said. "When you go through revitalization."

180

Revitalization. From what she understood, it meant how sphinxes changed when they aged. So, the winged sphinx who gave Oedipus the riddle was an older lioness. The answer finally came to Dina. What went on four legs in the morning, two in the afternoon, and three in the evening? A human being. Babies crawled on all fours. Humans with no aids or augmentations walked on two feet. In those days, elders often used a cane or "third" foot. Before the age of cyberprosthetics, and often even now, humans ended up hobbling or unable to walk in their old age, whereas sphinxes got magnificent wings and a second youth. Pah. The Markovians had a lot to answer for in their design of *Homo sapiens.*

"We've heard a lot," a male sphinx was saying. "And yet, what does it add up to? Maybe today was an anomaly."

A lioness gave a huge yawn, baring her substantial fangs. "Perhaps we should sleep on it."

More sphinxes yawned, starting a drowsy contagion that spread throughout the assembly.

"We can meet again tomorrow," Ra said. "Discuss this more."

"Oh, come *on!*" Dina couldn't take this anymore. How did she get these cats in touch with their inner bad-assery? She got up despite the growls that greeted her intrusion and strode to the front of the dais. "These monsters want your hex! They're sneaking in troops right under your noses. You won't solve this by taking a nap!"

"Um, Dina." Mehyt came up next to her. "Maybe you should—"

"No!" Dina roared at the crowd. "Send them back to their hex!" Wow, that sounded impressive.

Bast stepped over to her. "Young kit—"

"Dina," she growled. "My name is Dina Ramos."

"Well, Dina Ramos," Bast said. "You need to calm down."

"Why?" With exasperation, Dina added, "Do you really think your greedy neighbors will go away while you sleep?" She glanced at Ra. "Have they *ever* asked how you feel about them killing your animals and stockpiling weapons?"

"We do *not* aggress against our neighbors," he told her. "It is not our way. Ever."

"They aren't exactly being neighborly." Mehyt turned, showing a gash along her flank crusted with blood. Dina had been so worked up by the attack, she hadn't thought about her own wounds. But yes, she also had gashes everywhere.

"No one wants a war." Dina would have much rather worked on her family farm than join the rebellion. "Sometimes you have no choice."

Ra spoke with unexpected compassion. "Dina Ramos, I am sorry for the struggles and pain you have lived. And you do speak truly, I believe, when you suggest the Teliagins pose a danger." His voice became firm. "But we cannot commit violent aggression. Period."

"Well, you have to do something," Dina persisted. "They aren't going away."

He gave a roar, one that sounded like it barely accessed the volume he could call up, yet it still set the wooden floor vibrating. "We will not take up arms!"

The gathered sphinxes looked suitably impressed. Bast not so much, though. She frowned at Ra. "So then, what? This is our hex, not theirs."

He answered in a quieter voice. "Another way must exist to push them back across the border."

"They're larger than us," Anhur said. "Stronger, better organized."

"Ah, but we're smarter," Mehyt said.

"And you have wings," Dina said. "That's an air force."

Ra scowled at her. "What, you want us to fly over them and drop bombs? No."

"We have no bombs anyway," Anhur pointed out.

"It depends on what you call a bomb," Dina said.

"Meaning what?" Ra said.

Good question. An idea came to Dina, a way to reach them. Of course. Pose a riddle.

"Answer this," Dina said. "How will a mathematician go to war without violence?"

The shift in their posture showed immediately, an easing of tense muscles, a tilt of the head. Ah yes, they *liked* puzzles.

"By solving the equation," Anhur offered.

"Yes!" Mehyt said. "Develop a solution."

Ra regarded them with a distinct lack of enthusiasm. "Great. What equation?"

"Umm … I'm not sure," Mehyt allowed.

Bast considered them all. "They win by putting their enemy in brackets."

Ra looked more approving. "By putting their enemy in *closed* brackets."

Ho! Dina hadn't expected them to find an answer so fast. It made sense, though. Mathematicians often put numbers in groups enclosed by brackets that kept them contained within their own set. She nodded to Bast and Ra. "We need to bracket them. Separate them from this hex."

"Sure, good," Anhur said. "That still doesn't say how."

"But we have a start." Turning, Bast posed the riddle to the gathered assembly, together with the overriding theme: *How can we push out these hungry cyclopes without violent combat?*

They all got down to business then, hammering out ideas.

It took many days to organize the sphinxes. They worked in secret, keeping watch for any cyclops scouts who might discover their preparations and warn the others. Once the sphinxes started paying more attention, they discovered that Teliagin patrols often infiltrated the inner regions of Boidon. The intruders were mapping out the land, setting up secret outposts, even culling milk-cows when they found them in open spaces with good, stiff breezes. The sphinxes who understood the Teliagin language became cat spies, prowling in secret. The more they discovered, the worse it looked.

The intruders were indeed planning an invasion. It wasn't even because they had a shortage of food or considered Boidon nicer than Teliagin. They *liked* their cold hex. They wanted to take over Boidon and eat her sphinxes just because they could. Or so they thought. They planned to sneak in gradually, unnoticed by the blissful math cats until it was too late. The cyclopes figured their scrumptious neighbors would be too busy sleeping to notice.

On the sixteenth day, the sphinxes made their move. They'd needed that much time to spread the news throughout the hex and coordinate their communities. Dina had heard it was impossible to herd cats, but apparently when they had a mutual enemy, they were more than happy to cooperate, like lions working together in one big pride.

At dawn, the sphinxes headed to the border. The Teliagin camps there contained many cyclopes, but their numbers came nowhere near the total sphinx population in Boidon. And though the cyclopes were indeed huge, much larger than the sphinxes and with greater strength, the cats were nothing to sneeze at, either, or bellow at, given the cyclopes' preferred method of speech.

Wingless sphinxes converged all along the region where the cyclopes had settled. They didn't go right up to the camps; they stayed far enough away to avoid the reach of handheld weapons. The cyclopes could have thrown spears, given a reason, but none of the sphinxes attacked. They just sat on their haunches, tall and unmoving. They came in hundreds. Then thousands. As the day progressed, sphinxes converged on the camps. They made no threats. They just sat, shoulder to shoulder in ever growing lines, all watching the cyclopes with that inimitable, unwavering gaze that cats had perfected.

The cyclopes came out, standing around and looking confused. They didn't realize what was happening until it was too late to try running off the sphinxes. Nor could any cyclopes get past the blockade. The lines had no openings; they enclosed the camps—in sphinx brackets. Behind the main lines, another line of sphinxes turned in the other direction and sat staring at the cyclopes scouts that tried to get back into camp. The isolated cyclopes milled around, seeming at a loss for how to respond. No sphinx attacked or threatened them. They just, well, *stared*.

The cyclopes gathered to talk among themselves, gesticulating dramatically and bellowing. After a while, they started to pace along the line of sphinxes, staying beyond the reach of their giant claws. Some tried "talking" to the sphinxes, roaring about what the bloody hell were they doing.

The sphinxes sat and stared.

The cyclopes eventually formed a semiorganized pack of emissaries and approached the cats. Several knew the sphinx language and spoke in it, or shouted more accurately, demanding the sphinxes go home and stop bothering them. None of the sphinxes responded. They just continued to stare, line after line of them.

The cyclopes came closer, brandishing their weapons. In response, the sphinxes growled en masse, a ground-shaking thunder than sent the cyclopes stumbling backward. When the intruders tried again, the sphinxes *roared* in a huge chorus, shaking the trees, grasses, and especially the invaders.

The cyclopes retreated.

The sphinxes stared.

The cyclopes gathered in their camps, talking among themselves. Although they clearly had no idea how to respond, neither did they seem inclined to leave.

The sphinxes continued to stare. For hours. Not one of them went to sleep.

The cyclopes stayed put.

Stalemate.

At midafternoon, Ra and Bast called in the air force.

The airborne cats did indeed carry bombs, though not of the typical military variety. Cyclopes didn't like cattle. Well guess what? Only one other smell offended them even more than cow patties.

Sphinx shit.

Another reason it took the sphinxes so long to prepare was that they needed to eat like they'd never done before, producing supplies for their instruments of fertilizer warfare. They constructed many, many pouches filled with the output of their heroic caloric intake, which the air force now took aloft into the pristine blue sky.

Winged sphinxes soared above the cyclopes camps and dropped their pouches. The moment the flimsy bombs hit anything, they exploded in a chaos of cat feculence that splattered everywhere. The cyclopes shouted their protest and ran around in a melee of furious, panicked giants. Some of them rushed at the impassive lines of staring cats, then broke ranks when flying lions dropped more bombs, leaving the cyclopes staggering in a tumult of bumfuzzled monsters.

The lines of sphinxes moved forward just a bit, only a meter, and the cyclopes backed away just a bit, their ranks becoming disorganized as the aromatic air force kept up its onslaught.

The sphinxes sat and stared.

Gradually over the afternoon, the sphinxes moved forward, meter by meter, ever so slowly herding the cyclopes back to their own hex. The invaders put up a valiant resistance even when covered in shit shrapnel, but the cats drove them relentlessly. It wasn't until the great orb of the sun grazed the horizon that the cyclopes decided their half-baked plan for hex domination wasn't worth the trouble and ran for home. The cat brackets parted enough to let them escape into their own hex.

Two cyclopes remained, among the largest of the invaders. They stood facing the wall of sphinxes, a barrier that had almost reached the border. After a protracted period of cats and invaders staring at each other, Bast and Ra left the other sphinxes and strode to the two cyclopes. Dina moved to within hearing distance but stayed back enough so that Ra and Bast didn't notice her.

One of the cyclopes spoke in a rough voice, using the sphinx language. "You must stop this appalling and vicious attack."

Bast spoke coldly. "You must stop your invasion of our hex."

Silence. They continued to stare at each other.

The male cyclops spoke. "You destroyed our camps. They now stink."

Ra answered him. "Your camps are on our land. We never said you could come here."

"We spent years building those camps," the female cyclops said. "We never hurt you."

Bast gave a snort. "You've killed our livestock. And you've tried to kill us."

The female cyclops crossed her arms. "You are ugly, smelly neighbors."

"Then stop invading our hex," Ra said. "You have a perfectly good hex that smells just fine."

"Go home." Bast's eyes glinted. "Or we will send our air force to invade your hex."

The two cyclopes bellowed at her and Ra, and then at each other. Dina realized they were simply talking in their own language, but wow, it was *loud*.

The male cyclops finally said, "You stay out of our hex, we will stay out of yours."

Ra and Bast nodded their acceptance of the proposed treaty. "We agree."

"Done, then," the cyclops said.

"Done," the cats said.

With that, the first ever peace summit between Boidon and Teliagin was complete.

Dina lay in the sun with her paws in front of her, basking in the grass. Anhur settled on her right and Mehyt on her left. Before they'd shown up, Dina had worn herself out chasing her tail, but fortunately she'd stopped before they arrived to witness her undignified behavior. Now they just drowsed like the giant sphinx at Giza, being regal and looking intelligent.

"Nice day," Anhur eventually said.

"Hmmm." Mehyt purred. "Warm."

"I should go search the other hexes," Dina said.

Anhur yawned. "Whatever for?"

Dina opened her eyes. "To find what happened to the refugees who got caught here, like me."

"You could," Mehyt said. "But why? It will just remind you and them of lives you can never have again."

Dina doubted she would ever be that serene about what she'd had to leave behind. Mehyt had a point, though. She and her fellow refugees had little to gain from a reminder of what they'd lost. Did she even want that violent, desperate life back? The longer she spent here, the less certain she felt.

Her mind was becoming sphinxlike. She'd never before realized the beauty of math, to put it mildly. She used to rank it lower than getting her teeth pulled without pain killers. Now, she couldn't help but wonder what hypotheses remained unproven. She also felt like getting into trouble, creeping in the grass, pouncing on prey, real or imagined. She had a whole hex to explore! First, though, she needed a nap.

"You know," Dina mused. "In a way, we did defeat the Com."

"Really?" Anhur rolled onto his back and gave a luxurious stretch. "How?"

"They want us to be identical, the same, all forced into their mold." She huffed, her cat version of a snort. "Well, I gave them the ultimate finger. Or paw. I've become as unconforming as anything they'll ever see. I'm not even human anymore."

Mehyt and Anhur both chuckled at her thought, and Dina exhaled with satisfaction. The Markovians had set up a world that defeated everything the Com wanted to inflict on the universe.

She rolled on her side, fitting herself between Anhur and Mehyt, the three of them settling in for their drowsy afternoon. They'd make a good start on a pride. They could bring in more sphinxes to join their group. Someday, they might have little sphinx kittens running around.

For now, though, she would sleep.

Chapter Twelve:
THE WELL WORLD
David Boop

Above the Borgo Pass
Last day of the War of the Well

Nathan Brazil was a pegasus, and his quasi granddaughter, Marva Chang, was a horse.

Serge Ortega wondered, not for the first time, if the ancient Markovians had programmed a sense of humor into the Well of Souls. Especially when it came to Brazil or any who chose to fight alongside him. Last he'd seen Brazil, a thousand years ago, the man's soul had been transferred into the body of a stag. And as for Marva, when she last left the Well World, she'd been mutated into a grotesque donkey.

To find them in these forms was no shock to him. Despite their handicaps, they'd both beaten the odds and crossed half the Well World to reach the Avenue outside the Well of Souls. It was only here that Brazil could enter and reboot the universe. And rebooting it, effectively turning it off and turning it back on like some sort of computer technician, was the only way to save it.

Humanity had tried to play god and screwed the universe in the process. Now it was dying a permanent death, and the only thing that would survive such a catastrophe would be the Well World, because it sat on a different Markovian server. So, Brazil would go in, turn off reality, repair the issue, then turn it back on. The only problem being … nothing and no one in the previous universe would remain. Brazil in his position as care-taker, would seed the universe as the Markovians did, using beings from the many hexes of the Well World. That didn't sit well with the Council that ran the day-to-day operations, so they launched a war to stop Brazil and Chang from reaching the very Avenue they looked down on.

The Ulik used his six arms to pull his jacket tighter. His race might have layers of fat to protect them from normal cold, but high up in the moun-tains of Borgo, Ortega discovered the wind could reach even his old bones. He reflected, once again, that he'd had the option to stay in his ambassador's office, where he was warm and well fed, and continue manipulating the Council or the small minds of the short-lived individual hex leaders. He ultimately decided that beating Brazil to the Avenue and seeing the man's face, even transformed as it was, was worth the sacrifice of his immortality.

That look Brazil gave Ortega, horse-faced or not, made his life com-plete. Just when both he and Chang thought they'd lost, Serge revealed to them he'd switched sides and would make sure they got to the Well of Souls by midnight, when the gate opened. It was the ultimate victory to the old spacer, and Brazil's ultimate defeat in their millennium-old game of chess. Serge had won, Brazil was at his whim, and that whim, surpris-ingly was to see him succeed.

For as much as Ortega had stood in Brazil's way, he still respected and adored his friend. Probably the greatest one he'd ever have.

Unfortunately, the only way down to the Avenue from where they'd met up was via a pulley system Ortega's army set up. The winds were too strong for Brazil to fly down, and there were no clear trails to descend that wouldn't be spotted by Gunit Sangh's army. Sangh wanted nothing more than to take over Well World and, if possible, the whole universe. Enough madmen had tried that before, and the Dahbi was truly the embodiment of evil. No way Ortega would ever allow Sangh to win.

Ortega's people had just gotten the harness around Brazil. They'd al-ready lowered Chang, her descent being easier without wings, but they had to adjust and readjust the leather straps to accommodate Brazil's current form. Nate had asked Serge to come with him into the Well, and the old spacer considered it for half a moment, mostly because he wanted to see Brazil in his natural form again: a Markovian. The giant heart-shaped beings, who created everything, were a sight to see. Ortega had been too awed the first time he'd seen the true identity of Brazil, even if what Brazil had told him about him not *actually* being a Markovian but just a human who'd been recruited for the job after the last Watcher wanted to retire were true. Serge believed, in every cell of his body, Brazil planned to do the same thing to Marva Chang. If that was true, the Ulik decided he wouldn't be around to find out. No, he planned this to be his last stand. He'd go down fighting to save the universe. No better way to leave your legend intact.

"Hey, Serge!" The tone and inflection were Brazil's, even if the voice wasn't. The flying horse couldn't speak; instead, it was a Gedemondan who channeled Brazil's thoughts into words for him. "Before I head down, I have a question for you."

Ortega slithered his way over to Brazil as people continued to strap him down.

"What is it, Nate? I do have a destiny waiting for me, and we already said our goodbyes. No sense getting sentimental now."

The mysterious yeti-like being who telepathically communicated Brazil's words frowned. "I'm not getting sentimental, you old pirate. No, I wanted to ask you something, and this seemed like the last chance to do it."

Sitting back on his tail, Ortega crossed his six arms. "Ask away."

Brazil gave the closest approximation to a sigh the pegasus could. "About a thousand years ago, I was forced to make a choice, and I sent a bunch of people through an active Markovian gate without their knowledge. I wish I could say I had *no* choice, but it was the *best* choice I had at the time. Did you receive them?"

Serge put on a show of pretending to recall the event, but then punched Brazil in the haunches. "You bastard. That was a shitty thing to do to those innocent people."

"Ouch! And you're right, it was. It's one of the many decisions I've made, this one included, that I have to live with." Brazil bowed his head. "The guilt tore me up for a while, but then faded, as it does. Never gone. Always in the back of my mind."

Ortega studied his friend with empathetic eyes. "Can't say I haven't made a few thousand bad decisions myself." He drew a cigar out of his jacket pocket and lit it. "What do you want to know?"

Looking at Ortega with one of his eyes, Brazil asked, "Do you know what happened to them?"

Exhaling, Serge said, "Well, that was a long time ago, and you know, how easy it is to get lost on Well World. I never hear about most of the Entries, unless they stir up some sort of trouble."

"And did they?"

Smirking, Ortega said, "Oh, did they ever. Well, at least some of them."

Ortega went on to tell Brazil a truncated version of what happened to Bennitt Grimbel.

"A serial killing Wuckl?"

Ortega nodded.

"That spoiled son-of-a-sponge lord brought him to light?"

Shrugging, Ortega nodded again. "With some help, yes. He even went on to become a well-respected healer and lived the last part of his life as an ambassador to the Ecundo, their neighbors. Brought his spouse over to their hex. He said he preferred the higher tech zone."

"So, maybe not completely unspoiled." Brazil chuckled, which his translator tried to emulate, but failed. "Will the wonders of the Well never cease? Who else?"

"Let me think."

Brazil nickered. "You may be a walrus, but you look like the caterpillar from Wonderland, sitting back, smoking, and dreaming."

Raising a bushy eyebrow, Ortega looked ready to argue the point, then realized it was a bit of a compliment.

"Oh, there was that young man Jared. Ended up a Dunh'gran."

"Hey! I'm not a gelding!" the Gedemondan shouted for Brazil as one of Ortega's men wrapped a strap too close to a sensitive part of Brazil's body.

His translator blushed on the few patches of skin near his cheeks.

Brazil refocused on Ortega. "Those birds that are into racing, huh? What type of trouble did he get into?"

"Brought to light a whole conspiracy involving a member of his race seeking immortality by using that little trick you pulled with the Murithel."

"Soul switching? I didn't know they'd do that for anyone they didn't consider honorable."

The Ulik tsked. "Times change, Nate. Sooner or later, there'll always be a bad bunch that go rogue for profit."

Brazil hung his head. "I guess you're right. Seen enough of that in my life."

"Jared really did well for himself, though. He got into engineering school, despite being an Entry. After that, he started his own racing company with his wife and brother-in-law. The company still exists, run by his descendants. Think they've won more awards than any other racing team in the history of their hex."

"Good for him. What about the little girl who was running from her mother? Lita, I think her name was."

"Oh, that one … ." Ortega narrowed his eyes at Brazil. "You really put a burr up my ass with that one."

"How so?"

Brazil kept repeating, "What?" or "Really?" as the Ulik regaled him with the tale of Lita the Oolakash.

"A spy? An aquatic spy?"

Ortega chuckled. "Is it so odd, Nate? She lives her best life here: a double life of deputy ambassador and secret agent."

"She's still alive?" Even the Gedemondan seemed a little surprised.

"Oolakash have very long lifetimes, Nate. You should know that." Ortega raised an eyebrow, and asked the yeti, "Are you sure you got the right Nathan Brazil?"

The pegasus nickered. "You try being shoved inside the brain of a horse and see how well you retain fifteen-hundred species."

Relaxing, Ortega continued, "Yes, still alive, but not as active as she used to be. She's a Magistra now; administration more than analysis, plus she spends her free time maintaining the Markovian museum she built. She's having tadpoles, I bet, missing a chance to go into the Well with you."

"Why didn't she?" Brazil asked. "Certainly with her connections, she knew I was here."

Ortega shrugged. "She's built quite a mythology around you, and you know what they say about 'never meeting your idols.' Plus, how would she follow you from the Overdark Ocean on this damn crusade of yours? As a deep-pressure species, she couldn't just 'suit up,' right?" Taking another deep pull from the cigar, Ortega said, "She'll instead collect information from everyone whom you've been in contact with since your arrival and add whatever's appropriate to the museum, and be happy that she played some small part in the big picture."

That seemed to satisfy Brazil.

"I would've thought Dina Ramos would've been the bigger problem for you. In just the short time I knew her, I expected to come back here with her sitting in your place."

Ortega didn't have to think hard to remember *that* one. "Oh, she caused problems, all right, but not so much for me. The Teliagin, however, will never forget her."

Brazil chuckled. "Is that who she ended up as?"

The large walrus-man shook his head. "No, Boidon."

"The sphinxes? I can't tell you how much trouble they gave me on Earth when a couple snuck through the gate."

"Yeah? Seems like a lot of Well species stowed away to good ol' Earth. Care to explain?"

The pegasus eyed him. "Don't ask me. Wasn't my shift."

But Ortega doubted it was that simple. "Ramos led the Boidol in a peaceful war against a Teliagin incursion. Damnedest thing I'd ever heard. Drove those one-eyed bastards right out of their hex without a single drop of blood spilled. Never had trouble with them after that, and those Teliagin idiots even became model Ambassadors in the Zone. Something about threats of Boidon shit bombs." Ortega held out four of his hands in a "what are you going to?" pose.

"Hmmm," said Brazil's translator. "Considering her previous MO was death and destruction, that's saying something."

Drawing in air and puffing out smoke, Ortega agreed. "Her transformation went well beyond the physical, as you know it does. She formed a pride with a couple she'd met coming through as an Entry, rose through the ranks to lead the Boidon for nearly a hundred years. In that time, she became an adviser of sorts for many hexes at the Zone. She brokered peaceful resolutions to several potential crises, though I'm pretty sure Ramos also had a hand in a few, shall we say … quick turnover of powers that shortened actual conflicts."

"You sound like you respect her."

Ortega smirked, his thick mustache at an odd angle. "She worried the hell out of me. She played the game almost better than I did. I had only one thing going for me. Age. I wish I had time to tell you about her orientation. Had a lot to do with that body you dumped on me."

"The clone? If you remember the note I sent you, I was most concerned about her. Any idea if she survived?"

The Ulik let out a big laugh. "Survived! She nearly destroyed the whole Lamotien race!"

Brazil's eye widened. "What?"

"Hold your horses …"

"Ha, very funny."

Ortega sat back on his tail and let the smoke from his cigar act as a window to his memories. "She was quite a shock to the Lamotien, who'd not had an Entry in quite some time. In fact, many of the places your refugees ended up were hexes that hadn't been visited by the outside world in centuries. All the Entries struggled at first, but like Five, as she chose to be called, most made places for themselves until their last days."

"Five, huh?"

Ortega nodded. "The Lamotien, being a hive race, share all their thoughts, but Five's were alien to them. Feeling like she was just becoming a part of someone else, as was intended with her originator, caused her to push back. Well, she accidentally corrupted a large portion of the people trying to help her. It was a big mess."

"I … I hadn't intended that to happen. I wanted her to be free, her own person."

"Now, don't get all maudlin with me. Turns out she was perfect for them. Five came to understand the duality of her life, both as a piece of something bigger, and as an individual. In fact, many of the Lamotien fighting in this war are a direct result of her teachings. You could even say she still lives on through them."

"How so?"

"That's the weird part. While the Lamotien certainly were aware of the concepts of self and autonomy, as they can exist as individuals, their understanding of individual decisions had been limited, as their nature was to join with others of their kind. Five's human experiences touched them in a deeply personal way. When she melded with them, she showed the Lamotien not only what it was like to be a single being even when fully accepted by their friend/family group, but also how horrific it was to have that autonomy ripped away against your will and to lose control of your body without willingly giving it.

"This new understanding, while falling short of creating religions or even cults among the Lamotien, still created a movement toward understanding and acceptance of individuals, as well as a respect for their rights and desires, which led to the Lamotien being much more tolerant of the other races.

"Ironically, it also helped them to become even more perfect mimics and better spies when the battle of the Well World approached."

"Five did all that?"

Ortega nodded. "And more."

Brazil bowed his head a moment. The Ulik didn't know if Brazil thanked the Well, tried to cry, or just had pride in his decision to push that parted-girl through the Gate. But whichever it was, he seemed happy for the moment.

Ortega had a question for Brazil then. "That one young man Trake, what was his story? He was a slippery one. Reminded me in some ways of what Gypsy, I mean, Gil Zinder, can do."

"So, you figured it out, too."

Ortega nodded. "Are you going to tell Marva?"

Brazil shook his head, tossing his long white mane back and forth. "No need. If she hasn't figured it out yet, why complicate things? Zinder had his reason for hiding his identity after all. If he didn't want her to know …

194

But yes, Trake, or in reality, another runaway named Calum Brach, wasn't tapped into the Well of Souls or anything. He just developed the skill of not being noticed."

"Like you?"

"Like me. Of course, it annoyed me when he did it to me on *my* ship."

"Well, he stopped being able to be anonymous when he landed with the Arestol. Quite the opposite."

Brazil cocked his head, as did his Gedemondan translator, which was so comical, Ortega nearly lost his train of thought. "As you know, Nate, the Arestol start out as these fixed, rooted plants, but then leave that state once they've mastered the collective conscious called The Dreaming."

For the first time, the Gedemondan spoke for itself. "It is similar to what we do with our minds. It can be quite … unnerving at first for young without an adult to guide you, as we do. But the Arestol have no such ability. Their young must navigate The Dreaming on their own."

Ortega, slightly shocked that the yeti entered into the conversation, agreed. "Sort of like a chicken breaking out of its shell. Without surviving The Dreaming, the Arestol cannot evolve to the next stage."

"There are times I just wanted to slap those 'artisans' who created these species," Brazil said.

Ortega pointed his cigar at the pegasus. "Don't you mean slap yourself, Mr. Markovian?"

"Ha, ha. I'll remind you I wasn't there. I'm just IT, remember?"

"Sure, pull this one and it plays 'The Lady from Praxis 5.'" They eyed each other, then laughed. "Anyway," Ortega continued, "Once he reached maturity, this Trake, or Brach, or whoever, started working on exactly that: having his people send comforting messages just before their off-springs' 'hatching,' which allowed the Arestol children to retain more of the skills they'd learned in The Dreaming. Turns out they're brilliant at multidimensional math and almost never gassed and ate the people they worked with after that."

"That's a good thing, right?"

Ortega laughed. "Calum even found Ramos and communicated with her for years, exchanging high-order mathematic puzzles for them to solve. That came in handy later with that pair Conrad and Randolf."

That gave Brazil pause. "They ended up together? The dog and its owner?"

"Not only that, but the same species: Agitar."

Brazil snorted. "That's rare. I guess Randolf and Conrad's bond was stronger than I'd considered. Then again, I've seen the Well do some very weird things."

"You and me both. The pair stayed together their whole lives, though they ended up working slightly different jobs. Conrad, the computer genius, learned that Agitar electric abilities could read the Well of Souls language in a limited way, but not to the level of the Ivrom or the Murithel. More like they can sense it, follow it; not so much change it, but manipulate what was already there. That came in handy when a group of terrorists started a 'Hack the Well' movement. He really saved our behinds."

"And kept me from being called back earlier." Brazil looked as impressed as a horse could. "That's quite a talent he discovered."

"And unique. Conrad refused to teach anyone else how he did it, I suspect to make sure we didn't end up with the Agitar becoming the next Olborn." Nobody on the planet wanted another species that could turn unsuspecting beings into barely sentient donkeys. "Plus … ." Ortega took a long drag of his cigar, which was almost to the end, as was his recounting of the stories. "I think he couldn't do it alone. They've never said as much, but I suspect Conrad wasn't able to run the Well without the help of Randolf."

"Why so?"

"Conrad was a mess when he got here. Even after years on this World, he still had panic attacks. Those times I called on him as a troubleshooter, Conrad never came alone even though Randolf had taken on side work as a councilor of sorts, working with other races across the Southern hemisphere to teach meditation and calming techniques. He never left Conrad's side for long, but every time he did, he created a lasting impact."

"If there's one thing *this* war has shown me it's that we all need more tolerance and patience."

Ortega nodded. "He was a good boy—er, man, Agitar. Whatever. Conrad went first, thankfully. When Randolf died, the Agitar erected a statue to them in the capitol square."

That left only two Entries to be accounted for, and the Ulik knew this next one would cut Brazil the deepest.

Sensing what was coming, Brazil bowed his head, apparently steeling himself for the news he could tell was on Ortega's face.

"She didn't last long, if that's any blessing, but she didn't leave without doing something remarkable."

"Tell me."

"Elida Silduun ended up in Betared, where she lasted a week."

"That barbaric rite of passage where they force everyone to survive the winter elements alone, unarmed, and unprepared?"

Ortega shook his head. "They sent her out in that, all right, but no. After getting caught in an avalanche, she ran afoul of some Ambrezan traffickers peddling Glathriel slaves."

Brazil's Gedemondan helper didn't even bother translating the string of curses the spacer issued, but Ortega didn't need him to.

"A Betared named Faven went looking for her when she never arrived back in civilization. He found her body next to an abandoned watercraft near a couple dead Ambrezan. One had been clearly torn apart by her. The other looked to have fatally wounded her in turn, only to be offed by its slaves, taking advantage of the distraction." This was the kicker. "One of the Glathriel put her out of her misery, so it was a quick death."

Ortega knew Brazil well enough to see the torment he experienced even through the horse's eyes. He had to be questioning if he'd been better off leaving the woman in real space.

"A Betared search party found the lot of them trying to make it back home overland. We got them through the gate and to Glathriel. Evidence on the boat helped us break those mean little beavers' slaver operation, so that's not bad."

Brazil didn't say anything for a moment. Ortega's army engineers looked for advice on if they should keep strapping the pegasus down. The Ulik held up a hand for them to wait.

When he spoke, Brazil didn't say anything about Silduun, instead focusing, as he did, on things he *had* control over. "I've really got to fix Glathriel when I reach the Well computer. The Ambrezans have had their fun for too many centuries now. I need to put humanity back on course."

Ortega thanked the gods that he wouldn't be around to see how *that* turned out.

"I wonder why she did it?" Brazil mused finally. "She looked ready enough to die without any heroics. Why save a bunch of unintelligent humans?"

"Obviously, the Glathriel couldn't tell us, as they were barely able to understand what was going on in the first place. However, when we showed them a picture of a Betared female, a redheaded woman cried a tear, but we couldn't get a reason why out of her."

"Forever a mystery, I guess."

"I guess."

Ortega held off digging further into Brazil's psyche, instead telling the engineers to finish their job.

"That leaves only ..."

"The father and son, right." Ortega told Brazil what happened in the gate room. Brazil seemed to have some thoughts on the matter.

"In those early days of the Com, children with abnormal abilities where often taken to a research facility called 'The Hill' in an attempt to harness those traits into a new line of clones."

"Yikes," Ortega said. "Maybe it's a good thing you're wiping out this universe."

Brazil nickered. "The next one will have the same or a different set of horrible things we do to each other."

That gave Ortega pause.

"So, what about the boy?"

This time, the Ulik really did have to think about it. "Never knew 100 percent for sure, but there's a line in a song about all the Ivrom males who eventually mated with the queen after overcoming a grueling trial by fire. They add a new line to the song for each "king" of the species, to remember them after their death."

"What does this have to do with Thorn?" Brazil asked, trepidation in his voice. He'd had bad experiences with the Ivrom, and rarely did anything good come from the pixie species.

Ortega felt he already knew what was coming but said it anyway.

"I obviously haven't memorized the whole song, as there are tens of thousands of lines to it, but I do get the updates, and I seem to remember one verse that stuck in my memory ..."

Ortega sang a stanza that nearly broke Brazil's heart, it was so beautiful. To think those devil pixies could produce something so amazing left him feeling there was still much about the universe he had yet to learn. "For a being who swore he'd have trouble remembering any of them, you sure seemed to have a thorough recollection of a group of Entries some thousand years in the past."

Ortega opened his mouth to say something flippant but then changed tactics.

"I hate you, Brazil. Ever since your first visit back, when you showed me who you really were, I've hated the power you've had over me, the Well, and damn all reality. Maybe in part, that's why I made the deal for near immortality. Just so someday I could be here, at what could be the universe's last stand to tell you you're an arrogant son of a bitch."

"But ..."

"But," Ortega continued, "I can't help but still think of you as my old spacer buddy. Of the time you helped me break some of my crew out of jail."

"That came in handy, by the way."

"I heard." The Ulik crushed his cigar stub out under his tail. "And that's probably the reason those Entries stuck with me. You were alive out there, still helping people, even if it was in the worst way possible. Those refugees, mostly, they got to be their true selves in the end. Maybe that was the Well's doing, maybe it was your doing. Could even be a little of both. God or not. Markovian or not. You truly believe you're helping people, even if you have to kill them to do it."

"And …"

Ortega cursed. "Dammit, Nate. You're gonna make me say it, aren't you?" He stared at the winged horse for a good long moment. "That's all you can ask of a god, or a friend, is for them to try to do the right thing."

The rigging finished, Brazil was hoisted up off the ground and swung out over the ledge to be lowered down. He asked his translator to tell the crew to hold up.

"There is no owner's manual in there, Serge. You went in with me that one time. When I step through the Avenue Gate, I just have to follow my gut as if I were any other being in the universe."

"But you're not just any being, Nate. You're about to turn off all reality and start it up again, just like the technician you claim to be." The Ulik pointed down. "Sure, you'll have a helper this time, and maybe you plan to dump her with this responsibility, or maybe not, but you're the one leaving pieces of yourself all over time and space. Everyone you've touched here, or out there, owes you a kick in the dick, or possibly a hug."

"If it's the former, you better hurry. The war is waiting on you."

"Dammit, Nate," Ortega said again. "It's neither, but Marva doesn't have the experience to be your conscience. I do."

"So you're going to give me some unsolicited advice, then?"

Taking out another cigar and lighting it, Ortega blew a smoke ring toward his friend. "Don't screw this one up. Make better choices. Get rid of the stuff that made us turn on each other. Help us be the people we were meant to be. Isn't that what the Markovians wanted?"

Brazil said nothing. He motioned for the engineers to begin lowering him.

"I've tried that, Serge. I really have. If there's a formula for lasting peace, I haven't found it yet, but sure, I'll try again. Maybe, with Marva's help, we can figure it out together."

Ortega moved to the edge and watched Brazil descend. "See that you do! I'm not dying here just to have the same shit happen again!"

The Gedemondan started climbing down as well. "Brazil wanted me to give you the finger, but I think I won't. You're right. He knows it."

Ortega leaned back on his tail and laughed. The laugh continued until Marquoz and Gypsy came to get him to lead the charge against Sangh's forces.

"What's so funny?" Marquoz, a monstrous gray demon, who'd once been a small, fire-breathing dinosaur in a previous life, asked.

"Brazil admitted I was right about everything. They were his last words to me, but damn, if it wasn't good to hear."

Gypsy, the former human known as Dr. Gilgam Zinder and the only one to break the Markovian code, raised an eyebrow. He could appear as whatever he liked but currently appeared as his old friend Marquoz was most familiar with: a tall, lanky man. "I would've loved to have seen that; even more, heard it. Do tell?"

"On the way to the front," Ortega said. The trio moved away from the pullies which had finished lowering the pegasus Brazil, but then Zinder paused and looked back down to the Avenue Brazil and Marva would be taking into the Well.

"I'll be right back," he said and poofed out of existence.

Marquoz swore. "I'll never get used to that."

Ortega put an arm around the demon's shoulders.

"That's the thing about the Well World," he began with a grin. "You live long enough, you can get used to just about anything."

Taking out his last cigar, his actual last cigar, Ortega handed it to Marquoz and lit it for him.

As they walked toward their destiny, Ortega filled him in on Nathan Brazil and the ten passengers he once saved from the star-liner *Euphrates*.

BIOGRAPHIES

David Boop is a Denver-based speculative fiction author and editor. He's also an award-winning essayist, and screenwriter. Before turning to fiction, David worked as a DJ, film critic, journalist, and actor.

David's novels run the gamut, such as the SF/noir *She Murdered Me with Science*; *The Soul Changers*, a historical, dark fantasy TTRPG tie-in to *Rippers Resurrected*; and the Weird Western, *The Drowned Horse Chronicle Volume 1*.

David edited the bestselling and award-nominated Weird Western anthology series, *Straight Outta Tombstone*, *Straight Outta Deadwood*, and *Straight Outta Dodge City*. He's currently working on a trio of Space Western anthologies starting with *Gunfight on Europa Station*, *High Noon on Proxima B*, and *Last Train Outta Keplar-321c*. He's edited several pulp anthologies, including *Green Hornet & Kato: Detroit Noir*.

David is prolific in short fiction with many short stories including media tie-ins for *Predator* (nominated for the 2018 Scribe Award), *Kolchak the Night Stalker*, *The Green Hornet*, and *Veronica Mars*. His first comic, *Travailiant Rising*, coauthored with *NYT* bestselling author Kevin J. Anderson, is a giant mech series.

He's a summa cum laude graduate from UC-Denver in the creative writing program. He temps, collects Funko Pops, and is a believer. His hobbies include film noir, anime, the blues and history.

You can find out more at Davidboop.com, Facebook.com/dboop.updates, Twitter @david_boop, and www.longshot-productions.net.

Neal Asher: I was born in 1961 in Essex, Great Britain, and divide my time between there and the island of Crete. I've been an SF and fantasy junkie ever since having my mind distorted at an early age by JRRT, Edgar Rice Burroughs, E. C. Tubb, and many others. Sometime after leaving school I decided to focus on only one of my many interests because it was inclusive of the others: writing. Over the years I worked my way up through the small presses, wrote the inevitable fantasy trilogy (still in my files), and zeroed in on science fiction. Finally taken on by a large publisher, Pan Macmillan, my first full-length SF novel, *Gridlinked*, came out in 2001, and now in total I have over 30 books to my name, also in translation across the world.

http://theskinner.blogspot.com/ or http://nealsher.co.uk

Distinguished Silpathorn Artist of Thailand, **Somtow Sucharitkul (S.P. Somtow)** has been called, by the *International Herald Tribune*, "the most well-known expatriate Thai in the world."

Born in Bangkok, Somtow grew up in Europe and was educated at Eton and Cambridge. His first career was in music, and in the 1970s he acquired a reputation as a revolutionary composer, the first to combine Thai and Western instruments in radical new sonorities. Conditions in the arts in the region at the time proved so traumatic for the young composer that he suffered a major burnout, immigrated to the United States, and reinvented himself as a novelist.

His earliest novels were in the science fiction field, but he soon began to cross into other genres. In his 1984 novel *Vampire Junction*, he injected a new literary inventiveness into the horror genre, in the words of Robert Bloch, author of *Psycho*, "skillfully combining the styles of Stephen King, William Burroughs, and the author of the Revelation to John." *Vampire Junction* was voted one of the forty all-time greatest horror books by the Horror Writers' Association, joining established classics like *Frankenstein* and *Dracula*.

In the 1990s, Somtow became increasingly identified as a uniquely Asian writer with novels such as the semiautobiographical *Jasmine Nights*. He won the World Fantasy Award, the highest accolade given in the world of fantastic literature, for his novella, *The Bird Catcher*. His fifty-three books have sold about two million copies worldwide.

After becoming a Buddhist monk for a period in 2001, Somtow decided to refocus his attention on the country of his birth, founding Bangkok's first international opera company and returning to music, where he again reinvented himself, this time as a neo-Asian neo-Romantic composer. The Norwegian government commissioned his song cycle, *Songs Before Dawn*, for the 100th Anniversary of the Nobel Peace Prize, and he composed, at the request of the government of Thailand, his requiem: *In Memoriam 9/11*, which was dedicated to the victims of the 9/11 tragedy.

According to London's *Opera Magazine*, "in just five years, Somtow has made Bangkok into the operatic hub of Southeast Asia." His operas on Thai themes, *Madana*, *Mae Naak*, *Ayodhya*, and *The Silent Prince*, have been well received by international critics. His most recent operas, the Japanese inspired *Dan no Ura* and the fantasy opera *The Snow Dragon*, have gained him acceptance as "one of the most intriguing of contemporary opera composers" (*Auditorium Magazine*). He has recently embarked on a ten-opera cycle, *Dasjati—The Ten Lives of the Buddha*, which when completed will be the classical music work with the largest time span and scope in history.

He is increasingly in demand as a conductor specializing in opera and in the late-Romantic composers like Mahler. His repertoire runs the entire gamut from Monteverdi to Wagner. His work has been especially lauded for its stylistic authenticity and its lyricism. He has received the "Golden W" from the International Wagner Society. The orchestra he founded in Bangkok, the Siam Philharmonic, mounted the first complete Mahler cycle in the region.

Somtow's current project, *The Siam Sinfonietta*, is a youth orchestra he founded five years ago, using a new educational method he pioneered and which is now among the most acclaimed youth orchestras worldwide, receiving standing ovations in Carnegie Hall, the Konzerthaus in Berlin, Disney Hall, the Musikverein in Vienna, and many other venues around the world.

He is the first recipient of Thailand's "Distinguished Silpathorn" award, given for an artist who has made and continues to make a major impact on the region's culture, from Thailand's Ministry of Culture.

Keith J. Olexa began his career writing for entertainment periodicals, including *Starlog* magazine, before directing his energies to science and history articles and books. He has written on the histories of such things as the American militia, the rise of seaplanes, and the medal of honor, and has covered science topics ranging from exoplanet astrophysics to the effects of the paleolithic diet on the metabolism.

Besides writing, Keith edits for several publishing houses and authors. He has edited for reprint the works of the late Alan Drury and also books by Kevin J. Anderson, Mercedes Lackey, and Peter Wacks as well as several anthologies. He has written his first book, *The Gross Science of Lice and Other Parasites*, for Rosen Publications.

Sam Knight is the owner/publisher of Knight Writing Press and author of six children's books, five short story collections, four novels, and over 75 short stories, including three coauthored with Kevin J. Anderson.

Though he has written in many cool worlds, such as *Planet of the Apes*, *Wayward Pines*, and Jeff Sturgeon's *Last Cities of Earth*, among his family and friends he is, and probably always will be, best known for writing *Chunky Monkey Pupu*.

Once upon a time, Sam was known to quote books the way some people quote movies, but now he claims having a family has made him forgetful—as a survival adaptation. Find more at knightwritingpress.com.

Elektra Hammond emulates her multisided idol Buckaroo Banzai by going in several directions at once. She's been involved in publishing since the 1990s—now she writes, concocts anthologies, and edits science fiction for various and sundry. When not freelancing or appearing at science fiction conventions, she travels the world judging cat shows.

You can find her expounding on all things genre, writing, comics, TV, and Supernatural at Con-Tinual (the Con that Never Ends) on Facebook and Youtube.

Elektra is a graduate of the Odyssey Writing Workshop and a member of SFWA. She lives in Delaware with her husband, Mike, and more than the usual allotment of felines.

Find her at www.untilmidnight.com and expressing her opinions on Mastodon as @elektra@wandering.shop.

Davis Ashura is a bestselling author and a full-time practicing physician. He is best known for the Instrument of Omens series and the Castes and the OutCastes trilogy, both of which are part of the interconnected Anchored Worlds universe. His books are generally about heroes, family, friendship, and fellowship.

Davis shares a house with his wonderful wife, who somehow overlooked his eccentricities and married him anyway. They have two sons, both of whom have helped turn Davis's once lustrous, raven-black hair prematurely white. And of course, there are the obligatory strange, stray cats and a gnarly-toothed rescue dog.

Visit him at www.DavisAshura.com and sign up for his newsletter to learn the latest information on his books or simply follow him on Facebook, Instagram, or Twitter.

Marsheila (Marcy) Rockwell (Chippewa/Red River Métis) is an award-winning tie-in author and poet. Her work includes novels set in the Marvel Universe and in the world of *Dungeons & Dragons Online* as well as numerous short stories, poems, and comic book scripts. She lives in the Valley of the Sun with her husband, three of their five children, two rescues, and far too many books. You can find out more here: *https://marsheilarockwell.com/*.

Jennifer Brozek is a multitalented, award-winning author, editor, and media tie-in writer. She is the author of *Never Let Me Sleep* and *The Last Days of Salton Academy*, both of which were nominated for the Bram Stoker Award. Her *BattleTech* tie-in novel, *The Nellus Academy Incident*, won a Scribe Award. Her editing work has earned her nominations for the British Fantasy Award, the Bram Stoker Award, and the Hugo Award. She won the Australian Shadows Award for the Grants Pass anthology, coedited with Amanda Pillar. Jennifer's short form work has appeared in Apex Publications, *Uncanny Magazine*, *Daily Science Fiction*, and in anthologies set in the worlds of Valdemar, Shadowrun, V-Wars, Master of Orion, and Predator.

Jennifer has been a freelance author and editor for over seventeen years, and she has never been happier. She keeps a tight schedule on her writing and editing projects and somehow manages to find time to volunteer for several professional writing organizations such as SFWA, HWA, and IAMTW. She shares her husband, Jeff, with several cats and often uses him as a sounding board for her story ideas. Visit Jennifer's worlds at jenniferbrozek.com.

Samantha Chalker is the daughter of Jack L. Chalker and an information security consultant at IBM X-Force Red. The environment of science fiction and fantasy across the early part of her life fueled her creativity, turning it into short stories with themes of psychological exploration in fantasy settings and sharing them among her friends. Having been in the field for eight years and presented a tool at Black Hat, one of the world's most well-known hacking conferences, she brings her background of security and everything technical into her writing, breaking down security concepts in her stories and including them to create fun adventures. She is currently based out of the Seattle, Washington area.

As well as writing fiction, **Arlen Feldman** is a software engineer, entrepreneur, maker, con-runner, and computer book author—useful if you are in the market for some industrial-strength door stops. Some recent stories of his appear in the anthologies *Museum Piece*, *Particular Passages 4*, and Kevin J. Anderson's *Gilded Glass*, and in *Little Blue Marble* and *Nocturne* magazines. He lives in Colorado Springs, Colorado. His website is cowthulu.com. Mastodon: @cowthulu@mastodon.social.

Catherine Asaro has authored about thirty books, including science fiction, thrillers, and fantasy. Her novel *The Quantum Rose* and novella *The Spacetime Pool* both won the Nebula® Award. She is a multiple Hugo nominee and a multiple winner of the AnLab from *Analog* magazine. Her recent books include *The Down Deep*, Book 1 of the Dust Knights trilogy.

Catherine has a doctorate in chemical physics from Harvard and a BS in chemistry from UCLA. Her paper "Complex Speeds and Special Relativity" (*The American Journal of Physics*, April 1996) forms the basis for some of the science in her fiction. She directed the Chesapeake Math Program for many years. Her students distinguished themselves in numerous national programs, including the USA Mathematical Olympiad, the USA Physics Olympiad, and the Harvard–MIT Math Contest.

Catherine has appeared as a speaker at many institutions and as a guest of honor at cons across the US and abroad. She also appears as a vocalist at clubs and conventions. Her most recent single, the Celtic-themed song "Ancient Ages" (written by Arlan Andrews) placed on the Blast-FM top 100 in 2020. She served two terms as president for SFWA and is a member of SIGMA, a think tank that advises the government as to future trends affecting national security. Catherine can be reached at www.catherineasaro.net and has a Patreon page at: www.patreon.com/CatherineAsaro.

www.ingramcontent.com/pod-product-compliance
Lightning Source LLC
Jackson TN
JSHW022200140525
84468JS00001B/35